KIAN'S FOCUS

A
BRIGS
FERRY BAY
NOVEL

MISTY WALKER

Kian's Focus
Copyright © 2020 Misty Walker

Cover Design: K Webster
Photo: Adobe Stock
Editor: Lawrence Editing
Formatting: Champagne Book Design

ALL RIGHTS RESERVED. This book contains material protected under International and Federal Copyright Laws and Treaties. Any unauthorized reprint or use of this material is prohibited. No part of this book may be reproduced or transmitted in any form or by any means, electronic or mechanical, including photocopying, recording, or by an information and retrieval system without express written permission from the Author/Publisher.

This is a work of fiction. Names, characters, places, and incidents either are the product of the author's imagination or are used fictitiously, and any resemblance to actual persons, living or dead, business establishments, events, or locales is entirely coincidental.

To Kristi, the Daria to my Jane. Or are you the Jane to my Daria? Either way, you're my person.

PLAYLIST

"Something in the Way" by Nirvana

"supercuts" by Jeremy Zucker

"Gravity" by Sara Bareilles

"The Search" by NF

"Gone Too Soon" by Andrew Jannakos

"If You're Too Shy..." The 1975

"Motion Sickness" by Phoebe Bridgers

"A Thousand Bad Times" by Post Malone

"Breathe (2AM)" by Anna Nalick

"Runaway Train (with Skylar Grey feat. Gallant)" by Jamie N Commons

"Alaska" by Little Hurt

Welcome to Brigs Ferry Bay…
Brigs Ferry Bay is a steamy MM romance series.
While each book can be read as a standalone, to get the full experience, they're best read in order.
Enemies to lovers, friends to lovers, hurt comfort, age-gap romance, and so much more.
Fall in love with the charming small-town gay romances of Brigs Ferry Bay…

KIAN'S FOCUS

A
BRIGS
FERRY BAY
NOVEL

ONE

Archer

"I'll say it again, we should head back early. This storm is going to be ugly." Mason stares through the window in the cabin, studying the rolling waves of the Bering Sea.

"That's why we shouldn't. Everyone else probably is, which will make our haul that beyond valuable," I argue.

"I don't know. Everything I'm hearing is this one's going to be ugly," Adler warns. "But Archer's right. We'll be able to charge double if everyone else goes back to the port with a short load."

"Then let's do it," I say, zipping my coat and sliding my hands back in my gloves. I massage Mason's shoulders as we leave the cabin and step out into the miserable weather.

"It's going to be a rough one." Mason grabs hold of a giant crab pot and pitches it into the ocean. I can barely hear him over the wind and water slapping me from every direction.

"Not as rough as what's going to happen to you later," I holler back and throw him a wink he probably can't see with my raincoat hood drawn down over my face.

He grins at me devilishly. Even with the icy temperatures and being soaked to my bones, my body warms. He's a fucking gorgeous man with a penchant for danger. He's perfect and tonight, after we've put in a long day and have finally warmed up, both by showering and making love, I plan to ask him to marry me. I reach down and feel the square box in my pocket and smile.

His rubber boots slip out from under him and he falls flat on his ass, sliding toward the cutout in the side of boat. His features turn panic stricken and he scrambles to reach for the thick rope that's coiled next to him before he topples over the edge. I've only made it a few feet in his direction when he hops up in front of me. Our eyes catch and a million unspoken words are said.

Despite our earlier joking, we both know risks here are real. Temperatures often plummet to negative thirty degrees Fahrenheit, wave heights can top fifty feet, and winds can reach sixty knots. Yet day after day, we're out here throwing crab pots and bringing them back in. All to catch the elusive king crab and go home with a fat paycheck, while hopefully not losing our lives.

"I meant to do that!" he shouts and I shake my head. Not funny.

Hours go by. We strategically toss pots, bring others up, and if we're lucky enough to catch something, we empty the crab into a holding tank for processing when we're back on dry land. After nearly eight hours of taxing labor, we ready ourselves to throw out the few remaining pots we'll leave out all night.

"Last ten!" I say and use the lift to hook onto a pot sitting on top of the stack. I bring it down to the deck and unhook it while Mason braces himself to hurl it into the ocean.

"Cowabunga!" he shouts, chucking the pot and laughing at his lame Teenage Mutant Ninja Turtles joke. All of his white teeth are showing when he smiles brilliantly over at me.

"You're an idiot," I joke. I'd never admit this to him, but I love that he watches old movies from the eighties and nineties. It's our favorite thing to do back at our place in Homer, Alaska. If we're not fishing and hiking, we're cuddled on the couch with some cult classic movie on.

"You love me."

I listen to the whir of the thick rope rubbing along the edge of the boat as the pot sinks deeper and deeper into the ocean.

Something's off.

There's an extra sound, like the rope is brushing something

other than the boat. A sick feeling hits me in the gut. My eyes dart to the ground and see Mason's boot is inside a loop in the rope. God fucking dammit. He knows to watch his feet, but he gets lazy at the end of the day.

"Mason!" I warn, pointing at his boots.

His face falls and he looks down. He tries to pull his boot free, but there's no time. It's already tightened around his ankle. The last image I have of my almost fiancé is the absolute horror on his face as he's yanked off the boat and pulled into the ocean.

"Mason!" *I scream at the top of my lungs.* "Mason! No!"

I run to the edge of the boat, but there's no saving him. He's thirty feet underwater by now and there's no safe way to pull him out. It doesn't stop me from trying. I grab a life vest and secure a rope to the boat and loop it around my middle. I've almost dived in after him when Adler stops me. He holds me close. I try to fight him, but I'm unsuccessful.

"You can't do that, kid. You know as well as I do, he's gone."

"No. I can still save him. I can find him. Let me go." *I struggle against Adler's arms.*

"Won't let you do that. I won't lose both of my best friends in one day." *His eyes brim with tears.*

"Mason!" *I wail into the nothingness and sink to my knees, sobbing.* "Noooo!"

"Archer." Someone shakes my arm. "Archer. You're having a nightmare. Wake up."

I jolt upright and scan my surroundings. I'm in a bed, not on a boat. I'm in pajamas, not in rubber boots and a thick raincoat. It's my sister's tired face in front of me, not Mason's. But one thing's the same. Mason's dead.

"Sorry, Sara. Did I wake you?" I scrub a hand down my face, running my fingers through my beard.

"I think you woke the whole house." Her point is proven when I hear the sound of her three-year-old crying from a room down the hall.

Her brows furrow and she pinches the skin at the base of her throat. She's worried. She's always worried. The last thing I want to do is make things worse for her. I'm supposed to be here for her. Not the other way around.

I moved to Brigs Ferry Bay last week to help her when her loser ex-husband, Chad, abandoned her and their kids for a younger woman with no baggage. He emptied their bank accounts claiming it was his money since she was a stay-at-home mom, packed up all his things, and left without even a goodbye to their small children.

She called me crying, telling me she needed me. She didn't know I was barely existing back in Alaska. She probably wouldn't have asked for me to move here otherwise.

But she's my sister, so I packed up in a day and flew to Maine. I thought a change of scenery would help me escape the ghosts of my past. I hoped my demons only haunted the house Mason and I shared, the car we drove, the places we visited. I didn't know they'd taken up residence in my mind, not allowing me to escape them no matter how far I traveled.

"Shit. I'm sorry. Need me to help get the kids settled?" I toss the covers off, ready to solve the problem I caused.

"No. Stay here. Lou will fall back asleep. I'll bring Emmy into bed with me." She tucks me in the same way I did for her while we were growing up.

"I'm settling into a new place. I'm sure that's all this is. I'll be okay," I lie. I've relived my nightmare many nights since the accident. Though up until a week ago, I didn't have anyone around to disrupt.

Her lips turn downward. The same expression I've seen on her face since I got here. Not that I think I caused it. Fucking Chad is responsible for that look. I'm just not helping to change it. Yet. It's something I plan to remedy.

She pats my shoulder and leaves my room, closing the door behind her. I cover my eyes with an arm and blow out a breath.

I need to get my shit together. Not for my own well-being, that ship has sailed. But for Sara. I've always been the person she can rely on. Losing Mason doesn't change that.

It's not surprising that the Warren kids are reunited and back to being the ones who everyone pities. Sad and only having each other to rely on. The difference now is, we have the two innocent souls she brought into the world to take care of. Emmy and Lou, named after Emmylou Harris, and who are our silver lining.

I roll onto my side and hug my pillow. I needed some sleep tonight. I start my job at the BFB Fishing Company tomorrow, and I want to make a stellar impression.

I'm only qualified for commercial fishing and this is a one shop town, so I'll do whatever it takes to keep this job. I've been living off mine and Mason's share of the money from the sale of the boat and crabbing company for well over a year now, but it won't last forever. Not to mention Sara is relying on me to help out with her bills.

I flip over onto my back and spin the ring on my finger. It's the only thing of Mason's I kept. I'd planned to give Mason the gold band with a Koa wood inlay on the night he died. He would've loved it. The perfect mix of traditional and outdoorsy, just like him. He wanted everything *normal* people wanted. To be married, have kids, a house, a dog, all of it. But he wanted to do it in Alaska, living off the land. I was ready to make all his dreams come true, even if I wasn't sure I had what it took.

Since I'm the one who raised my sister, I know what you have to give up in order to have a family and I wasn't sure I wanted to make the sacrifice again. But when you love someone as much as I loved Mason, you don't care what the future looks like. Just as long as they're in it. And he would've been the best dad ever. I couldn't take that away from him.

I bring my phone to life and see it's four in the morning. There's no point in trying to sleep now. The early bird gets the worm and if you want to catch the fish, you need the worm.

I climb out of bed feeling exhausted, but ready to see what fresh hell my new life has to offer.

The fog is so thick, it's as though I'm breathing in water as I step onto the wooden pier. The sun is on the horizon and preparing to make its ascent into the sky. I tug my beanie down further to keep my earlobes warm. Plumes of steam billow out of my mouth with my breaths and the salty air settles on my tongue in a familiar way. I missed being out on the ocean. She's a bitch, but she's a bitch I know, and I've been landlocked for too long.

As I step onto the long wooden dock, I spot a guy with a clipboard in his hand, directing the fishermen to their boat for the day. I'm assuming he's my boss. I tuck my hands behind the bib of my orange shoreman pants. The neoprene is stiff because I had to buy a new pair. I burned everything that reminded me of Mason after the accident. Surprisingly, it was comforting to put them back on this morning. They'd been a staple in my wardrobe for so long, I didn't realize I'd missed it.

"You Henry?" I ask the man, setting my backpack on the ground.

He tucks the clipboard under his arm and holds a hand out to me. "I am. You must be Archer?"

"That's me. I'm ready to be put to work."

"That's what I like to hear. I'm sending you out with Oliver. He's been around a long time and he'll help you get the swing of things." He points to a white painted wooden boat named Lucky.

"Thanks, man. I'll see you later." I toss my backpack over my shoulder and approach Lucky. She's a beauty.

I step on board and find Oliver at the bulkhead, starting the engine to warm it up. It roars to life, sending vibrations through my body. I look around and see the traps are already loaded on deck, so we'll be able to push off soon.

"Oliver?" I shout over the loud motor.

He turns and flashes a smile. He's an older guy, probably late fifties, and has the average fisherman appearance. A beard to keep your face warm, bib overalls, a beanie, and a pair of duck boots.

"You the new guy?"

"Yep. Archer."

"Nice to meet you, Archah. You fish for lobstah before?" he asks in a thick New England accent.

"No, I'm a king crab guy, but I'm a fast learner."

"Great, 'cause I'm a fast teachah. Let's go make some money." He walks up the side of the boat, gaffs the mooring rope, and unhooks us. Then we're off.

It's been over a year since I've felt the massive rolling waves of the open ocean. It's this motion that tends to make people queasy, but for me, it's like the swaying of a rocking chair. It's comforting and I feel as though I'm finally at home. I didn't realize how much my sea legs missed staying fluid. I immediately unlock my knees to keep my balance and roll with the motion. It's like dancing, you have to follow your partner's lead. My partner is this body of water and I'm ready to bust a move.

"You wanna bait the traps?" Clemens calls out.

"On it." I find the mesh bags of oily herring and tie them to each trap. It's stinky and gross, but like everything else about the day, it's like breathing to me. It comes naturally.

The day goes smoothly. Throwing traps, picking up others, banding the claws of the lobster and tossing them in a holding pen over and over again. The repetitiveness gives my mind time to wander because if I look out at the vast expanse of the ocean, memories try and sneak up. But I'm careful to reel them back in before visions of the angry Pacific take over and it's not the calm Atlantic I see.

That memory doesn't belong anywhere near here.

TWO

Kian

I gaze out the windows of my wine bar, Focus, that overlooks Mainstreet. Dante and Jaxson walk past, hand in hand. *Barf on a cracker.* My closeted high school sweetheart refused to claim his sexuality when he was with me, but Dante rides into town with his giant checkbook and suddenly Jax's parading around town waving a rainbow flag.

Whatever. My ass is so much better than Dante's.

I peer over my shoulder to make sure. Yep. Still perky and bubbly. *My best ass-et, really.* I chuckle at my own joke. I know I'm a catch. I have a fabulous sense of humor, amazing taste in clothing, and I own two successful businesses. What more could anyone want?

"Are you going to stare at your own tush all night, or can you pass over that glass of wine?" Jarrett Sullivan, the owner of Jarrett's Antiques, asks. He and our friend, Fernando, stop in for a glass of wine most every night.

"Sorry." I push two glasses down the bar, depositing them in front of my friends. "I just don't get it. No one wanted that B&B here, but suddenly the sheriff gets a hard-on for the big shot New Yorker and we're supposed to conform?"

"Sweetie, jealousy was so two years ago. It's not a chic look." Jarrett swirls his wine and takes a sniff. This bitch wouldn't know Two-Buck-Chuck from Dom Perignon.

I roll my eyes dramatically. "I'm not jealous. I just don't

want our quaint town to be taken over by big businesses. You two are lifers, too. You should be just as worried."

"We are. But I have to admit, the man has impeccable taste. That has to count for something," Jarrett says.

Dante bought all the B&B's furniture from Jarrett, earning himself goodwill from my friend. And yes, I may have benefitted from the B&B as well, but it takes more than purchasing a few bottles of wine for a Lobster Crawl to win me over.

"I guess." I reach into the countertop dishwasher and pull out clean glasses to polish before putting them away. It's early still, so Focus while is open for small bites, tasting plates, and wine, my dance club next door, Blur, won't be open for another couple hours.

"Did you hear about the new guy?" Jarrett tucks an invisible strand of hair behind his ear.

"New guy?"

"Your employee's brother moved to town." Fernando fills me in.

"Who? Sara?" I rest a hip against the bar. I only hired the sad girl two weeks ago and she's never mentioned a brother. Then again, she doesn't mention much. She's a hard worker and always on time, but she's closed off and I'm not one to pry.

Okay, I am one to pry, but she's wound tighter than a ball of yarn.

Now that I think about it, I don't know much about her and none of it came from the horse's mouth. Paul, the local newspaper owner, told me when she arrived to town with a husband. They set up house and had kids. Appeared to be the perfect family for many years. Then last week, Fernando told me he left her for his secretary.

Soon after, my friend Cato, the owner of *And Puppies!* came in asking if I had any job openings for her because she had inquired about a job with him, only he didn't have the need for an employee. I shuffled my employees around and gave her a bartender position at Focus since she doesn't exactly have the right equipment for Blur. Namely, a dick. A giant, gay dick, to be exact.

She's been with me ever since. Now, there's a brother. *Interesting.*

"Yep. I guess he moved in with her to help out and whatnot." Jarrett leans in. "He's hot, Kian. Big, burly, and bearded. I saw him walking to the docks this morning."

"Sounds like he's probably straight."

"I don't care, I'm not looking to marry the guy. I just need some new eye candy around here. The selection is stale."

"I'm not stale." I argue.

"You're also not my type. Unless you suddenly changed your mind and like to be on the giving end of a pound session." His eyebrows rise.

"Bitch, I'm not made for manual labor." I motion up and down my thin frame. "But you're right. It's been a while for me, too."

"You know I'm always down for a friendly fuck." Fernando offers. Our *desperate times calls for desperate measures* relationship has worked in the past, but we've gotten to be close friends lately and I don't want to rock the boat.

"Soft pass," I say gently, patting his hand. "It would feel a little incestuous at this point."

Fernando rolls his eyes but moves on. "Anyway, new guy got a job at the fishing company."

My lip curls. "Disgusting. I wouldn't want my lover to smell like fish. That's one of the perks of being with a man."

"Slap it here." Jarrett holds up a paint stained hand and we slap fives.

Eventually, Jarrett and Fernando leave, and Sara arrives for her shift, doe-eyed and depressed. She has permanent dark circles under her eyes and bags big enough to pack luggage in, but her hair is in a perfect bun and her clothes are neatly pressed.

"Hey, honey," I greet.

"Hi." She flashes me a fake smile. "How's it going?"

"It's been busy. Actually, I was hoping you could stay late tonight. We're having a foam party next door and you know how that goes. I need to babysit all the disorderlies who think just because the foam is waist deep, they can get frisky."

Her eyes bulge and her jaw drops. She's so innocent, I can't help but shock her now and then.

"I, uh, yeah. I can. My brother is living with me now, so I have a babysitter all night."

"Oh, a brother." I sidle up next to her, pretending I knew nothing. "Do tell."

"Nothing to tell. I needed help and he didn't have any commitments where he was living, so he offered to move here."

"Where's he from?" I ask nonchalantly, busying myself with rearranging wine bottles, but commit every detail to memory so I can spill them to Jarrett tomorrow.

"We both grew up south of here, but he was living in Alaska before coming to Brigs Ferry Bay."

"Ooo," I drawl. "Alaska. The undiscovered wilderness. How exciting."

"I guess." She moves to the time clock. "I should clock in and get started."

"Okay, honey." I grab my set of keys. "If you need anything, I'll have my phone on me."

"Thanks."

I step outside, inhaling the fresh spring air. It's still nippy from winter, but I can smell the change coming. Flowers are sprouting, new leaves are budding. Spring is my favorite season. There's just something about it. Like Mother Nature is going through a rebirth, rewarding us for making it through another doom and gloom winter.

I walk next door where the peaceful, calm, orchestral music and romantic light from Focus is left behind, and I'm greeted by loud, bumping beats, flashing strobe lights, and gays. Lots of gays. Well, at least for a small town. Brigs Ferry Bay is the self-proclaimed gay capital of Maine. For whatever reason, we collect here. I'm proud of our little community. I don't think many small towns are so lucky.

I nod to the bouncer, Steve, who's collecting the cash and stamping hands. The large man is wearing black leather shorts, a black tank top, boots, and nothing else. He's hairy everywhere except his bald head and has a dainty diamond nose ring. I'm sure Steve is a top, but he's definitely not my type. I prefer understated men. *Closeted men*, my mind shouts at me. I shake my head, disagreeing with myself.

I haven't been with a closeted man since Jax and we all know how well that went over. As in, it didn't go over well at all considering he's now warming the bed of another man. I'm happy for him, I am. But sometimes, late at night, when the lights turn on and the magic of the club is gone, I feel the letdown. Like I wasn't enough for Jax. Maybe I won't be enough for any man.

I step onto the dance floor to take in the scene. Although Blur is known for being gay friendly, men and women frequent my club. Currently, the dance floor is crowded with couples and groups bumping and grinding. I usually have a foam party once a month, a technique I picked up that kills two birds with one stone. My customers have fun slipping and sliding all over each other. Then, after everyone goes home, a cleaning crew comes in and uses the suds to deep clean the place. I'm all about an efficient use of resources.

Everything seems to be under control, so I slip away to my office to complete some paperwork. My office overlooks the dance floor via a one-way mirror, making it easy for me to do business while also keeping an eye on things.

I flip through the day's mail. Bills, bills, more bills, and one envelope that looks like a letter, but when I open it, it's just another bill. I purchased this wine bar and club at twenty-five years of age. I thought it would be a party every night. Now, I'm twenty-nine and the party is over. Although I wouldn't change it for the world, the magic of the nightlife is gone.

A few hours in, I get a message from Sara telling me there's been an emergency and she has to go. I want to be annoyed, but Sara is a star employee and she has kids, so I get it.

I rush next door and find Sara clocking out. "Everything okay, honey?"

"Yeah, but my brother didn't know Emmy is lactose intolerant and gave her ice cream."

I cringe. "I'm guessing big brother doesn't know how to clean diarrhea from the carpet?"

"Worse. She was crying when her tummy started hurting, and so he brought the kids by, thinking she just missed me and not knowing what was wrong with her."

"Uh-oh." I'm lactose intolerant myself. I can predict the next string of events.

"She had diarrhea in his car. He's now in the parking lot, unable to get the kids home because every time he gets in his truck, he gags over the smell."

"No." I gasp.

"Yeah. So, I've got to let him take the kids home in my car and figure out how to clean the mess from his."

"Yikes. Want some help?" I offer. The last thing I want to do is clean up kid feces, but I'm dying to see what this mysterious brother looks like.

"You don't have to do that."

"It's fine. I've got some vinegar, a bucket, and rags. We can do this."

"Actually, that would be nice. My initial plan was to take his truck to the car wash and start hosing."

"Excuse me, everyone," I call out to the customers while gathering supplies. "You're in charge of yourselves for a while. I've got to go help Sara out."

The few patrons sitting at the bar and the intimately spaced tables nod back and then return to their conversations. This is what I love best about small towns. Not only can I trust they'll leave cash on the bar for whatever wine or liquor they consume, they'll also leave bigger tips because they'll assume Sara's problem will cost money. We take care of our own around here.

I follow Sara out to the parking lot that's only illuminated by two streetlights. Sure enough, a beat-up truck is parked next to Sara's Corolla. Three figures stand next to the tailgate, two tiny people and one hulking man. A sexy, beefy, hunky hulking man. His hair is dirty-blond and unkempt, he has an overgrown beard, and he's wearing a Death Cab for Cutie T-shirt with worn in jeans.

Might not be gay, but he's very easy on the eyes.

"I'm sorry," he starts. "You didn't tell me she was allergic to milk. *She* didn't tell me she was allergic to milk." He accuses Emmy with a point of his finger.

The panic on his face and the way he's quick to blame a little kid is comical. I cover my smile.

"You think a three-year-old is going to turn down ice cream?" Sara rushes over to her daughter and hugs her, despite the brown dripping from her pants down. "But you're right. I should've told you. Where did you even get ice cream? There was none in the house."

"We went to the store earlier and picked up snacks because we were going to watch some movie about elves," the brother explains.

"Trolls." Lou, the five-year-old, corrects.

"Pretty much the same thing, little man." He ruffles Lou's hair, then turns his attention to me. "Who are you?"

Okay. He's direct.

"Oh, right. This is my boss, Kian," Sara says.

I reach my hand out. "And you are?"

"Archer. Sara's big brother." He takes my hand and shakes. He appraises me for a second too long.

There it is, that tiny little glint of interest in his eyes. This man is gay. I'd bet my ass on it.

A flush spreads from my chest to my cheeks and my heartbeat pounds in my ears.

"I came out to help clean," I say dumbly, holding up my supplies. What the hell is wrong with me? I'm not one to lose my mind, no matter how attractive the other person is. Then again, I've never seen anyone this outrageously handsome.

"I don't want to put her in my car seat all covered in poop, ruining two seats. You didn't pack a diaper bag, did you?" she asks Archer.

"We were just stopping by. I didn't pack anything. Plus, she's potty trained. Why would she need a diaper?"

"For accidents. Like this one."

"Here." Archer lifts his shirt off and hands it to Sara. My tummy does a somersault and my jaw drops. His shoulders are broad, and his waist is tapered. Ripples of muscles scroll down his abdomen and frame that stupid V thing that makes girls and gays drool.

"Thanks." Sara takes the shirt and peers over at me, probably knowing I'd salivate over the man. She's right. He is delicious. "Come here, sweetie. I'll set you on the tailgate, and we'll get you changed."

She takes her daughter around to the back of the truck for some privacy, leaving me, a half-naked God of a man, and Lou. I bend down to the little boy's level. "Hey, little Lou. How are you?"

I've met both Sara's kids before, but only briefly.

"Emmy shit herself," he deadpans.

My wide eyes go from Lou to Archer, who awkwardly chuckles and tucks the boy into his side. "We talked about this, remember? I used a naughty word and you shouldn't repeat it."

"Sorry. I forgot."

"Kids say the darnedest things." I snicker and Archer scrubs his fingers through his beard sheepishly. "Don't worry. Your secret is safe with me."

Sara brings Emmy back to the front of the truck. "There we go. She'll need a bath when you get her home, but at least she won't dirty up another car seat."

Archer leads the kids over to Sara's car and begins to strap them in, but Emmy doesn't want to go. She cries and begs for her mommy.

"It's okay, sweetheart," Sara coos. "I'll be home just as soon as I clean up Uncle Archer's truck."

"No! I want you! My tummy hurts."

"It's fine, Sara. You can take them home. I'll stay here and clean this up."

"Are you sure?" she asks Archer, but her eyes are on me. She knows how awkward this will be for two strangers.

"I've got it. Get them home. I'll be right behind you."

"Okay. See you tomorrow, Kian?"

"I'll be here," I reply.

She gets in the driver's seat and pulls away, leaving me, a shirtless wonder of a man, and a truck full of doo-doo. This should be fun.

THREE

Archer

I'm going to kill Sara. I know I said it was fine for her to take the kids home, but it is so *not* okay. I don't know this guy. Kian, I think is what he said his name was. It suits him. Quirky and cute. I can't deny the attraction that sparked when we shook hands, even though I want to.

He's shorter and much smaller than me, and he dresses kind of nerdy with suspenders and a bow tie on. He's cute, in an adorable kind of way with his big hazel eyes and slicked back brown hair. But it's his grin that gives the most pause. Sideways and toothy. Like he has a joke on the tip of his tongue at all times that he's holding back.

He's nothing like Mason. Mason was big, like me, and he smiled with his whole face, his cheeks swallowing his eyes with the hugeness of it. Not that I'm comparing the two. They're incomparable. Mason was everything and Kian, he's just a guy who owns the bar my kid sister works at.

"So, I guess we should get to scrubbing," Kian says.

"You don't have to help. Just leave the supplies and I'll have Sara bring them back tomorrow." I offer because cleaning up shit requires a level of intimacy we don't share.

"I'm actually a pro at cleaning up bodily fluids." He shoots me a pointed look. "Don't ask."

"I wasn't going to." Because, gross. But I still smirk.

We take our positions on opposite sides of the truck, me

on the driver's side and him on the passenger. It's an older model with one long bench seat. Lou's booster chair is on the passenger side and Emmy's shit-stained car seat is in the middle. It wouldn't be a big deal if the car seat had caught all of the shit. I could throw it in the bed of the truck and Sara could hose it down and wash the padding at home, but the shit was very liquidy, and it seeped clear into my fabric seat.

"Good God, that smell." Kian retreats a few steps.

I gag and choke, backing up. "I can't do it. I'll have to get the truck towed to the junkyard."

"No, don't do that. We've got this. One step at a time. I'll climb in and unhook the seat. You pull it out and throw it in the back." Kian lifts the neckline of his shirt over his nose. It reminds me I can't do the same because I'm topless. Fuck, how did I get myself into this situation?

I nod and watch as Kian climbs in, audibly breathing through his mouth. I don't know how he isn't barfing all over the place. My niece is cute, but dammit, she's toxic. He hastily undoes the seat belt and pulls it out from where it's latched. I grab it and hurl it into the truck bed.

"Oh my God." Kian looks down at the stained seat, his eyes watering. "Okay, we can do this. Grab the bucket of water and pour about a cup of vinegar in it." The way he says water and vinegar sounds almost like watah and vinegah. He must've grown up in Maine, but worked on losing the accent.

We spend the next ten minutes taking turns scrubbing and choking on fumes. It's disgusting and even though I didn't want his help originally, I never would've been able to make it through this without him.

I can't help but notice Kian takes an interest in me while I clean. I regret not keeping a spare change of clothes in my truck.

Sara said her boss was gay when she told me about her job. She hinted about setting me up with him, which led to further conversations. One, being how I wasn't ready. And another, about how even if I were ready, her trying to set me up with a guy simply because he's gay is like me trying to set her up with a man simply because he's straight. It's ignorant and rude.

"Thank you," I say when all the cleaning supplies have been collected and there's a dry towel sitting over the wet spot.

"No problem. You want to come in for a drink while that airs out a little?"

I think about it. A drink sounds fantastic after an experience like that, but I also haven't done any socializing in over a year. I'm rusty. And he might ask questions about my past. I'm not prepared for that conversation with anyone. I barely even talk about it with Sara.

"I don't have a shirt." I motion to my naked torso, thinking I've found the perfect excuse.

"That *is* a problem since we have a *no shirt, no shoes* policy, but it's one I can solve. Follow me." He waves over his shoulder and I trail behind. We go through a back exit and into a small kitchen where a tall, thick, and kind of scary man is preparing a cheese plate.

"About time you came back," the man says and then looks up. "And you brought your own snack."

"Not exactly. Duke, this is Archer, Sara's brother. We were cleaning up a little mess in his truck." Kian digs through a bin on a metal shelving unit. He pulls out a black tee with Focus written in gold fancy script. "Here we go."

He tosses it over to me and I hold it out. It's a large, so it'll be tight, but whatever.

"A mess, huh? Is that what you kids are calling it these days?" Duke waggles his brows.

"Get your mind out of the gutter, Duke." Kian walks over to a hand washing station and dumps half a container of soap into his palm. "You want to get in on this?"

"I do." I pull the shirt on, thankful to not feel so exposed anymore, and step up to the sink, shoulder to shoulder with Kian. I pump a few squirts of soap on my hands and scrub the shit out of them. I go to rinse at the same time Kian does, and our hands meet. I'm the first to jerk mine away.

"Sorry. Hand washing hazard," he jokes and rinses. When he's pulled out a couple paper towels, I rinse my own. "All right. How about that drink?"

"Take this cheese plate to table four while you're out there," Duke says.

Kian huffs, but takes it through a swinging door. I follow him. It leads to the space behind the bar. The vibe is chill in here. Rich woods with emerald green and gold accents. It looks expensive and swanky. I take a seat on one of the barstools.

Kian delivers the cheese plate, his eyes staying on me the whole time as I try not to notice. When he returns, he takes his place behind the bar. He looks comfortable and at ease. Unlike me, who can't stop shifting in my seat and looking around. Anything to avoid his scrutiny. I know he's trying to figure me out.

"What'll it be? We mostly have wine, but I also have Jim, Jack, Johnny Red, Johnny Black, and Jose." He reaches down and pulls up five bottles. "All my favorite men."

He laughs at what I think is a joke. But I don't understand the reference, so I stare at him blankly.

"Oh, come on. Haven't you seen *Coyote Ugly?*" he asks.

"Coyote what?

"Ugly." He huffs out a breath. "It was a joke. I keep a stocked bar. What'll you have?"

"Can you make a whiskey ginger?"

"Sure can." He busies himself opening a can of ginger ale and squeezing a wedge of lime into the highball glass. When it's done, he proudly places it in front of me.

"Thank you." I take a sip. It's perfect.

"I prefer a glass of Chablis myself, but whatever floats your boat." He pours himself a glass of white wine and holds it up to me. "Cheers. On a shitty job well done."

"Cheers." I can't stop a smile from showing and I clink my glass to his. The man is charming and easygoing; it makes me forget my life is in shambles.

"So, why did you move to Brigs Ferry Bay?" he asks.

"My sister's loser husband left her alone with two kids. It was only right I help her out."

"That's very noble of you. I heard it was a bad situation."

"Sara hasn't told me too much yet. I think she's still processing." I think about how every time I've asked her what happened, she shuts down completely. She gets this vacant stare and asks me to watch the kids so she can be alone for a while.

"It must be hard to have your life take a sharp turn when you thought you were going straight."

"Yep." I understand that completely.

"I'm sure she'll come around. Are you two close?"

"We were close growing up. We had shit parents, so I took care of her. But she went off to college and I moved to Alaska. We spoke on the phone a lot, but I always felt like I wasn't getting the full story. It was weird, you know. She only blabbered on about all the good things going on, when no one's life is that perfect," I say before realizing I'm saying too much.

This mere stranger has something about him that makes it easy to talk to him. I've never met someone who makes me feel like I've known them a thousand years when we've only met. But that's bullshit nonsense, and I need to shut the hell up. I'm probably just tired.

"Maybe she knew you would worry, and she just wanted you living your best life without her problems weighing you down." He shrugs. "I don't have any siblings, so maybe I'm talking out of my ass."

I think about that. He's probably right. I spent my entire childhood and teenage years taking care of her since our parents couldn't or wouldn't. She probably felt guilty and my selfish ass was in love, truly living a happy life. I should've taken a stronger interest in her life.

"Maybe. I'm sure she'll tell me in her own time." I take another swig of my drink.

"You didn't have any ties where you were living before?" he asks nonchalantly, but I know this isn't a nonchalant question. Too bad for him, I'm not going to give him the answers he's looking for. It's one thing to spill secrets about my sister. It's another to talk about Mason.

"Nope."

"And now you're working for the fishing company?"

"Yep. I'm a fisherman by trade."

Of course, he already knows where I work. The rumor mill in Brigs Ferry Bay is very much active and running. I realized this the first time I popped into the grocery store and everyone knew me by name. It's why I need to keep my secrets close. The last thing I need is a bunch of meddlers.

"You should be used to foul smells then," he quips.

I can't help the chuckle that bubbles out as the seriousness of the conversation dissipates. He's funny. It makes me wish Kian and I could be friends. It would be nice to have someone to share or drink with once in a while, someone who is over three feet tall and doesn't want mac and cheese for every meal. But friends are never satisfied with one-word answers and gaps in history you refuse to speak of.

"I'm immune to fishy smells. Not what happened in my truck. That was something different." I screw up my nose at the memory.

"Right?" he says around the lip of his wine glass. I know this move. He's drawing attention to his mouth. My skin heats. I feel flush, and not from arousal. I'm not prepared for this. I can't be the object of anyone's flirtation. No matter how innocent.

I need to get out of here.

"I should go. Thank you for the drink. And for helping me out." I try to take the last swallow of my drink, but my throat constricts, so I leave it. I stand up and remember I have his shirt on. "I'll wash this and get it back to you."

"Don't worry about it. It looks good on you. Plus, it'll remind you of how we met." He's definitely flirting and that always leads to being asked out. I can't do this. Not now and maybe not ever.

I don't answer, just give him a tight-lipped smile and walk out. I shove my hands into my pockets and keep my head down on my way to the truck. I'm losing my shit and I don't want to risk anyone talking to me.

I hop into my truck that smells heavily of vinegar, but at least it doesn't smell like shit. I crank the window down all the way. My engine roars to life and the tires squeal when I accidentally press a little too heavily on the gas.

I can't go home feeling like this, so I drive down the main drag and away from the town. My eyes sting just thinking about how disappointed I am in myself. Mason's only been gone a year and I put myself in the situation where someone could hit on me. I should've told Kian I didn't want his help and not allowed him to stay.

I slam my palm down onto the steering wheel. Fuck, I miss Mason so much.

I think about what Mason would've thought about me being hit on. A sad smile creeps across my lips. He probably would've laughed.

Actually, I know he would.

Back when we had our boat, we would always dock at Dutch Harbor to sell our load and there was this buyer for a restaurant in Seattle who would come to purchase our crab once a month. He flirted with me relentlessly, begging me to go out with him. No matter how many times I told him Mason and I were together.

It was awkward as fuck and I begged Mason to meet with him so I could avoid the guy, but he got a kick out of how uncomfortable it made me. Each time he would joke about me going to see my "boyfriend" when we pulled up to shore. It annoyed the fuck out of me.

The last time it happened, the dude actually handed me a key to his hotel. Then he leaned in to kiss me, while his hand grazed my dick. I marched back to the boat, pissed as all hell that I couldn't punch the guy out seeing as we needed his business. I told Mason what happened, and he laughed his ass off.

However, the last time we saw the guy, Mason did come with me. I thought he'd stake his claim, hold my hand and kiss me, show the asshole that I was taken.

He didn't.

He strolled up to the douche canoe, grabbed his ass, and said, "I heard you like my slave. I was thinking maybe you'd like to join us. I've got shoes that need to be polished and an extra-large butt plug that would look amazing in your ass."

Dude ran away so fast. We lost the business to another boat, but it was worth it seeing the look of horror on the guy's face.

That was Mason, though. He had a unique way of dealing with things.

A tear slides down my cheek at the memory. Fuck, I miss him so much.

FOUR

Kian

It's been a week since Archer ran out of Focus like his ass was on fire. He's hiding something. I can feel it. I've been trying to pry info from Sara, but she's as tight-lipped as her sullen brother. All I get are one-word answers and avoidances. I want to know more, damn it.

So, as I left my condo this morning, I decided to do a little recon. It just so happens, I live ocean front, right next to the Fishing Company. I'm not brazen enough to go up there, but I do walk my happy ass across the street to Fran's Coffee House. I know for a fact all the fishermen stop in there throughout the day for their caffeine fix and maybe if I'm lucky, I'll run into my mystery man.

I find a chair near the front entrance and sit down. I pull my laptop out so I can get some work done and not look suspicious for sticking around a while. After I get myself settled, I walk up to the counter to get a drink.

"It's nice to see you so bright and early, Kian," Fran says. "I don't normally see you until evening before you go to work. I see you've set up shop over there."

"Needed a change of scenery while I do some budgeting. Can I get my usual, plus a cranberry orange scone?"

"Of course. I'll bring it over in a minute." Fran takes my money and I make myself comfortable at my table.

I try to focus on the numbers filling up my screen, but

every time someone walks through the door or walks past, I look up. So far, no Archer. Maybe he's already been in today, or maybe he doesn't even like coffee. I dismiss that idea. Men like him love coffee. The dark bitterness speaks to their souls.

"Here you go." Fran sets my citrus black tea and scone down on the table. "Someone special you're keeping an eye out for?"

"No. Just distracted today, I guess."

"You wouldn't be wanting to check out Brigs Ferry Bay's newest resident, would you?"

"No." I gasp in mock incredulity.

"If you were, I'd tell you he comes in at ten-thirty every morning when he takes his first break."

I sigh, looking at my watch and seeing it's only ten.

"Ah-ha! I knew you weren't here just to work." Fran cackles.

"How did you know?"

"You forget I've known you since you were in pampers."

"Don't I know it." I playfully roll my eyes.

"Remember, I used to babysit you. You and Jax both. You boys were always thick as thieves. Whatever happened to you two?"

We fell in love and had sex. It was such a magical experience I wanted to come out as boyfriends, but he chickened out and then stopped talking to me and ignored my existence. At least until recently when he apologized.

"Just grew apart," I say.

"Such a shame. Well, anyway. If you need anything else, you let me know."

"I will, Fran. Thank you." I watch her walk away, but then get an idea. "Do you know anything about him? Archer, I mean."

Fran places a hand on her hip and thinks. "Not much.

Probably no more than Jarrett knows, and I know Chatty Cathy has already spilled his guts to you. But I can say one thing, he's sad, just like his sister."

"You got that, too, huh?" I guess I wasn't the only one who saw Archer carries the weight of the world on his shoulders.

"He's not like you, so go easy on him."

"What's that supposed to mean?" I huff.

"I just mean you're an open book, you say whatever's on your mind and don't care who knows."

"I do not," I argue.

"Son, how many times has that mouth of yours gotten you in trouble? I'm not saying it's a bad thing. I think it's good for people to know where they stand and be called out on their bologna when they spout it. I'm just saying, some people keep things closer to their heart and you can't always pry information from them."

I try to speak, but nothing comes out. Do I do that? I think about all the spats I've gotten into around town. Damn it, Fran's right.

"I just like to keep an open and honest line of communication," I sputter.

"For some people, that requires trust."

"I can't help it if I have no filter." I defend my own honor. "Plus, I'm only being friendly with Archer. Moving to a new town where everyone is so close already, it's bound to be intimidating."

Fran shoots me a look and then effectively ends the conversation by escaping behind the counter, leaving me to rethink my entire dating career.

I'm so absorbed in my thoughts, I don't even look up when I hear the tinkle of bells on the entrance door. But I snap out of it the second I hear Archer's deep bass voice.

"Can you fill this up with regular black, please?"

"Of course. How are you today, Archer?" Fran asks.

"Can't complain. Been bringing in a decent haul," Archer says.

"That's good work you boys do. Our economy depends on you catching those sea bugs." Fran giggles at her own joke.

"Happy to do it. It feels good being back on a boat."

I lean back in my seat and crane my neck so I can hear every word of this conversation. Despite what I told Fran, I'm interested in this man. I want to know everything about him.

"Oh? You were a fisherman before coming to our quaint town?"

Archer hesitates. "Um, yeah. I fished crab in Alaska."

"That's a dangerous job. I'm glad you made it out alive," Fran says, concern in her tone.

"I need to get back. The coffee, please?" His voice turns flat, like he's no longer interested in their casual conversation. Interesting. He shut down when I started questioning him about his past too.

"I'll get right on it."

I chug my still-hot tea, burning my tongue, but needing an excuse to go over to the counter.

"Archer. Fancy meeting you here," I say, stepping into line behind him. I forgot how tall and beefy he is. I'm five-foot-eleven and nowhere near eye level with him.

"It's funny how everyone says Archah around here." He chuckles.

"Isn't that your name?" I ask, confused.

"My name is Archer." He emphasizes the R sound. I grew up here. I know what locals sound like. It bothered me that tourists would mock our accents. So I worked at hard to rid myself of the nasty habit, but it still comes out when I'm flustered.

"Okay, Archer," I say pointedly.

"That's better."

I roll my eyes playfully. "Don't get used to it."

His expression changes from amused to suspicious, like he's suddenly not so happy to see me. "What are you doing here?"

It's a stab to my ego, but I can't let it stop me from trying to win him over. Although I don't know he's gay with any certainty, my gay-dar is very rarely off and although he was affronted by my flirting the other night, he wasn't disgusted. It was something else I haven't figured out yet.

"Yep. Just doing some work." I hook a thumb over to my table.

"Here you go." Fran hands Archer his thermos.

"Thanks, Fran." He turns to me. "Well, I better get back."

"Why don't you come join me for a minute? Surely your break is longer than just enough time to get coffee."

He drags his meaty fingers through his beard, expelling a breath. "Sure."

I internally fist pump, but very cooly drop my cup off with Fran and ask for a refill before leading Archer over to my table and pulling a chair out for him. He eyes me warily but accepts and plops his large body down.

He was sexy in the dim light of the parking lot and the romantic ambiance of Focus, but in the daylight, he's absolutely breathtaking. His hair is combed and styled and his beard is tame. I think he even has beard oil in it.

"How's Emmy feeling?" I ask.

"She's better and I threw out the ice cream so there won't be a repeat."

"Smart."

An awkward silence falls between us. I'm flustered and I never get flustered. I rack my brain trying to think of something to say.

"Can I ask you a question?" He leans back in his chair, stretching his long legs out in front of him.

"Anything," I say, way too hurriedly.

"Last night you said Sara is tight-lipped with you, but do you think she's okay?"

"What do you mean?"

"From an employer's perspective, is she okay at work?" His leg bounces up and down. I can tell he's concerned for her.

"She's great. She's a hard worker, mostly on time, and is friendly with customers."

"That's good. I'm glad. After I got home last night, I heard her crying. I don't know if it's normal for her to be so down. I don't have anyone to talk to about it and I know we just met, it's just—"

"You're worried."

"Yeah."

"She had a shitty thing happen to her. I didn't know her well before she came to work for me, so I don't know how she was before the breakup, but I can tell she's down in the dumps." I shouldn't be talking about Sara behind her back, but if this is the only conversation Archer's willing to have with me, I'll set aside my ethics.

"You think so?" He blows out a breath and his face falls, like this was the worst news I could tell him.

"Yeah, I mean, I can't imagine the betrayal she must feel," I say gently.

"You're right. I just want her to be happy, you know?" He's having this conversation with me, but I know I could be anyone at this point. He seems to just need to talk. "I think she does a good job at shielding the kids from it, but she's not the same person she was when I moved away."

"I'm sure it's hard being the older brother, watching her go through all of this."

"Honestly, I'm more of a parent to her than a brother."

"Where are your parents?"

"Not in the picture. They never were." Our gazes lock, and it's like it hits him that he's admitting his secrets to me.

He stiffens and grips tightly onto his thermos. "Sorry to dump all that on you."

"It's okay. People say I'm a good listener."

"I'm not normally so honest with a stranger."

"Just with your friends?"

"I, uh, don't have any of those," he admits sheepishly.

"Moving to a new town can be hard. Especially a small town like this." An idea pops into my head and I lean in. "How about you let me give you a tour this weekend?"

"I don't know. I need to check with Sara."

"That's fine. Let me see your cell phone." I hold my palm out flat. He stares at it for a minute, making me think he's not going to hand it over, but then he seems to make his mind up and reaches into his pocket. He reluctantly places an older model iPhone in my hand. I quickly send myself a text message and hand it back. "There. I'll text you later tonight and you can let me know."

"I better get back."

"Okay. I'll see you around?"

"Sure. You're a good person, Kian. I hope we can be friends." He walks out and back in the direction of BFB Fishing Company.

I close my laptop and fall face first onto it. Friend zoned. He's either not gay or isn't interested. I choose to believe he's not into men because if he were, there's no way he could resist me.

I'm irresistible, damn it.

FIVE

Archer

Saturday morning, I wake up and groggily step into the shower. After going around and around about whether or not to let Kian take me on a tour of the town, I finally gave in.

My first week working has my mind and body drained. Then there was picking up the slack with Sara and the kids. Their house hadn't been properly maintained and I spent every free moment fixing busted cabinets, unclogging drains, mowing her lawn, and all of the other tasks that had been overlooked since Sara's douche of an ex left. And that's on top of babysitting every night.

I love Sara and the kids, I do. But I spent the last year barely able to take care of myself and now overnight I'm suddenly responsible for three more. I'm sure Sara wouldn't see it that way. She's stubborn and thinks she's got everything under control. She doesn't know I hear her in the early hours of the morning breaking down. When I should be asleep myself, but I'm too worried I'll have a nightmare and scare her again.

Quite the pair, the two of us are. Both of us trying not to alert the other about what we're going through and desperately trying to prove to the other that we're fine.

That's why, when I got Kian's text message asking me to take him up on his offer for a tour, I accepted. I need to get out of this house and away from responsibilities. At least for a few hours. But as I scrub my body and wash my hair, I have an internal conversation with myself about oversharing. I don't exactly know why I feel the need to blurt shit out to Kian, but I need to stop that shit.

I dry off and dress in my usual beat-up jeans and band tee. The only other clothing I have in my closet are a couple pairs of bright orange, rubber bib pants and hoodies, so my decision was easy.

I walk into the kitchen and find Emmy and Lou tucked up to the kitchen island, happily eating frozen waffles. Sara's standing in front of the kitchen window that overlooks the backyard, cup of coffee in her hands. She has a faraway look in her eyes and her brows are bunched together. I wonder what she's thinking. It's not good, whatever it is.

I open the cupboard next to her and pull out a mug. It startles her and coffee sloshes over the side of her cup.

"Shit. Sorry." I take the mug from her hands and grab a paper towel to clean up the mess.

"No, it's my fault. I zoned out." She turns on the faucet and rinses her hands off, then notices I'm dressed with shoes on. "Where are you headed off to?"

"Kian asked to show me around town. Thought it might be a good way to get my bearings. I kind of hit the ground running when I moved in last week."

"Sorry about that. I should've taken you around and introduced you to people."

"It's not like you have an abundance of free time." I squeeze her shoulder and then pour both of us coffee. "Here."

"Thanks. Do you know where he's taking you?"

"No. I don't think he planned anything. Probably just the main points of interest." I shrug.

She tips her chin down and raises her eyebrows. "You don't know Kian very well if you think he didn't make charts, graphs, print out a map, and create an agenda."

"Really?"

"Definitely. He's a planner. You should see our staff meetings. It's ridiculous." The first real smile I've seen since I got here creeps across her lips. She likes Kian too.

"Maybe I shouldn't go. You probably need help with the kids anyway."

"Oh, no. You're not canceling on my boss last-minute. You made your bed."

"Uncle Archer doesn't make his bed. It's always messy," Lou comments.

I ruffle his hair. "It was a figure of speech."

"I no wanna make my bed." Emmy pouts.

"Everyone will be making their bed. Even Uncle Archer." Sara pins me with a glare, like I better not argue.

"Your mom's right. We all need to do our part to keep this house looking nice." I kiss both kids on the head. "I'll see you guys later, okay?"

"Okay," they chirp in unison.

I leave out the door and decide to walk to Kian's condo instead of drive. Sara lives in a housing development on the southwest side of town next to the elementary school, but nothing in Brigs Ferry Bay is far away, so it's barely four blocks to the waterfront condos he told me he lives in. Which is also right next to the fishing pier, so I know I won't get lost.

The morning air is cool and I wish I'd grabbed a hoodie, but I know by afternoon the sun will warm things up enough for me. After working in Alaska for so many years, I don't tend to chill easily. Ten minutes later, I'm taking the stairs up to the second level and then finding unit two-ten.

I hear music on the other side of the door, but even louder than that is Kian's singing voice. He's listening to some pop song I've heard on the radio, but don't know the title. I chuckle and listen for a few seconds before beating my knuckles on the paint chipped door. This place could use some updating.

The music stops abruptly, the door flies open, and Kian appears. He's wearing a wool knit sweater with leather elbow patches, tan slacks that are cuffed at the ankles, and shiny brown shoes with a square toe and no socks. He has way too much style for such a sleepy town, but I like it.

"Good morning. Come on in," he greets me with a huge smile.

"Nice place." I walk into a large open floor plan I wasn't expecting for such an older complex. The walls are a pale teal textured wallpaper and the floors are done in gray, wide planked wood. His furniture is tufted light gray leather with a modern white coffee table, and a large white bookcase. The kitchen looks brand-new and is clean. Really clean. I doubt you could find a stray coffee ground anywhere in there.

"Thanks. I just remodeled. It seems like there's a ton of developers just itching to knock down all the old buildings around here and change them into tourist attractions. I figured if I updated this place, I'd have a leg to stand on if they try to buy out this building."

"Is that a possibility?"

"I don't know. With the new B&B, there's been talk that Dante will want to expand into other developments around town."

"Dante?"

"You probably haven't met him. He dresses in thousand-dollar suits and walks around like he has a stick up his ass. Or maybe it's my ex-boyfriend's dick that's up his ass. Whatever. Same thing," he mumbles.

"You hate him because he's with your ex?" Suddenly, I don't like either of these men. Dante, out of solidarity and Jax, because what kind of guy wouldn't want Kian? He's cute and kind. He helped my sister out with a job when she needed it. I'll always be grateful to him for that.

"No. I hate him because he wants to change things around here. The fact that he's dating Jax is just the cherry on top."

"That sucks." I don't know what else to say. That was too much information.

"It's fine." He waves my comment off. "Anyway, ready to go? We've got an agenda." He pulls out his phone and shows me a list.

"I thought this was a casual stroll through town."

"You don't know this about me yet, but nothing is casual with me. Now come on. We've got places to go and people to meet."

"Okay. Let's do this, I guess."

We start out walking past the fish market where we sell our daily catch, Fran's Coffee Shop, and Beacon Island Gifts. Kian chatters on about who owns what and who to avoid. There's no way I can keep up, so I nod and let him yammer on.

We turn up on Main Street and stop for a coffee at the Seaside Café. It's cute and obviously there for tourists because little trinkets no local would want line the entrance. I order a black coffee and Kian orders some kind of citrus tea.

Drinks in hand, we continue our tour.

"This is the Daily Harald, owned by Paul. Stay away from him unless you want to make the front page with some kind of headline like, *New Guy in Town, What's He Hiding?* or something equally annoying. It's more of a gossip tabloid than a real newspaper," he grumbles. Without taking a breath or giving me time to figure out if he's being serious or joking, he continues, "Across the street, you'll remember my wine bar and club, Focus and Blur. I'm a little biased, but I like to think we're the shining star of Brigs Ferry Bay."

His prideful smile and the way his chest puffs up is cute. It reminds me of the way I felt when Adler, Mason, and I bought our boat. The world felt like our oyster, or king crab, since that was our currency.

Things can change so quickly. But I won't bring it up and

rain on his parade. Not everyone's stories end as tragically as mine.

"You're kinda young to own two bars, right?"

"I'm not *that* young. I turn thirty next month."

"You're a baby. I'm forty and have nothing to show for myself. You should be proud of all you accomplished."

"Age is just a number, old man. But you're right. I am young. I inherited some old money when my parents passed. When I turned twenty-five and this building went up for sale, I guess I thought why not? This may come as a surprise, but I'm gay." He watches for my reaction before finishing his thought.

"I knew that." I chuckle.

"Just being transparent." He tosses his empty coffee cup in a metal trash bin on the sidewalk. "Anyway, there weren't many establishments for the younger gay community. So I decided to change that. We're open to anyone, obviously, but I made sure everyone knew we are gay friendly."

"That's commendable." I still haven't disclosed my sexuality. I'm not embarrassed. I've been out since I was a teenager. I guess I'm worried once he knows, this mild flirtation between us will amp up and I need a friend right now, not anything more.

"I'm proud of it."

"What's with all these rainbows painted everywhere?" I point at a vandalized building.

"Oh, that's just the Rainbow Vigilante."

"The what?"

"We don't know who does it, but every now and then a new rainbow pops up. Although he's been quiet for a while." He appraises a colorful painting on the side of one of the buildings.

"I kind of like them. They're cheerful and fun."

"And destruction of private property," I add.

Kian rolls his eyes dramatically. "Don't be on the wrong side of this battle, Archer."

"You might change your mind if you end up with one."

"I could be so lucky." He sighs. "Fernando at the diner got one. I'm green with envy."

We continue our stroll, stopping in front of a building that says BFB PD *And Puppies!*

"This is the police station?"

"Police station and a grooming salon my friend, Cato, owns. You can meet him later. Let's keep walking." He grabs my arm and tugs me farther down the sidewalk.

"Kian, is that you?" A man steps out from the building. He looks about Kian's age and is wearing a ballcap with Sheriff stitched across the front.

"Fuck," Kian mutters under his breath and then does a one-eighty. "Fancy running into you."

"Who's this?" The guy eyes me speculatively.

"My new friend, Archer. He's Sara's brother."

"Right. I heard you were moving to town. Nice to meet you. I'm Sheriff Bell." He holds a strong hand out and I shake it.

"Sheriff Bell? Please. You can call him Jax." Kian argues.

Jax. So this is the ex.

"When I'm on official business—"

"He can still call you Jax," Kian interrupts. "If you'll excuse us. I'm taking Archer on an official tour."

"Nice to meet you, Archer. If your sister needs any more help, you let her know she can call me."

"More help?" I ask.

"With that jerk ex. I think I scared him off, but if he comes back, I'm around." Jax disappears back into the police station.

I'm quiet as we return to our walk. Kian continues telling me stories and introducing me to people, but my mind is racing. Sara didn't say she'd had problems with Chad. She made it sound like she found out about his affair and he happily left her. I need to know what the real story is. The only reason she wouldn't tell me is if she were worried about my reaction. And I'd only react badly if he laid a hand on her. That fucker better not have touched my sister.

"Let's eat at Comida's. He has the best huevos rancheros." Kian opens the door to a diner, and I follow him in.

We're seated by a flippant teenager who looks like he wants to be anywhere but here. We sit on opposite sides of a booth and I open my menu, but I still can't focus.

"Okay, what happened? You were fine and now you're all broody and spacey." Kian shoves my menu down to the table.

"Sorry. Something that Jax said about Sara got me thinking."

"What did he say? I swear, that man went years keeping his trap shut about everything and now suddenly he's so open and honest," he rambles.

"He said if Sara needs help *again*. Did something happen with Chad I don't know about?"

"Honestly, I have no idea. I didn't know Sara before she came to work for me. I only heard rumors."

"What kind of rumors?"

"Well, Jarrett told me that when she caught her husband cheating, she threw all his things out. He didn't like that too much, so he…" Kian trails off.

"He what?" I growl.

"The rumor was he got physical. I don't know if it's true, though," he rushes out.

"I've gotta go." I stand up from the booth and rush out of the restaurant. Kian runs after me, calling my name. But I don't stop. I'm seeing red. Why would she keep this from me? I need answers. And then I need to find that asshole Chad and teach him not to fuck with my baby sister.

"Archer. Wait." Kian's short steps are no match for mine. I eat up the entire street length before he's even made it halfway.

Shop owners run to the windows of the businesses to find out what's happening. I see their curious looks, but I don't slow. No one attacks my sister without consequences. No one.

I've just turned up Sandpiper Way when an out of breath Kian pops out of an alleyway between the grocery store and the Fish Market.

"Why are your legs so long?" He bends over, panting and clutching his side. I want to walk right past him and get home to Sara, but he's clearly in distress.

He's one determined man to run after me when he clearly doesn't get much cardio, judging by the fact that he looks as though he's going to pass out after running a couple blocks. The anger at Chad still sits on the surface, but it's knocked down a peg or two by the out of shape man in front of me. The humor of it all hits me and I can't stop the bellow of laughter that comes out at the sight of him.

"This isn't funny. I need water. And a bench." He looks up, scanning the street. Seeing neither, he makes a pained noise. "Cramp. In my calf. Ouch."

I snicker and help him to standing. I duck under his arm and wrap a hand around his waist. He uses me as a crutch to limp along, but it's not easy considering I'm more than a foot taller than him. We trip over each other and stumble more than we make progress.

"This isn't working. Hold on." I turn to him and lift him over my shoulder.

"What are you do—" He starts to protest, but then changes his mind. "Actually, this is good. Anyone ever tell you that you have a bitable ass?"

"If you're okay to comment on my ass, then maybe you're okay to walk." I prepare to set him back down.

"No, my calf really is cramping. I'll be good. I promise."

I shake my head and get us to Sara's house, where I set him down on the sofa.

"Kian!" Sara rushes over. "What happened?"

"Just a cramp, honey." He winces.

I push the coffee table closer and elevate his leg. I leave Sara to dote on him and get a bag of frozen peas. I lift his leg and set the bag underneath his calf. In all the chaos, my hyper focus on confronting Sara is pushed to the side.

And Kian looks all too pleased about it.

SIX

Kian

Did I exaggerate a cramp in order to get Archer to stop his tirade? Maybe. The second I told him what the rumors were about his sister, he freaked the hell out. I don't know much about abuse victims, but I'm sure having your brother get in your face and demand answers would be a triggering experience.

I thought if I could talk to him, I could calm him down so he didn't traumatize the poor girl, but he's fast for being so dense. You'd think his muscle mass alone would slow him down.

So I did what all damsels in distress do. I faked a more severe injury than what really happened, and it worked. I wasn't expecting to get tossed over his shoulder like a sack of potatoes, but I'm not angry about it. I got up close and personal with the juiciest ass I've ever seen. I'm talking two honey hams sitting side by side, screaming to be devoured.

"Do you want an ibuprofen?" Sara asks. She's such a mom. The second Archer tossed me onto the couch, she was all over me. I love her for it.

"No, I'm fine now. Just a charley horse from hell." I readjust the peas under my leg.

Archer takes a seat across from the couch on a wingback chair. He crosses his legs with an ankle on his knee and studies me. He knows what I did. He probably knows why, too. His intense eyes meet mine, making me squirm.

"How was the tour?" Sara takes a seat next to me.

"We didn't get too far, but I think Archer will be able to find his way around now."

"Did you stop in and see Cato? He has the most adorable little puppies in there right now."

"That's actually about as far as we got because we ran into the sheriff," Archer says.

"Oh yeah? How's Jax?" The muscles in Sara's face tense. She senses where this is going, and I don't know whether I should excuse myself or stay to deflect some of Archer's anger about her keeping this big secret.

"He's good. He told me to pass on a message to you." Archer's legs uncross and he leans forward, his forearms resting on his thighs. "Something about if you need him to stop Chad from beating on you again, to let him know."

"That's not exactly what he said," I mumble.

Archer ignores my interjection and proceeds to dig into Sara. "But that can't be right, because I know you wouldn't keep something like that from me."

"We should talk about this later. I'll go check on the kids in the backyard." She stands to leave.

"No. You're going to tell me what happened."

"It wasn't a big deal. He got a little handsy on his way out, but my neighbor called Jax and he came right over. He got Chad sent on his way and helped me change the locks on the house."

My eyes dart from sibling to sibling. I absolutely hate tension. I think I'm allergic to it. It's why I say whatever's on my mind and don't hold back. You can't build up animosity if you're honest one hundred percent of the time.

"Not a big deal? Are you kidding me? Do you know where Chad is right now?"

"I don't know for sure. I know he isn't in town." She sinks back into the couch and her shoulders curl forward. She's retreating, feeling threatened. "He hasn't tried to get in touch."

"I think I heard Lou call for you. Why don't you go see?" I suggest to give her a way out of this interrogation.

Sara always strikes me as such a delicate person, like one wrong word and she'd disintegrate into nothing. Archer's being an asshole and he doesn't even see what his words are doing to her.

"Yeah, okay." She pushes herself up, but it's forced and slow. She's weak mentally and emotionally.

I wait until she's gone before laying into the big oaf of a bully across from me. "Was that necessary? Can't you see she's not handling all of this well?"

"You've known my sister for five minutes. I've known her her whole life. You don't understand."

"I understand completely. Whatever she's going through, she's in a bad place. You can't attack her like that. You should be supportive and optimistic."

"She's tougher than she looks."

"Are we talking about the same person? Because I may have only known Sara for five minutes, as you put it, but I know her well enough to know she doesn't make eye contact with people. She's polite, but never personable. She works hard and never complains. Who doesn't complain? Scared people who are afraid of what response they'll get by expressing how shitty something is. That's who." I jump to my feet, unable to control my frustration.

"That's just her. Some people don't need to waste their time whining."

"And some people are depressed," I whisper. Either not wanting to say it loud enough for Sara to hear, or because I don't want to perpetuate the argument. Probably both.

"You should go." He gets up and opens the front door.

"Fine. I will. Just please be gentle with her."

"Don't tell me how to take care of my family, Kian." His eyes are dark and stormy. Whatever he and his sister have been through in their lives, they're not trusting and open people. It makes me sad.

"Okay, I won't. But if you ever need anything, I'm here for both of you." I offer. Archer nods and unceremoniously closes the door after me.

Well, that could have gone better. I turn toward home, but realize I don't have time before Focus opens, so I turn in that direction instead. I replay the day over and over, trying to figure out what I could've done differently.

I'm a problem solver. I'm the fixer of the town. It's what I'm known for. Everyone comes to me for advice.

Not big, bad Archer. Nope. That wolf blew my house down and knocked the wind right out of me.

My first customer of the day is one of my best friends, Cato.

"I'm so glad to see you." I run out from behind the counter to hug him, but realize he's still covered in fur from his dog grooming business and stop short. "You couldn't change before you came?"

"I didn't have time. I heard a rumor about you and the new guy spending the morning together and rushed over after my last client."

"Was your last client a bear? Because you're fuzzy."

"I thought he was before I got my shearers out. But nope. Just an unruly Chow Chow." He produces a lint roller from his back pocket and proceeds to de-fur himself. "So, what's up?"

"Rough day," I whine and lead him to a barstool.

"I can see that. You look out of sorts." His perfectly sculpted brow arches over one of his beautiful golden-brown eyes.

"First thing's first. Want to try a new rosé I just got in? It's a bit fruity and more of a summer wine, but it's delicious." I pull out the pale peach bottle of Jolie Folle.

"Sounds delicious. I'd love some."

I pour two generous glasses of wine and set one in front of each of us. I don't always drink while I'm working, but somedays it's inevitable.

"I took Archer on a tour of town. Being neighborly and all."

"Uh-huh. You're a regular Mr. Rogers. Go on," Cato prompts.

"It started out fun, but then we ran into Jax."

"Uh-oh," he singsongs into his wine.

"Exactly. But not for the reason you're thinking. He mentioned what happened with Sara and her creepy husband." I go to take another swallow of wine, but it's gone. I pour one more glass. If it's going to be one of those nights, then so be it. "Only Archer didn't know about it, so he flipped out."

"I would've flipped out too. I heard Jax recounting the story when he got back from the call. I think it's the most action he's seen in a long time. At least since Hank."

"Except it's Sara," I say in explanation. Cato and I both agree that girl is as delicate as the stem of a wine glass.

"Aw." He sighs. "Poor Sara."

"Exactly. He stormed back to her house and was all up in her face about it. I tried to intervene and he kicked me out."

"He didn't," he says on a gasp.

"He did. And now I feel bad. I'm a fixer, Cato, and I couldn't fix this. He wouldn't even let me try."

"You can't save them all, sweetie. Especially when you don't know him. He could be dangerous."

"I don't think he is. He just doesn't understand her."

"You need to stay out of it. Tell Sara you're there if she needs you and then avoid that Archer guy like the plague." Cato takes his last sip of wine and pushes it to me for a refill.

"Maybe." I can't explain why I'm drawn to Archer. It's not logical, but I know Cato's right. I should butt out. Instead, I change the subject so I don't have to think about it anymore. "What's going on with you?"

"Brooks asked me to go by the fish market to bathe a box of flea infested kittens today." He smiles softly. "It's kind of cute how he takes in all these strays."

"I think you have a little crush." I joke.

"Whatever. He's not gay. He's divorced. With kids," he emphasizes.

"You never know."

"With Brooks, I know." But he can't hide the tiny little hearts in his eyes. My poor friend, chasing the unattainable.

"You want to come dancing tonight? I'm in the mood to forget about the stack of paperwork and shake my ass." I turn around and bend over to do a little twerk.

"You know it. I'll go home and change now. Be back around ten?"

"Perfect." I spin, feeling a bit lighter now that I know a night of fun is ahead of me.

I work alone for the next few hours, well, not including Duke who's in the back putting together the few food items we offer. It's been a busy night and by the time Sara arrives for her shift, I'm glad to have a second set of hands for a while before things slow down and I can escape next door to hang out with Cato.

"Hey, honey. How are you?" I ask as I pass by to deliver a glass of wine to a table.

"Good," she replies. That's her go-to answer. Everything's always good, even if I know it's not.

I make it back to her side by the time she clocks in and ties her black apron around her waist.

"Sorry about today. I didn't mean to butt in."

"It's okay. Really. I should've told him what happened. I just knew he'd be upset," she says dejectedly. She looks out over the bar, assessing each patron, predicting what they might want next. It's what makes her such a good employee. Always on top of my customer's needs.

"It was your story to tell. Jax should've kept his mouth shut." I grab a knife and a small cutting board so I can prepare enough garnishes for the rest of the night. "Were things okay after I left?"

"Yeah, fine."

"He's not going to hunt me down and kill me, right?" I joke.

"No. I know he puts up a big front, but he's really a giant teddy bear."

"I'll take your word for it. Listen, I'm heading to the club now." I scoop up a handful of candied lemons and put them in a container. "If you need me, text."

"Yeah. Sure," she says, but she's chewing on the inside of her cheek.

I place a hand on her forearm. "Anything you need. Ever."

"I know, Kian. Thank you." She looks down uncomfortably.

I say goodbye to a couple regulars and walk next door. I enter through the back tonight, hiding from everyone until Cato arrives. Despite not wanting to delve into paperwork, I get lost in timecards until a knock sounds on my office door.

"I thought we were dancing?" Cato's head pops in. He's covered in body glitter and has on his signature ultra-glossy lips.

"We are. Just doing payroll. For some reason, they like being paid every two weeks." I roll my eyes.

"Silly people. Let's go!"

"I'll change and meet you down there." I motion to my casual attire.

"Okay. See you in a minute."

I step into the adjoining bathroom and assess the outfits I always keep on hand for the nights I want to party and not work. I hold out a short-sleeved button-down that has a red and black rose pattern on half the shirt and solid black on the other. I pair it with perfectly tailored black slacks and black loafers. It's darker than my usual outfits, but my mood matches, so I find my black eyeliner and smudge it into my lower lash line to fit with the theme. I lengthen my lashes with some mascara and apply a clear gloss to my lips.

Perfect.

I meet Cato downstairs where we order fruity shots and some specialty drink my bartender has come up with.

"Cheers, bitch." Cato holds his shot glass up. "To us."

"To us." I clink his glass and shoot.

From here, things get fuzzy. We dance. A lot. Grinding on each other, on whoever steps up to us, and on the wall when the other has found someone else to dance with. There are more shots, more drinks, and an insane amount of debauchery. It's a black-out kind of night and I don't fight it.

By one in the morning, I'm seeing double and I know it's time to go home. I dig through the crowd until I find Cato flirting with my bartender, Keith. I wonder if I should tell him not to waste his time. Keith is straight.

"I'm going to head out," I slur.

Cato looks from me to Keith, wondering where his loyalty should lie right now. His dick or me. I don't fill him in on the attractive bartender's sexuality, so he doesn't try and follow me home. I need to stumble my ass home and crash. I don't need him to babysit.

"Stay. I'll be fine." I assure him.

"Really? I'm okay to leave if you want me to walk home with you."

"No, it's okay. Promise."

Cato hugs me. "Call me tomorrow."

"You know it."

I push through the crowd until I'm outside. The air is

chilly, but I'm hot and sweaty, so it feels amazing. I know, as a business owner, I should stay and help close up. But that's what my managers are for. I never wanted to be married to my business, only have a friendship. I'll be there every day for it, but I also need to have a life outside of the responsibilities.

I stumble my way home, my mind reverting to the grumpy man I spent my morning with. I can't get him out. Not even top shelf liquor could erase how terribly things went. He wasn't listening to me earlier. He dismissed my take on the situation simply because I haven't been around Sara's whole life like he has.

I have valid opinions, dammit. Everyone knows that about me. Maybe I need to tell him everyone in this town uses me as a sounding board and values my opinions. Surely, he'd feel differently about me.

Genius plan.

I pull my phone from my back pocket and find Archer's contact info. In the process, I trip over a crack in the sidewalk. I stumble but regain my balance before I crash to the ground. *This is too dangerous.*

I find a curb and take a seat. *Much safer.* I click on his number and listen as the phone rings. He doesn't pick up until the fifth ring, when I'm certain his voicemail is going to kick on.

"Hello." His voice is gruff and sleepy… and sexy. Really sexy.

My dick grows painfully hard. How am I going to get this all out when he has a growly bedroom voice?

Abort mission. I hang up.

SEVEN

Archer

The call ends and I pull it away to see who it was. My eyes are blurry from sleep. I blink until my vision clears. Kian? Why is he calling me at one in the morning? My mind and body jolt awake. Sara. Something happened with Sara.

I flip on the bedside lamp and click on his name to return the call. It rings a few times before he picks up, but all I hear on the other end is breathing.

"Kian, is Sara okay?"

"Who?" he slurs and hiccups. Great. He's drunk.

"My sister, Sara. She works for you."

"Oh, she's great. She's such a good employee. I'm lucky to have her."

"Then why are you calling me at one in the morning?" I grit out.

"You called me."

"Jesus Christ." I run a hand through my beard, tugging on the ends. This conversation is painful. "I called you back, Kian. You called me first."

"Hold on, let me check." The line goes quiet except for his incoherent muttering while he checks his phone. "I *did* call you," he gasps as though he's surprised at this revelation.

"I know. Why?"

"I've been drinking."

"I know," I repeat.

"I wasn't finished. See? That's your problem. You don't ever let me finish. You jump to conclusions before you know the whole story."

"What are you talking about?"

"Today. I'm talking about today. Or, yesterday? Whatever day it was. You told me I don't know your sister and I don't have a right to an opinion. That's bullshit." It's hard to follow along when his words are running together, but I try to keep up. "Where were you last week right after it happened? Because I was with her every day. When someone's depressed, you can't get in her face and demand she tell you everything that's going on. I don't know much about much." He starts laughing. "That's a funny sentence. Much about much."

"Kian. Focus. What's your point?" I'm on the verge of hanging up. He isn't making sense.

"My point is, I know people. They come to my bar, they sit down, they tell me their problems, and I help them. I know people, Archer. And your sister needs help. The professional kind. She's too skinny, she doesn't sleep judging by the circles under her eyes, and she won't talk about how she's doing. I'm worried about her and your aggressiveness will push her away. *That* is my point and it's a good one." He breathes heavily from the effort of stringing so many words together.

"She's a newly single mom who got cheated on. Of course she's sad. She'll pull through. That's why I'm here. Don't worry about her. I've got it."

"Do you? Because you're sad, too."

"You're drunk, so let's forget this conversation ever happened. If you remember anything about this call tomorrow, remember this one thing. I don't need your help. We're fine." I hit the end button and toss my phone on the nightstand.

I wake up to crying. Emmy's probably giving Sara a hard time. It's Sunday and I don't have to work, so I planned to sleep in, but not if I'm needed to help with the kids.

I throw on a pair of sweats and walk into the living room. It's empty. So is the kitchen. Emmy starts crying again and I follow the sound to her room. I open the bedroom and find her on her little toddler bed, clutching a stuffed animal and sobbing.

"What's wrong?" I lift her up into my arms and settle us both back on the bed. She clings to my neck.

"Mommy won't get up. And Lou called me a baby," she whines.

"Why won't Mommy get up?" My hackles rise. Even though Sara works until two in the morning, she always gets up with the kids.

"She's sleepy."

I'm opening Sara's bedroom door in seconds to find her curled into a ball on her bed. I reach down and shake her shoulder. She groans and opens her eyes, but just barely.

"What's wrong? You sick or something?" I look around to see if maybe she'd been drinking or took a sleeping pill, but there's nothing on her nightstand.

"I'm just tired. Can you handle the kids this morning, please?" Her eyes close and she's back asleep before I even answer.

I step out of the room and close her door quietly.

"All right, little miss. Looks like Uncle Archer's in charge of breakfast. Where's your brother?"

"He's playing his video game." She points to the bedroom next to hers.

"Okay, let's go get him and we'll take a walk to the restaurant around the corner. Give Mommy some time to rest."

I get the kids dressed and their shoes on, not bothering

to change out of my sweats. As we walk to the restaurant, the kids chirp happily about all the things they see along the way. I nod and smile, but my mind's focused on Sara. I've been working on hiding my own sadness, so maybe I missed something bigger going on with her.

That seems crazy, though. She's been doing fine. This is the first time she's slept in since I've been here and I can't fault her for that. She works hard. She deserves a morning to herself. I dismiss my concern. She needed some extra rest.

I never did speak to her about what happened with Chad when Jax chased him from town. After Kian left, I was too angry about how intrusive he is to dive into the other reason I was pissed off. So, I left it alone. I wonder if that was a mistake.

Kian said Comida's Diner was good when he took me for a tour, so we turn up on Main Street and head that way. The kids must know the place because they get excited when we walk inside.

The same obnoxious teenager that sat Kian and me leads us to a booth and hands us menus without a word or smile. He returns with water cups and tells us our server will take our orders.

"I want bacon and eggs," Lou says.

"I want tacos," Emmy chitters.

"I don't know if they have tacos this early, but we'll ask, okay?" I open the menu, but before I can scan it, our server appears.

The man I see when I look up is sexy. He's Hispanic and probably around my age. He has deep brown, soulful eyes, and a trim goatee. A tattoo of three crosses peeks up from the collar of his shirt on the side of his neck. It gives him an edgy vibe that feels progressive for such a sleepy town. This place breeds beautiful men. If I'd lived here in my early twenties, it would've been like living in Disneyland.

"Welcome to my diner," he greets with a blinding smile. Jesus Christ.

"You must be Fernando?" I ask.

"I am. *You* must be Archer."

"Yep. And this is—"

"Emmy and Lou, my favorite little munchkins."

"This small-town thing is going to take some getting used to. I forget everyone knows everyone," I say.

"I was born and raised here, so I don't know any different." He crouches down to the kids' eye level. "I think smiley face eggs and bacon for Lou and Emmy. You want the breakfast tacos?" The kids cheer and he turns to me. "And for you?"

"What do you recommend?" I ask since I didn't have time to look at the menu.

"I'll bring you the huevos rancheros."

"Sounds good. Kian told me that you have the best."

"Kian's right." Only the voice doesn't belong to Fernando, it belongs to the drunk dialer himself. He steps around Fernando, looking worse for wear. He has on dark sunglasses, his hair's mussed, and he's wearing the most casual outfit I've seen on him, running shorts and an oversized T-shirt.

"Should I bring you the same? You're looking rough, my friend." Fernando squeezes his shoulder.

"Yes, please. And coffee. Lots of coffee."

"I'll get right on it," Fernando says and returns to the kitchen. I'm almost certain he's the owner and chef, so I don't know why he's the one who took our order, but I'd imagine it was to scope out the new guy. Like everyone else.

"Kian!" The kids squeal in delight and he winces at the sound. "Sit with us."

He looks at me for approval and I nod, scooting over to make room since both kids occupy the other side of the booth.

I reach into my backpack and hand the kids their devices.

I'm getting better at this whole kid thing, making sure to have a change of clothes and activities no matter where we go. The kids happily take them and quiet down with their battery powered entertainment.

Kian and I awkwardly eye each other. I don't know if he remembers last night, but if he doesn't, I'm not going to be the one to remind him.

"I'm glad I ran into you. I was going to call later anyway." His eyes drop to the table where he picks up a saltshaker and spins it around on it. "About last night…"

"I wasn't sure you'd remember. You were pretty—"

"Loaded. I know. I just wanted to say I'm sorry."

"It's cool."

He flashes a half smile that I have no business thinking is cute, but it is. "Really? I thought you'd put me through the ringer."

"No, not going to put you through the ringah," I say exaggerating his New England accent that isn't as pronounced as Oliver's but is still there.

"Oh, you're mocking me now?"

"Just a little." I show an inch between my forefinger and thumb.

"So, what are you kids doing today? Where's your mom?" he asks Emmy and Lou.

"Mom's asleep." Lou doesn't even look up from his game to answer.

I see a brief look of concern on Kian's face. I know he's thinking, but he's wrong.

"She was tired from her shift last night, so we let her sleep in," I chime in.

"I see. What are you doing after breakfast?"

"No plans. I was thinking about taking them to the boardwalk to play some games." This news to the little people is clearly exciting because their electronics hit the table and they chatter animatedly about what carnival games are their favorites.

"Would you mind some company?" Kian asks hopefully.

"Sure." Despite our recent fights, I like spending time with the guy. He's funny and charismatic. He's the calm to my anxious mind. When he isn't judging my family, that is.

Fernando appears with huge plates of food that we devour. Kian was right, this place is good. Even the picky kids eat most of their meals. Well, what they don't spill down the front of themselves, anyway.

In no time, we're outside and walking toward the Boardwalk. The sun is eating through the rich fog that blankets the area most mornings and the air smells damp and clean. It's still a little early for the vendors to be open, so we walk down the pier where the kids peak over the edge and point out all the sea creatures they can spot.

"There's a starfish, Archer." Emmy tugs on my hand.

"Good eye, Ems." I compliment. "Why don't you and Lou race to see who can get to the end the fastest?"

They take off in a sprint.

"Wanting to get me alone?" Kian eyes me flirtatiously.

"I want to burn off some energy. Those kids, man. They're exhausting."

"It's embedded in their DNA to be tiring. Does that mean you don't want any of your own someday?"

"I don't know. I thought I'd have a couple at one point in my life. Now, I'm not so sure."

Mason used to gush relentlessly about finding a way for us to have kids. He didn't care if they were adopted or from a surrogate, he just wanted them. Eventually, I just accepted it into my reality. It was a small concession since I wasn't necessarily against them.

"What changed?" He stops and leans over the railing that runs along the pier. I stop next to him but keep my eyes on the kids.

I could lie, come up with some other reason. But I'm tired of hiding and Kian seems to do well with drama. I'm realizing I can't run from my reality forever and if I want friends and people in my life I can turn to, this is something I need to get over. Even if it hurts.

"I lost my partner in an accident."

Kian's hand flies up to cover his mouth. "I'm so sorry that happened to you."

"It's okay." It's my trained response, and I regret saying it immediately because none of what happened is okay. "Anyway, we planned to have kids someday. But now that he's gone, I don't know."

"How long were you together?"

"Almost three years, but we worked and lived together. I think that makes you grow closer a lot quicker than just dating." The sadness I usually get when I talk about Mason threatens to overtake me, but I stop it. We were happy. I shouldn't let every memory be overrun with heartache.

"Yeah, that's a whole lot of togetherness."

I laugh. "It was. We actually owned a company together. We had a crab boat and would be out to sea sometimes for a week at a time, so it was even more closed quarters than normal. We didn't fight often, though. Mason was perpetually optimistic. He didn't razz easily."

"You love him a lot. I can see that." He doesn't say "loved" like most people do. Like somehow the day his heart stopped beating was the day my love turned into the past tense.

"I do."

Kian holds my gaze for a long moment until we're both smacked on the leg by small people screaming, "Tag. You're it!"

We chase the kids around for a while, laughing and goofing around. Then we take them over to play overpriced games that promise huge toys as prizes, but we end up walking away with tiny little stuffed animals. The kids don't mind. They're just happy they won something.

"So, we're friends now, right?" Kian asks as we walk toward our respective homes, all of us with ice cream cones in hand. Lou and I with a scoop of bubble gum and Kian and Emmy with sherbet so there will be no diarrhea in our future.

"Yeah. I guess we are." It feels juvenile to have a conversation like this, but I'm also glad he's spelling things out.

"Good. Then come over tomorrow for brunch. I'll cook."

"I would, but I hate to leave Sara in the morning since she's been so tired lately."

"Okay, then I'll come to you." He takes a long lick of his sherbet, his eyes locked on mine. If he hadn't just said we're simply friends, I'd think it was intentional.

"Sure. Sounds good." I break our gaze and turn to the kids. "What do you say, guys? Should Kian make us pancakes tomorrow?"

EIGHT

Kian

As I prep the bar for Sara, the morning replays in my mind. I didn't expect Archer to open up enough to tell me about his partner dying. I knew he had a dark cloud looming over him, but I never thought the reason would be so tragic. It's no wonder he's all brooding and somber.

I've just finished stocking the bar when Sara walks in. In the almost three weeks she's been here, she's always been perfectly groomed. But today, her hair's in a messy bun instead of the sleek one I'm used to. Her shirt is untucked and her pants are wrinkled. It's her red, puffy eyes that give me the most concern, though.

"Hey, honey. You okay?" I ask as she clocks in.

"I'm good. How are you?" She steps around the corner and I follow her. She shoves her shirttails into her pants and ties her black apron on.

"I'm well." I watch as she smooths her hair back and uses a couple bobby pins to secure it.

"Sorry. I took a nap this afternoon and it was hard to get back going."

"Been there." I try to comfort her frazzled state with my smile.

She rushes to the bar and takes in the occupied tables the way she always does. I study her, noting her energy is off.

She's like the canister of a vacuum cleaner. Her strong

exterior contains the chaos on the inside. She appears orderly, her emotions spinning in one direction, no one the wiser to just how gross she feels inside. The problem with that is, eventually she'll be full to the brim. And when that happens, all the messy feelings will spew out and go all over the place.

It's better to empty yourself after every shitty thing that happens, that way it doesn't fester. And I'm really worried she's got something festering.

I don't know nearly enough about the situation to feel like I can intervene, and I don't want to get my head bitten off by an angry Archer again, so I decide to get to know my employee for a while before leaving for the club.

I allow her to go about her business, flittering from table to table, taking perfect care of my guests. But when everyone is taken care of, I grill her.

"You and Archer are close, huh?"

"Yeah." A soft smile crosses her feminine lips. "Our childhood was horrible. My mom wasn't one to be tied down, so she'd take off whenever she met some handsome man who promised her the world. It would make my dad sad. Then, he'd lose his job and take up drinking. A few months would pass, money would get tight, but Dad wouldn't leave his recliner to take care of us."

"Then what would happen?" I ask.

A table catches her eye and she leaves to take the order, but gets right back into the story when she returns.

"My mom would come back, beg my dad to take her back in. Which he would, of course. Things would get better for a few weeks. My dad would get a job. My mom would pretend to be Suzy Homemaker." She pauses, counting her pour of wine. It's her first bartending job, so everything she does is by the book. "And it would start all over again. My mom would start hanging out at the bar until she met some other guy and so on and so forth."

"I can't imagine having such instability growing up."

Sara disappears for a minute to deliver wine, then comes back and presses some buttons to add the drinks to the customer's bill. "It was hard, but also it wasn't. I had Archer. He took such good care of me. He made sure I got on the bus in the morning, he made sure I had food." She chuckles. "He even learned how to braid my hair so the kids at school wouldn't make fun of me."

"Really?" I laugh too because I can't imagine it.

"He wasn't very good at it in the beginning, but after a few months, he'd even taught himself to French braid."

"You realize I'm going to give him a hard time about this, right?"

"I'm counting on it." She winks.

"Will you be good without me for the rest of the night?" I ask.

She waves me off and gets back to work. She seems to have everything under control, so I head next door.

I sink into my chair behind my desk at Blur. I try to lose myself in paperwork, but my new, sad sibling friends keep popping into my mind. I bring my phone to life and shoot a text to Archer.

Me: How's babysitting going?

Archer: These kids are insanely busy. All the time.

Me: I don't even have enough energy to own a cat, so kids are out of my wheelhouse.

Archer: Don't recommend them. Messy. Loud. Exhausting.

Me: You sure you don't want to come to my house tomorrow so you can get a break?

I ran to the store before work and picked up a lovely brioche to make French toast, some fresh fruit, nuts, and vegan cheese. I plan on making a charcuterie board so we can snack all morning and afternoon tomorrow. I don't know if kids are into that, so I also grabbed donuts.

Archer: I'd actually love that. Let me check in with Sara after she wakes up. If she's not too wiped out from working tonight, then I'll take you up on that.

Me: Okay, talk to you in the morning.

Later that night, as I lie in bed, I rethink about all the new information I've collected. I picture a little girl who looks like Emmy and a little boy who looks like Lou trying to fend for themselves. It's such a depressing image.

My parents weren't the most enthusiastic. They were older when they had me and didn't know quite what to do with all my enthusiasm and charm, but they were always there for me. When I came out to them in high school, they were worried for my safety, but they were supportive.

I got backlash from some of my friends, and being a small town, not everyone understood, but I knew my home was a safe place. My parents were retired by the time I was a teenager, so they were always there. Mom crocheting and discreetly reading romance novels, while Dad tinkered around in the yard, complaining about how the salty air was ruining his fence. I swear he replaced every slat on that fence once a year. They were good people and they gave me a good life. They didn't spend their inheritance from my grandparents, and they had quite a few savings of their own, so even in their death, they took care of me.

I can't imagine growing up in a home where the most responsible person is an eight-year-old. It makes me understand Archer more. He's so protective and so hesitant to admit something bigger is going on with Sara. If she's having a hard time, I'm sure he will think it means he failed.

This is too heavy for late night thinking. I get out of bed and pad to the bathroom. A hot bath will help me relax. I slap on a face mask and fill my claw-foot tub, sprinkling salts and oil into the water. I grab the tray that clips to the edge of the tub and grab my iPad. If there's one thing I picked up from Mom, it was her love of dirty romance novels, but I doubt hers were of the gay variety. I flip through my e-books until

I come across the new gay romance I picked up. Then I settle into the water and begin reading.

A few pages in, I'm obsessed with the plot. It's a cowboy romance about a ranch hand and cowboy. The ranch hand knows he's attracted to the cowboy, but doesn't understand why. He's always been with women, even though he was never truly into it.

Oh, sweet ranch hand. That cowboy will figure you right out.

In my head, I picture my own face on the young ranch hand, and of course, it's Archer playing the role of the big, strong cowboy in ripped Levis and boots. It only takes a few chapters for the ranch hand and cowboy to be alone in a barn. The cowboy steps behind the ranch hand, close enough they almost touch.

My dick hardens under the water. My imagination has gone wild and I'm completely lost in the fantasy. It's ridiculous. I've never even stepped foot in a barn personally, but in my mind, Archer and I are there and he's going to do all sorts of dirty things to me.

The cowboy reaches around the ranch hand and grabs his junk, stroking him over the fabric of his jeans. The ranch hand's head lulls back on the cowboy's shoulder. I picture it perfectly in my mind. I'll bet Archer's big strong hand would have a tight grip.

I realize my growing problem will soon need to be taken care of. I dry off and climb back in bed. After another couple of pages, I'm imagining it's Archer unbuttoning my flannel and tying my hands behind my back with rope.

I reach for my nightstand and grab my vibrating, black silicone prostate massager. I slather it in lube and lie back with my legs spread. I insert it slowly and then turn it on. *Fuck, that feels good.* Having to abandon my book, I continue the fantasy in my head while pumping in and out with the massager and with my other hand, stroking myself.

I'll bet he has a big dick with thick veins and a large crown. It'd probably hurt at first, but I wouldn't care. I'd welcome the burning stretch because the one giving it to me is the sexiest man alive. I picture him fucking me from behind, using my roped hands as leverage.

My body shudders from head to toe and I come all over my hand, calling out Archer's name. I clean up and climb back into bed, my mind and body exhausted.

Archer may have friend zoned me, but my fantasies do not care even a little.

NINE

Archer

"**G**ood morning," I say when Sara comes out of her room. I got up with the kids this morning so she could get a little more sleep. I was also hoping it would ease my guilt when I ask if I can take off for the day. I know she doesn't expect me to be here all the time, but she shouldn't be alone in this.

"Hey. Thanks for taking care of these guys." She kisses both syrup coated kids on the cheek. "You didn't have to get up with them."

"I know. But you work late and we actually got to bed early last night, so I was up anyway."

Sara pours coffee and takes a seat at the kitchen island. The bruising under her eyes has gotten worse since I arrived and I've felt her pull back a lot since the day we fought about what Chad did to her on his way out. I decide now is as good a time as any to have the conversation I've been dreading.

"Kids, go wash up and head out back to play." I clear their plates and like the awesome kids they are, they do as I ask. When they're gone, I take a seat next to Sara. She keeps her eyes downcast into her murky coffee cup. "I think we need to talk."

"About what?" She spins her cup in circles, her leg bouncing rapidly.

"About what that Jax guy said. Did Chad hurt you?"

"He got a little out of control. It was my fault. I shouldn't have dumped all his stuff on the front lawn. It was hasty and dramatic."

"Did he hurt you?" I place a hand on her leg to stop the motion.

"Obviously he did or Jax wouldn't have been called out."

"Was it the first time?"

"Why does this matter? He's gone. Do you know he hasn't even tried to call the kids? Poor Lou keeps asking when his daddy is coming back to play basketball with him and I don't know what to say." A giant tear tumbles down her cheek and lands in her coffee.

"You tell him that his dad is making bad choices and you don't know if he's coming back. But, Sara, if he does, I swear to God, I'll beat his ass." The rage I have for any man who lays a hand on a woman is nothing compared to the man who laid a hand on my sister.

"I just don't know where he went. Or what I even did to make him leave in the first place. I thought everything was good. I mean, I know I could've been a better wife, but—"

"Don't give me that shit, Sara. You have two small kids. Whatever happened, he didn't have to step out on you and lock you out of your bank account. That's seriously fucked up." I jump to my feet. Needing something to do, I take her tear infused coffee and dump it. Then I pour her a new cup and set it in front of her. She's crying even harder now.

"You know he cancelled his cell phone? I don't even have a way of reaching him."

"You tried? Why would you do that, Sara? The best thing that asshole could've done is leave."

"No, it's not. I can't do this on my own. Taking care of the kids all day, working all night, laundry, cooking, shopping, it's too much for one person." She rests her head in her hands, full-on sobbing now.

"That's why I'm here. We survived our childhood and we'll survive now."

"You don't get it. I don't want to *just survive* anymore. This was supposed to be my happy ever after. You and I suffered so much as kids so we could have happiness as adults."

I sit down next to her and clasp her hands in mine. "This is one more hurdle we have to jump. It'll get better, I promise."

"I don't think it will. I think this is my life and I don't want it anymore."

I study her, trying to figure out just how serious she's being. People tend to say things like that, but don't mean it. They're just overwhelmed. Sara wouldn't leave Emmy and Lou motherless, so it must just be the hurt talking.

"I know it feels like that now. Just hang in there. Those kids need their mom to fight for her happiness."

"I've fought my whole life, Archer. Now? I'm just really tired." Her shoulders slump, like even the small amount of energy to keep her body upright is too much.

"You trust me, right?" I tip her chin up.

"You're the only one I trust in this whole world."

"Then believe me when I say it'll get better. I just got here. You haven't given me a chance to fix anything yet."

"Okay," she agrees.

"Okay? You'll hang in there? Keep going?"

"Yeah. Besides, someone has to stop you from buying dairy. I saw cheese in my fridge." Her lips tip up, but just barely.

"I told Emmy it was spicy so she wouldn't touch it." I walk over and tear a paper towel off the roll and hand it to her.

"Smart thinking." She blows her nose and dabs her eyes.

"Kian wants to have brunch this morning."

"You should go."

"He said he'd bring it here and make enough for all of us." I offer because if she doesn't want to be alone, I'll make sure she has company.

"No. You go. The kids have eaten and I'm a mess. I think I'll put some laundry in and then have a lazy day. I don't work tonight, so I have nowhere to be."

"You sure?" I look for any sign of dishonesty.

"I'm positive. Matter of fact, I'm going to stay in my pajamas all day." She brushes down her flannel PJs with the palms of her hands.

"Okay. I'll go say goodbye to the kids before I leave." I open the back door, but Sara calls me back.

"Thanks, big brother."

"Anytime."

Brunch with Kian is an experience. He has wooden boards with sliced fruit and French toast sticks, dipping sauces, cheeses, nuts, and I don't even know what else, sitting on his kitchen island when I walk in. It looks way too pretty to eat.

"This is something else," I say, taking in the immaculate spread.

"It's too much, isn't it?" He pops his hip out, crosses his arms over his chest, and taps a finger on his bottom lip. He looks comfortable in a ball cap pulled low, cotton cut-off gray sweats, and he has on some kind of a man crop top. A sliver of his abdomen is showing between his shirt and shorts.

It surprises me how attractive I find him. I've only dated men who have been equally matched in size and personality. I'm a switch and I tend to be most attracted to men who have that preference as well. Kian gives off bottom energy.

I need to stop thinking about him like that. We're friends. Just friends.

"What do you even call this?" I motion to the table.

"Charcuterie. You don't like it?"

"No, it's not that. I just don't know where to begin."

"Well, it depends. Are you a germophobe?"

"Not particularly."

"Then start eating. We don't even need plates." He approaches the platters that are decorated with sprigs of rosemary, a whole ass honeycomb, and edible flowers. He snags a slice of French toast, dips it in a fruit syrup, and pops it in his mouth.

"Okay." I hesitantly take a seat on a barstool and pick up my own French toast. I smear some roasted fig and drizzle it with honey before taking a bite. Goddamn. This guy may be insane, but he knows his finger foods. "This is beyond good."

"Right? I wasn't sure if it would be hearty enough. I debated adding bacon or whatever else you mammoths eat, but it would throw off the aesthetic, so I decided not to. I did buy some, though, if you want me to cook it up." He stands up, but I rest a hand on his forearm to stop him. Sparks prickle at our connection and I jerk my hand away.

Kian stares at his forearm, like he felt the jolt too. I immediately release him and tuck back into the food, ignoring what happened. This chemistry we share has to be ignored. I'm no good for anyone right now, let alone someone like Kian. He's good and pure and kind. He doesn't deserve to have my mess dirty him up.

"It's fine. This is plenty."

"So, are you adjusting to Maine? It must be such a change from Alaska."

"Yeah. It's good, though. I spent the last year of my life having a massive pity party for one, so it was good to get out. There wasn't anything left for me there."

"Still, must've been hard to walk away from everything that reminded you of your partner." His eyes turn downward as he absently plays with a blueberry that won't stay on his toast.

"It was." So hard, I bawled like a fucking baby. Not that I'll admit that to anyone, least of all the happiest guy in the world.

"Can you tell me about him?" He looks up through his lashes.

"Mason?"

"Yeah. I'd like to know more about the man who won over Archer Warren."

"He was a lot like you, actually. Not physically. Physically, he was more like me. But you have to be for the work we did."

"Okay, okay. No need to rub it in that I'm built like a noodle." He holds his skinny arms out.

"It's not a dig. Besides, you have your own attributes that make you attractive." *Particularly, your bubble butt that I find myself checking out more than I should.* I don't say that, though; it's not a friendly thing to say.

"Let's circle back around to that after you tell me about Mason." I like that he doesn't press me for specifics. It shows me he's interested in my life.

"It wasn't until she made it to college that I felt I could have my own life. I wanted a big adventure, something to make up for all the time I'd lost becoming a parent to my sister. I saw a wanted ad looking for a fisherman in Alaska. I didn't have experience, but when you apply for one of the most dangerous jobs in the world, they tend to let anyone in who's crazy enough to do it.

"I spent three years moving around from boat to boat, not fitting in until I met Adler and Mason. They were looking for a third person to pitch in on a boat and to build a company with. I handed over my entire savings and things were good for a long time. Really good. I made all my money back and kept a hefty amount in the bank. And I fell in love."

Kian smiles softly with his sideways grin, completely absorbed in my story. This is the part I like talking about, so I grin and pop an olive in my mouth before continuing.

"Mason was the nicest person you'd ever meet. One time he saw our neighbors broken down on the side of the road. I didn't want to stop because these people were terrible to us. There isn't much diversity in Alaska and they made it clear they weren't okay with having us living next door to them. But Mason insisted. He said the only way he was going to change their opinion was by showing them we're just regular guys." I grin, lost in the memory. "That was Mason, though. He didn't want to simply exist. He wanted to make a difference."

"He sounds like an awesome guy."

"He was also a little shit. Working out on the boat, we'd be out to sea for a long time on this tiny ass boat with our captain. We didn't argue often, but when we did, there was nowhere to escape. Our last trip out, he wanted to cut the season short because the weather was predicted to be rougher than normal. But I knew that meant our haul would be worth more since most other boats headed back early and supply would be low. We argued and I told him he was being dumb. Then I yelled at him to go away, that I'd finish banding the crab alone just to get a minute to myself. He stormed off the deck. When I was done, I went inside to find holes cut out of the big toe of all my socks. I was pissed and asked him why he would do that. Know what he said?"

Kian's leaned over, his chin propped in the palm of his hand, looking amused. "What?"

"He said he was so mad I wouldn't listen to reason. He wanted to do something mean, but his idea of cruel and mine are different. He didn't want me to get frostbite, but he also wanted to remind me of what an ass I was." I'm laughing so hard my eyes water now. "If it were me, I would've slashed the socks, made them so his feet would be frozen solid every day, but not Mason. He was such a nice person, the meanest thing he could think to do to me is make my big toe cold. Enough to make me uncomfortable, but not enough to hurt me."

"I love that. He sounds like my kind of person." We laugh together for a minute until I remember what else happened that trip. The smile falls from my lips in a blink of my eye. "What's wrong?" he asks.

"If I had listened to him and cut the trip short, he'd still be here. A week after that, he got twisted in a rope and was pulled out to sea." My lower lip quivers and I take a deep breath, fighting off the tears.

"Oh, honey." His lanky arms are around me in an instant and I tuck my face into his neck. I don't sob. I don't even cry. I just let the feelings of overwhelming heartbreak wash over me while this almost stranger comforts me. "You didn't know, Archer. There was no way to predict. And hearing about who Mason was, he wouldn't want you to feel guilty."

"It was one stupid decision," I say against his skin. "In my head, I know it wasn't intentional and it was just a dumb coincidence. But in my heart, I'm just so bitter with myself."

He pulls back and holds my shoulders at arm's distance. "Hearts are dumb. They feel without logic. They lie to us and convince us of things that aren't true."

"Every time I close my eyes, all I see is his expression. I've never seen such terror. The guilt that I'm still here and he's not eats up at me," I whimper. Kian doesn't deserve all of this being dumped on him, but he exudes understanding and caring. It draws my secrets out and makes me feel safe admitting it all.

I'm sure he's like this with everyone, but in this moment, he feels sent to me by a higher power to help me heal. It's a stupid thought, but I can't deny the strong pull I feel toward him. I haven't felt this kind of immediate connection to anyone since Mason.

"Of course you do. Anyone would. That was a hellish experience. But from what you told me, Mason wouldn't want you to spend every day of your life beating yourself up. You didn't die with him and he wouldn't want you to live like you did."

He's right, of course. Mason was full of life and vitality. He would hate to see me dwelling on his death day in and day out. I gently pull away from Kian and pull the neckline of my T-shirt over my face and dry my eyes.

"I'm sorry for all this. I didn't mean to ruin brunch. There's just something about you. I feel weirdly at ease."

"Because I remind you of your dead boyfriend?"

"That was very Rent of you." Picking up on his reference to the musical right away.

"You're a musical guy?"

"No. Not at all. More into action flicks. But Mason—"

"Of course he was. I think Mason and I would've been good friends," he says quietly.

"Me too." In a different life, I can imagine them being two peas in a pod. I take a look at the half-eaten boards. "Can I help you pack this up?"

"Sure."

We spend the next little while putting food in Tupperware. Some of it, he sets aside to send home with me for Sara and the kids. Including a dozen donuts he bought for in case he were to see them today.

"Can you stay for a while? I've got Minecraft on the Xbox," Kian suggests. "And I don't have to work tonight."

"Minecraft? Isn't that for third graders?"

Kian gasps. "That is the most offensive thing I've ever heard you say. Take a seat."

We sit side by side on his stupidly comfortable sofa, controllers in hand, and Kian takes me through the ins and outs of survival mode. Pretty soon, we're joking and laughing and I've forgotten how I almost ruined the day.

"The mob is coming for me." My fingers rapid fire on the controller, trying to kill the monsters before they get me.

"Go melee on his ass!" Kian stops what he's doing and cheers me on.

"How do I do that?" I scramble with the different functions.

"Here, let me help." Kian reaches between my arms, entwining us together. His thumbs cover mine and he dictates my movements. He's so close, I can smell the sweetness of the figs and honey on his breath. He's focused on leading me away from the monsters, but I'm focused on him. He didn't shave today, so he has a slight stubble on his cheeks and chin. His brows are knit in a serious way that has me grinning.

Suddenly his fingers stop moving and he slowly turns to me, our faces inches apart.

Oh shit.

TEN

Kian

I'm trying to kick some mob ass, when I realize Archer isn't even trying anymore. I feel his eyes scrutinizing me. I want to look over, but I also don't. He'll either freak out at our proximity, or something more will happen. I'm so attracted to this man, I can't stand it. But especially after today, I know he isn't ready.

Even if he's able to forget about his ghost for a few hours, he won't forget forever. And then where will that leave me? Heartbroken and with a rejection complex. My ego isn't fragile, but I'm smart enough to realize he has the power to hurt me.

Even so, I slowly turn toward him. The temptation is just too strong. I dare anyone be this close to Archer Warren and not do the same. It wouldn't be possible. We're magnets and our poles are drawn together.

That sounded dirty.

"You stopped playing. I think the mob got you," I say at a level just above a whisper.

"I think you're right," he says in the same tone.

"Are you going to kiss me?" My eyelids drop to half-mast. I hate myself for it, but the intimacy between us is a thick fog and I can't find my way through it.

"It's a bad idea." His thumb reaches up and brushes along my lower lip. "There was a speck of raw sugar."

I lick my lips. "It's a horrible idea."

"I hope you understand it's not because I don't like you."

"I know." And I do. He's fighting this thing between us as much as I am, but just because two people want to bone doesn't mean it should happen. Still, I find myself asking, "One kiss might not hurt."

"It would if it meant we couldn't be friends." His large hand wraps around my calf that's now folded in front of me.

"I can still be your friend. And it might just hold me off until maybe someday you're ready." I sound desperate. Maybe I am.

"What if I'm never ready?" I see the war in his eyes. He doesn't want to make a bad choice and here I am force-feeding it to him.

"Then a kiss is all we'll have." That's a sad thought.

"Are you sure?"

"Just do it." I barely get the last word out before his lips are on mine and his hand is cupping the back of my neck. I don't open for him and he doesn't demand entry. That's not what this is about. It's about him taking a small step in healing. I can be that guy for him. Even if it was only a kiss, I can help him.

Our lips press in a tight lock, our breaths mingle, and our noses mash together. It's the tamest kiss I've ever had, yet it's packed with so much more emotion than I've ever felt. Sadness, excitement, grief, longing, desire, it's all there even though we're not moving, not progressing. He holds me to him for what feels like an eternity and mere seconds at the same time.

He pulls away and rests his forehead to mine. "Thank you, Kian."

"Anytime." I smirk.

"I think I better go now." He stands up and grips my shoulder, facing away from me. "It was a good day."

"Don't forget to take the food." *Internal facepalm.* I just had the most intense experience of my life and I remind him about Tupperware. For fuck's sake.

I don't watch him pack up and leave. I only know he does by the sounds. The refrigerator opening and closing, his shoes scuffing across the tile, the squeaky hinge on the front door, and finally the click of the latch when it shuts.

I throw myself back on the couch and cover my face with a throw pillow that had been tossed on the ground. I scream into it, not from anger but frustration. I'm sporting a chub and while I'd like nothing more than to release the pressure, it won't matter. What my dick really wants just walked out the door.

After two full days of no work, I'm ready to be back. Time off isn't good for my chaotic mind. I unlock the door to Focus and flip on the lights. Duke follows me in and without a word, making his way to the kitchen.

"Hello to you, too," I call after him, but only get a grunt in return. He's so cranky.

I check my phone to see if I have any new messages before going through my opening duties. Surprisingly enough, Archer didn't disappear after our kiss. He texted me that night and throughout the day yesterday. We didn't mention what happened, but chatted about what we were doing, sending pics back and forth. He sent me a snap of Lou pushing Emmy on a swing and I sent him a pic of a new plant I picked up that I named Brenda.

It was fun and casual. And friendly. Extremely friendly. Which is good because I predicted Archer having a massive freak-out and never talking to me again after our lip-lock.

I smile when I see a waiting text.

Archer: How's Brenda?

Me: She's a sassy bitch, but she's settling into her new home.

Archer: You at work?

Me: Yep. Just got here. Prepping for Sara and then going to the club. It's too bad you're on gunkle duty or you could come hang out.

Archer: Maybe later this week, I could ask the neighbor to come babysit for a few hours.

Me: You'd want to do that?

Archer: Sure. I haven't been out in ages. If BFB is going to be my new home, I might as well get familiar with the locals.

Me: That's a whole can of worms you're opening. The men of Brigs Ferry will be all over your fresh meat.

Archer: Is that a euphemism?

Me: Yep.

Archer: I'll talk to Sara about it. Surely the owner of the club could keep me safe.

I'm tempted to tell him I can't keep him safe if I'm the one who wants his meat, but that goes against our friendly boundaries, so I shoot him a ninja emoji and lock my screen, tucking my phone in my back pocket.

I've just flipped the neon sign to open when Jarrett comes in, Fernando in tow.

"Just the guys I need to see," I greet.

"First, pinot, then talk," Jarrett says, both of them taking a seat at the bar.

"On it." I take out three wine glasses. I'll need it to get through this conversation. I give us each a healthy portion, watching Jarrett's eyes widen.

"This must be juicy if you're being generous with your pour." He accepts the glass and takes a long drink. "Now spill."

I explain every detail of what's been going on between Archer and me. Of all my friends, Jarrett is the most levelheaded and Fernando is the most loyal. I can count on them to give it to me straight. When I'm finally done, I drink half my glass of wine in one gulp, readying myself for the honesty about to smack me in the face.

"I don't know, Kian. This sounds like a bad idea," Fernando responds first. "But I think you're aware of that."

"I know what I'm getting myself into. It's not ideal, but I can handle it. Besides, it was one kiss and now we're back to being strictly friends."

"Pfft." Jarrett huffs. "Can we just get beyond all the bullshit? You have feelings for this guy."

"He has feelings for me too," I defend.

"It doesn't matter. You're in a place in your life where you're ready for feelings. He's not. That puts you on an uneven playing field."

"I agree with Jarrett," Fernando says. "You're playing two different games with two different goals."

"Can we stop using sports references? I don't understand them." I distract from the conversation. I know what they're saying, I just don't want to hear it.

The door opens then and Sara walks in, head down with the same disheveled appearance from last week. Archer said she's been sad, but he's not concerned. He's being naive to her situation, but like he's pointed out to me more than once, I don't know her like he does.

"Hey, honey. How are you?"

"Fine. Good," she rushes out.

"It's our favorite bartender," Jarrett calls out and I scowl at him. "Don't get your panties in a twist. She's nicer than you. More attentive."

"That's because you guys are shit tippers."

"They always tip me well," Sara adds in with a tiny grin. It's good to see, so I let the jab slide.

"Obviously I'm not needed here anymore. Time for me to

escape to the den of sin." I wave at my friends. "Let's do coffee soon."

"Okay. Stop by the store, I got a new plant stand I think you'd like. I stripped it and painted it baby pink," Jarrett calls after me.

"Will do." I direct my gaze to Sara. "Call me if you need anything."

"I always do."

Next door, the place is bumping, but I lock myself in my office after making the rounds and checking in with my staff. The front of the house takes care of itself between managers and solid employees. I rarely am needed at all, the only reason I choose to open Focus up each night is because that's when my friends usually pop in. Otherwise, I'd hire someone to work that shift too.

I touch the screen of my phone, planning to answer some emails, but find a waiting text. It's a picture from Archer. He has a fort made in Sara's living room and he and the kids are tucked in, waving at the camera. Archer's smile is blinding, even from underneath his thick beard. It reminds me of what it felt like to have those whiskers pressed against me. They're rough and prickly, but not in an uncomfortable way. In a way you hope it leaves abrasions on your skin so you can remember them for a few days.

I decide to call versus text back.

"Hey," he answers on the first ring. The background is chaotic and that's coming from someone who owns a gay club.

"Hey yourself. That's a badass fort you guys made."

"It is. We've just added cardboard boxes to the sides for stability. Emmy kept yanking the sheets down."

"Did not," a tiny voice hollers.

"Did too," another tiny voice hollers back.

"Guys, quit. We've gone over this. Emmy, you did pull it down. Lou, it wasn't her fault. That's why we put up the walls," Archer chides.

"Oh, daddy. Your stern voice is super sexy," I tease.

"If being a part-time gunkle, as you put it, has shown me anything, it's that I don't want to be a daddy." I can almost hear him running a hand through his hair.

"I hear ya. Kids are cute and all, but they're dirty and mouthy."

"Yep. Both of those."

"I'm calling to see if you made any progress on finding a free night this week. I need to make sure I get all my work done, so I can hang out with you and protect you from the locals." It's the truth. There's no way I'm setting him free on the dance floor without me. We may only be friends, but he's still mine.

"Yep. I got the neighbor to agree to Thursday. That work for you?"

"Perfect."

"See you then. Bye, Kian." There's amusement in his voice. I love the way it sounds.

"Bye."

I dive into work, only going home after the lights in the club turn off and the music quiets. Nothing like a little Archer induced motivation to get my ass in gear. One more night and I'll be completely caught up and ready to introduce him to my world.

Hope he's ready.

ELEVEN

Archer

When I say I only have band tees, jeans, and rubber overalls in my closet, I mean it. So when I wake up on Thursday, I go to town in an attempt to find something more stylish for a club. I've never actually been to a club. I spent my teen years taking care of my sister, and my twenties and thirties in remote Alaskan villages where their idea of a fun weekend was assembly line preparing muktuk to store for winter months when fresh food was harder to come by.

Sara informed me the only clothing shop around here is Belle's Boutique. The name alone tells me I can't expect too much. Still, I'm not prepared when I walk in the door. Sequins and sparkles in all colors assault my eyes. Dresses and pant suits hang from every surface. This was a mistake. I turn around to walk out, prepared to resort to wearing jeans and a tee tonight.

"Yoo-hoo," a high-pitched trill calls out to me. I flip back around to see a large and colorful woman walking right for me. She's wearing a glittery baby blue pant suit. She doesn't have a shirt on underneath the buttoned-up blazer, so her massive tits are on full display and bounce with each step she takes. It's a lot to ask of the buttons holding those things in. "Oh my. You're a tall drink of water."

"Oh, hi. I'm sorry. I think I'm in the wrong place."

"What were you looking for? A sixty-year-old woman who's in her sexual prime?"

I choke on my own spit. "Men's clothing."

"That's too bad, but you're still in the right place. We have a whole section in the back just for men." She points in the direction. I can faintly see some clothing with more muted colors. "I'm Belle. This is my shop. Follow me, I'll show you around."

I follow Belle through racks of clothes that I think would fit in more if we were in Texas. Definitely not a sleepy town in Maine that has an overwhelming amount of gay men.

"How's this?" Belle motions to a small section of closet staples.

"Might work." I flip through the first rack I come to.

"What's the occasion?" She chomps down on a wad of gum, bringing my attention to her shiny red lips. Everything about this woman is flashy, from her colorful eye makeup to her long, fake eyelashes.

"I'm checking out a club tonight, but I only own this." I motion to my underwhelming outfit.

"You must be talking about Blur. I just love it there. Me and my girlfriends go at least once a month."

"Cool," I drawl out dumbly.

"We don't run into men like you, though. Maybe I'll have to call the ladies and make a trip out tonight, show you how it's done." She shimmies her massive bosom. I'm positive those things could suffocate a man.

"I'm meeting someone there. A man." I specify.

"That's too bad. Oh! You should find Kian when you get there. He's the one who owns the club. Tell him Belle sent you and he'll take good care of you. He's the sweetest. Maybe a little on the gossipy side. He always knows everything before everyone else." Her face falls slightly. "Like when my cheating ex-husband was sleeping with that hussy from Bar Harbor." Except it comes out Bah Hahbah. Maine locals must have a vendetta against the R sound.

"That's actually who I'm meeting." I admit because while Kian knows a lot about me, I can't say the same about him. This lady seems like she'd tell me anything.

"Wicked." She claps her hands. "Kian always has been a man's man. Does that mean the same thing as a lady's man?"

Interesting. So Kian gets around, huh? My duplicitous mind feeds me thoughts like, *maybe we could be friends with benefits.* And, *you haven't been laid in so long, wouldn't it be nice to at least get sucked off?*

"I'm not sure if it means the same thing, to be honest." I ignore the rest of what she said.

"Either way, cute boy like him has been known to break a few hearts." She watches me flip through the hangers of clothes. I have no idea what I'm looking for. My style is absence of style. On a linear chart, I have negative style. "Can I make a suggestion?"

"I guess."

"You work at the fishing dock, right?"

"How did you know?" I ask, but immediately want to take it back. Small town.

"I could pretend I knew because of your rough hands, but won't lie. Jarrett told me about you when I went hunting for an antique clock for my mama last week." I look down at my calloused fingers and palms. They're dry as fuck from working with saltwater and fish. "Anyway, this looks like something you might feel comfortable in."

I take a plain white button-down and brown distressed leather vest from her. Surprisingly, she's right. I do like it. "This actually might work."

"I know it will. It's manly and stylish. Kian will love it."

"It's not like that. We're friends."

She flashes me a discerning look. "You kids are always keeping things casual these days."

"Do I just wear jeans with it?" I skip right over her comment. I don't think she'd believe me anyway.

"Yeah. Blur isn't fancy or anything."

"Okay. I'll take them."

I check out and wave goodbye to the eccentric woman.

I walk into Focus first, wanting to catch Sara in action. She's busy jotting down an order from a couple at a bistro table by the window, so I take a seat at the bar. I was impressed with the bar the first time I saw it, but now that I know Kian better, I'm even more in awe that someone his age could pull off something so classy.

"Hey." Sara appears from behind the bar. She looks like shit. She didn't even put on her normal makeup to cover up the circles under her eyes. I feel like an asshole. She's so tired and worn out. I should be doing more to help her. "Come to check up on me?"

"No. Just wanted to say hi before going next door."

"Were the kids okay when you left?"

"Yep. They were on the couch watching a movie. I think they'll be perfect angels."

"Good. You want a drink while you're here?"

"Sure."

She doesn't even ask what I want; she knows I only drink Scotch whisky. I'm thankful Kian keeps it stocked. She watches me curiously while she pours. She didn't say much when I told her my plan for the evening.

"What?" I ask.

"This thing between you and Kian, is it more than friendship?"

"No," I say right away, but the kiss we shared flashes through my mind. It was stupid. I shouldn't have done it. I was so desperate to feel something for another person, I lost myself. It's all on me, though. I don't blame Kian one bit. If anything, I feel guilty for doing that to him when I know he feels more than friendly toward me. I tried to make it up to him by purposefully not letting things get weird.

"Does he know that?"

"Yes, mom. He knows."

"Maybe it should be more." She suggests. "You deserve happiness."

"I don't think I'm ready for that."

"I don't think you'll ever be ready if you don't push yourself. You were happy once. You can get there again."

"I'll think about it."

She shakes her head disappointedly as she wipes down the bar, then says, "I've got to get back to my tables. Let me know if you need anything else."

"I mean it, Sara. I won't fuck this job up for you."

"It's not the job I'm worried about. It's you that has me concerned."

"You're one to talk." I deflect, but realize my mistake when her face falls.

"My husband left me a month ago. I don't know where he is or if he's coming back. We had years together, Archer. Years," she bites out through clenched teeth. Her eyes well with tears, making me feel like the asshole I am.

"I'm sorry. That's not what I meant. I just mean, you should get out. Find some friends. Do something for yourself besides sleep."

"I'm not having this conversation with you. Please just go and have fun. I'll see you later." She takes a calming breath and walks over to a table of customers.

I chug my drink, mentally kicking my own ass. I don't know how to talk to her. Every time I mention how depressed she seems, she snaps at me. She's withdrawing from life more and more. She's short with the kids, which makes them sad. The atmosphere in the house is full of doom and gloom, and I don't know how to fix it. Especially when I'm a contributing factor.

I leave without saying another word, walking the few steps next door. The second the door opens, I'm hit by the rumbling bass of the music. A large man stands at the door, shirtless, behind a podium. He lift his chin at me.

"There's a ten-dollar cover," he advises me. I reach into my pocket, but before I can hand over the cash, Kian is rushing from behind two thick black curtains that separate the entrance from the club.

"It's cool, Steve. He's a guest." Kian smiles hugely at me. My mouth waters at his appearance. He's wearing a tight tan T-shirt that shows just how trim his chest and arms are and tan plaid trousers that are just as fitted and hug his package like a glove. For a slight man, he's either stuffing or he's endowed.

Fuck. I miss sex.

"Hey," I say.

"You look good. I love this." He tugs on the end of my vest.

"It's new."

His eyes widen. "Please tell me you went to Belle's."

"I did."

"Oh my God, I'll bet she loved you. That dirty old woman." He chuckles and pulls back the curtains. "Come on in. I saved us a booth."

I step through and take in the space. The club is small, lined with booths along the perimeter except for one side that has a long bar stretched down its length. Behind the bar are backlit panes of neon-colored glass that illuminate the bottles of liquor that sit on the shelves. Simple black stools line a shiny black bar with the same backlit panels of neon glass. Strobe lights blast flashes of neon-colored lights and a barely-there fog floats around the dance floor in the center of the room. An electronic mix of Madonna's, "Like a Virgin" plays loudly.

I lean into Kian and say, "This is cool. I love it."

He beams at me. "Thank you. I love Focus, but this is my pride and joy. Follow me."

We make a stop at the bar where he orders some kind of pink bubbly champagne with floating fruit for himself and a whiskey ginger for me. He remembered my drink. Then I follow him over to a booth with a comfy padded bench. He takes one side and I take the other.

I people watch for a minute, taking in the dancing crowd. It's not packed, but there's enough people that you could be on the dance floor without feeling self-conscious. It's mostly men, but there are a few groups of girls, too. They all look so free, like the world isn't a shithole for them. I remember that feeling.

Kian says something, but I can't hear him over the music. I hold a hand to my ear in the international sign for *I can't hear you*. I lean in, but I still don't catch what he says. He rolls his eyes and moves over to my side of the booth.

"That's better," he shouts. "You must be losing your hearing in your old age."

"Hey, a couple days ago you were telling me I wasn't old."

"That was before I knew you needed a hearing aid." He smirks.

"You won't be saying that when you see my moves."

"Oh really? You ready to show me those moves?" His eyebrow quirks challengingly.

I lift my drink to my lips and throw it back. It goes down easy and I motion for him to get up from the booth. He grabs my hand and tugs me to the center of the floor. Everyone we pass gives Kian a greeting ranging from a hug to a kiss on the cheek. He seems to know everyone personally, especially the men. A pang of something hits my gut. I don't like it. I wonder how many of these men he's slept with. It's none of my business and I don't ask. It's just petty curiosity.

When he's done saying hi to everyone, he faces me fully and motions up and down my body. "I'm ready."

I shift from side to side, feeling dumb. I give up the ruse and lean into him. "I was lying. I don't dance. I thought I could figure it out, but I have no idea what I'm doing."

He laughs. "Well, guess you're about to get a lesson."

Kian moves with the music, rolling his hips provocatively. His hands roam around his body from his neck, down his chest and around his hips. It's sexy as fuck. I completely forget he's trying to teach me and just watch him. He's so at ease with his movement. Like with everything he does, he exudes confidence.

"Your turn," he shouts, pointing at me.

Awkwardly, I sway to what I think is the beat. Kian looks like a mix between amused and horrified. I freeze, not wanting to embarrass myself. I move to walk off the floor, but Kian stops me with a hand to my forearm.

"Come here," he says. I allow him to pull me close, his hands resting on my hips. We aren't touching, but almost. I feel the heat coming from his body, smell his sweetly spiced cologne, and see the twinkle of mischief in his eyes. "Follow what I do."

His hips move in a figure eight and he guides me to do the same. I still feel dumb with my arms hanging limply at my side, so I place them on his shoulders. He works himself closer until our pelvises are pressed together. I pray I don't get a hard-on. It's been too long since I've been this close to anyone.

"That's good. Now try this." He bends at the knees and rolls his body until he's upright again. This doesn't seem like something I should try for the first time with an audience, but the drinks have loosened me up, so I give it a try. Kian bites his lower lip and drags his teeth slowly across the flesh in a move so sexy, I lose my balance. I take a step back before I fall over.

I rock from side to side and watch as he goes all out with his movements. He could be on a stage with his facial expressions and the way he moves his body. He's beautiful and sexual and fucking enticing. The way his hips thrust and his torso rolls. Kian is a goddamn visual orgasm.

After a minute, the song turns into a slow and sensual beat. He breaks his dancing queen character and smiles over at me. I move to stand behind him, intoxicated by the whiskey and his body. I wrap an arm around his middle and pull until his ass is nestled against me. I don't know what I'm doing, but when do I ever when it comes to this man.

I let his movements guide us. I palm his hard abs while his hands reach behind him and roam every inch of my body he can touch. With a slower song, it's so much easier for me to keep up. Beads of sweat pop up on the back of his neck and along his hairline. I get the urge to lick the droplets up, but I use every last ounce of self-control not to.

I'll bet he tastes like sex and sin. Like a drug I'd never quit once I started.

TWELVE

Kian

Archer is the king of mixed messages. His lips tell me just friends, but his body? His body tells me we'll be fucking within the next ten minutes. And because I'm a horny idiot, I ignore his words and believe the hard-on that's currently pressed against my ass.

He can't dance. At all. Even right now while he's following my lead, he's jerky and uncoordinated. It would be a pity if that translated to the bedroom. I always thought you could tell a lot about a man's performance by the way he dances. I've never wanted to be wrong more than in this moment.

He grips the fabric of my shirt in one hand, while the other clutches my hip, pulling me even closer to him. His nose brushes the shell of my ear, causing goose bumps to rise all over my body. I don't want this moment to end. I want to live in this imaginary world where he's not going to change his mind and push me away.

It's a stupid game I'm playing because I know this ends with him hurting me. It's like videos I've seen of people running with the bulls. They know it'll most likely end with horns puncturing their spleen, but those idiots show up anyway. That's me right now. I'm aroused and excited, but my proverbial spleen is about to get obliterated.

I turn around, circling my arms around his neck. Our eyes meet and hold. I try to read where his mind is at, but all I see are more lies. His brown orbs dance with mirth and sparkle with slight intoxication. His palms rest dangerously low on my lower back. A couple centimeters and he'd have a handful of my ass.

Like he knows what I'm thinking, they slip lower. Tingles of anticipation claim my lower half.

"What are we doing?" I ask before I give myself permission to feel all the things barking at my door, begging to be let in.

"I honestly don't know," he shouts, not looking away and finally exposing the uncertainty he's been hiding.

"Want to go to my office and talk?"

"Sure."

I lead him up the stairs and punch the code into my office door, letting him enter first. There's nothing special about the space. A desk, a laptop, a bookcase, a file cabinet, and a leather sofa are the only furniture. I had the walls painted the deepest of blacks throughout the entire club, including my office, making them feel like they're not there at all. Like oblivion is the only thing surrounding you.

The door clicks shut, silencing most of the pounding bass from the club. The instantaneous sound change is striking. Archer saunters over to the large window that looks down at the dance floor. It's a one-way mirror, so while we can see out, no one can see in.

"I feel voyeuristic watching everyone," he muses.

"It's kind of a thrill, right?" I stand next to him, our shoulders touching.

"It is. I didn't know I was into this sort of thing." He chuckles.

Our eyes meet at the same moment and whatever conversation we have, we must come to the same understanding because in less than a heartbeat, we're on each other. He backs me up against the window and grips my jaw between his thumb and forefinger, bringing our lips together. Unlike the other day when we just held them there, tonight, we don't stay still for even a second. It's a race to experience each other all at once. He tastes of sweet Scotch whisky and spicy ginger from his drink and like a desperate alcoholic, I suck it from his tongue.

I touch him everywhere over his clothes, but I need more. I already know his hands are rough from labor, but I'm desperate to know what the rest of him feels like. I reach under his shirt, letting my fingers explore his strong abs and run through the patch hair on his chest. Every inch of him is hard and muscled. If I weren't so lost in sensation, I might get a little self-conscious about how thin and soft I am. In this moment, though, I don't care.

Still squeezing my jaw, he turns my head to the side and latches onto my earlobe, flicking it with the tip of his tongue. I imagine him doing that same move on the tip of my dick and I harden even more than I was before. He kisses down my neck and then lets go of me completely. I'm a little stunned, but not for long because he yanks my shirt over my head and tosses it behind him.

He bites his lip and regards me with lust in his eyes. His fingertips drag down my chest. He brushes his thumbs over my nipples and then moves lower. With the waistband of my pants in his grip, he pulls me back to him.

Our lips meet again, our tongues dancing and dueling in harmony. But if I'm shirtless, giving him full access to me, I want the same.

"Take this off," I murmur against his mouth, tugging on the hem of his shirt.

With a cocky smirk, he yanks it over his head, letting it join mine. Skin to skin, our torsos meet and it's sexy as fuck. I kiss and touch my way down his chest and abdomen, slowly lowering to my knees. I unbutton and unzip his jeans, not daring to look up. If I saw anything but undeniable lust, I'd lose my confidence and call this whole thing off.

"Kian," he says breathily. "Look at me. You have the most

gorgeous eyes I've ever seen. I want to see them while your mouth is wrapped around my cock."

Well, shit.

I slowly raise my eyes, scanning every inch of him on my way up, and goddamn it, what I see has me wanting him to bend me over and fuck me six ways from Sunday.

After the loss of his partner, I was worried if we ever got in the place where we were intimate, there would be three of us in the room together. But Mason isn't here with us at all. Archer's one hundred percent here with me.

I get back to work, first pulling his jeans down to his thighs, followed by his gray boxer briefs. His hard cock springs free and it's everything I expected. Long, thick, and with a fat head oozing with pre-cum. I take it in my hand and lick up the underside until I reach the tip. I swirl my tongue around it, savoring the salty taste.

"Fuck. You have no idea how incredible that feels," he moans.

His praise urges me on and I wrap my lips around him. He rests a hand on the back of my head, letting me know what he wants. He doesn't have to ask twice. I bob up and down, taking him as far as I can without choking. A growl escapes him from deep in his chest. It's music to my ears. So much better than what they're playing downstairs. This song I could never tire of, no matter how often I heard it.

He thrusts his hips forward once and then takes a step back. "Your skilled mouth feels like heaven, but any more and I'll coming in your mouth. That's not what I had in mind."

"What did you have in mind?" I flirt.

"Take off your pants." He commands while kicking his shoes off and removing his jeans and underwear completely. He's like a Greek god, chiseled from stone.

Like a soldier following orders, I hastily divest myself of my shoes and pants. I don't wear underwear, so I'm left fully nude. He stalks toward me, spins me around, and pushes me toward the glass. He takes my hands in his and flattens my palms on the cool surface. My eyes scan the crowd. I know they can't see us, but with how clearly I see every detail of them, it plays tricks on my mind and heightens my arousal.

"You have lube and condoms in here somewhere?" he speaks softly against my ear.

"Top drawer of my desk."

He's back within seconds. I hear the cap of the lube pop open and then a squirting noise. He kicks my legs apart and pulls up on my hips, popping my ass out. Then, his fingers are working their way between my cheeks and rubbing circles around my hole. I gasp. It feels exquisite. He's so dominant and forceful.

"How long?"

"Um." I look down at my dick, not knowing what else he could be talking about. "I've never measured before, but maybe six or so inches?"

He chuckles. "I mean, how long has it been since the last time you fucked?"

My cheeks heat. I'm such an idiot. "Oh, uh." I do mental calculations. "Six months, maybe? But you won't hurt me. I, um, like to play with toys."

"Fuck, I need to see that sometime." One finger enters me slowly, pumping in and out. He must be satisfied, because then there's two. And then three. His cock is girthy, so I appreciate the preparation.

He pulls out and I hear the foil of the condom wrapper being torn open and then again, a squirt of lube. The anticipation is killing me. I need this now and he's taking too long. I drag my hand down the glass and then over to my aching dick. I need stimulation. Now.

"What did I say?" He places my hand back on the glass. "When you're alone, this is yours. But when you're with me, it's mine."

He wraps his calloused hand around my dick and pumps

me a few times. My eyes roll back into my head in ecstasy. With his other hand, he guides himself to my asshole and at a snail's pace, inches forward. It burns a little, but I associate that feeling with pleasure, so all it does is excite me.

When he's finally balls deep, he says, "You okay?"

"No, not okay. Amazing," I keen.

He thrusts in and out, slowly picking up speed each time he enters me. All the while, he jerks me off, staying in rhythm with his fucking. Then he does something that makes me lose my mind. He bends his knees to reach an angle that has him bumping against my prostate. I moan and whine. My balls tighten, preparing to release.

"Shit. When you clench like that, you strangle my cock. You're making me want to come," he grits out.

"Do it. I'm almost there."

He picks up the pace, his grip tightening around my dick. It's all I needed. I come. Hard. My eyes squeeze tight and my head falls back, and my breaths coming out in short spurts. Archer lets out a series of expletives that tell me he's coming too, and it intensifies my orgasm to know we're experiencing the same thing at the same time.

He thrusts into me three more times, holding himself deep inside each time and grunting from deep in his chest. When he finally pulls out, I sink to the floor, collapsing onto my back. He does the same, falling next to me on the tightly woven carpet. He drapes his arm over my stomach and strokes my sweat damp skin.

"That's a sight." I turn to the window and see my cum dripping down the glass.

Archer takes notice too. "I'll get it. I've got to ditch the condom anyway. You have cleaning supplies in here?"

"On the bottom shelf of the bookcase." I'm glad he offered because I'm boneless and sated.

Groaning, he peels himself from the ground and disposes of the condom. I watch as he finds window cleaner and a paper towel. With him facing away and bending, I get a delightful view of his ass. Next time, I'll make sure we fuck face to face so I can get a handful.

If there is a next time.

"Thank you. I guess I better get up, too."

Nothing is said while we dress, but our thoughts are loud enough to cause hearing loss. I just wish I could read his mind. I don't want to say I can't wait for next time if he's going to tell me that can't happen again, and I don't want to tell him we should just be friends if he wants to keep going.

Being gay isn't a choice, but if it were, I'd choose girls. They don't let you go too long before telling you exactly how they feel while men leave me guessing all the time.

"We didn't get a chance to talk." I pull on my T-shirt.

"Our bodies had a lot to say." He shrugs.

"True. And I loved it. Don't get me wrong. But I was hoping we could use some words, too."

He rubs at the back of his neck, looking uncomfortable. "What should we talk about?"

"Want to sit?" I motion to the sofa and take a seat. He reluctantly follows. "We agreed to be friends, but we had sex."

"I noticed." He rests his ankle on his knee and leans back.

"What does this mean?"

"What do you want it to mean?"

"I like you, Archer. A lot. I know you're kind of a mess and probably not ready to hear that, but I do."

He blows out a breath, uncrossing his legs and leaning forward on his knees. "I like you, too. I don't want to and the timing is all wrong. That's why I'd like to keep this casual."

"Okay." The disappointment hits me right in the heart. I was expecting it. It was stupid to hope for anything else.

"I mean it, Kian. You're a great guy and I'm obviously attracted to you. It's cliché, but it really is me, not you." He takes my hands in his. "I can't make promises. If that's not something you can handle, I understand. If it is, I'd like to keep seeing you. Hanging out and if more occasionally happens, then it does. You have to know it won't lead to anything, though. At least not in the foreseeable future."

I think about it for a long moment. Why do I think I want a commitment anyway? I'm the casual king. Ever since what happened with Jax, I haven't wanted anyone for more than a night or two.

"Good thing for both of us, I'm an expert at casual. I haven't had a boyfriend since high school." The confidence I'd been lacking, fills me once again and I'm back to myself. I'm not relationship material. I'm young, I'm hot, and I shouldn't want to be tied down anyway. This will work. I've got this.

Archer smiles, stealing my breath with his full set of white teeth and sparkling eyes. "Then we agree."

"We do."

"Unfortunately, I've got to go relieve the sitter." We both stand and he leans down, kissing me soft on the mouth. "Text me tomorrow. We can make plans."

"Okay."

He leaves and I fall back onto my couch, an ache in my ass and a happiness in my heart.

THIRTEEN

Archer

"Archer." A tiny hand shakes my shoulder, waking me up. "Wake up!"

I pry my eyes open. "Lou. What time is it?"

"It's morning time. The sun is awake."

"I see that." I look at the time on my phone. Six-thirty. "Is your sister up?"

"Not yet. Want me to wake her up?"

"God, no." I grab his hand and drag him into bed. "Why don't we snuggle for a minute?"

He makes it all of two seconds before he's squirming to get away. "This is boring. Let's go make pancakes."

"How about you watch a show on my phone for a minute?" I try, pulling Netflix up and clicking on a kid's show.

He greedily accepts the device and is instantly sucked in. I sigh in relief. Mornings have gotten hard for Sara, so on the weekends, when I'm not working, I wake up with the kids to give her more time to sleep. I hope by resting more, she'll snap out of this ongoing depression and feel more like herself.

It's not normally an issue for me to be one to wake up first, but after a few drinks, fucking Kian, and then coming home and lying awake for hours beating myself up, I'm exhausted.

With a liquid confidence flooding my system, being with Kian wasn't even a choice. He was so responsive, like putty in my hands. However, when it wore off and I was alone, I wasn't so sure. I scoured my memories of Mason, looking for a conversation that'd give me a clue about how he'd feel in a situation like this. There wasn't anything there. We didn't talk about death, we only talked about our life and our future.

How stupidly optimistic of us.

Then, I thought about how I'd feel if the roles were reversed. I think I'd want him to move on. I'd want him to fulfill all of his dreams, especially if the one of us growing old together would never come true.

That was the only thought that finally allowed me enough peace to fall asleep. Unfortunately, that was only three hours ago and now I'm playing fun gunkle until Sara wakes up.

I doze on and off for another hour with Lou entertained next to me until Emmy joins us. After that, all bets are off and they grumble about breakfast nonstop until I agree to get up. We make pancakes, get dressed for the day, and even play in the backyard. Still, Sara doesn't come out of her room.

By lunchtime, I'm knocking on her door. She's not in bed, but her en suite bathroom door is closed. I stick my ear to the door and hear her crying. It kills me she's still hurting so much.

I knock and hear her blow her nose before responding. "Just a minute."

I set the kids up in the living room with a show and a snack, then return to Sara's room. She's sitting on her bed, wad of tissues in her fist, papers resting on her lap, and she's staring out her window.

"Bad morning, huh?"

"Yeah. Sorry. I'll just take a quick shower and then I'll take over."

I take a seat next to her and wrap an arm around her shoulders. "The kids are fine. It's you I'm worried about. You've been sleeping more and more. You hardly ever smile."

"I'm sad, Archer. I try not to be, I do." She rests her head on my shoulder. "I got these in the mail yesterday. I couldn't bring myself to open them until I got home last night."

I take the papers from her and quickly read through them. "Divorce papers?"

"Yes. He doesn't even want parental rights, Archer. It's like he wants to walk away from his entire life and start over. How can he do that?" Her voice trembles.

"It's probably for the best. You don't want the kids growing up with his influence." I try to reason.

"You don't get it." She jumps up, pacing. "We had a life together and now we're trash to him. He's throwing us out for a new model."

"I do get it, but if he's going to walk away, it's best he doesn't do that with the kids."

"It's my fault my kids are going to grow up without a dad. If I'd tried harder, made him more of a priority."

"Sara! Listen to yourself. This wasn't your fault. He's an asshole. If he wanted to find a way out, he would do that regardless of what you did."

"I just need to be alone for a while. Can you please take care of the kids?" She wraps her arms around herself and turns back to the window.

"Maybe you should do something fun with them today. Get out of the house." I suggest.

"Not right now."

I know I'm not going to change her mind. Instead, I pack the kids a lunch and we walk to the park for a picnic. While they chase each other around and go down the slide a hundred times each, I think about how to best help my sister.

We've discussed finding a therapist. She objected and turned it around on me, telling me I should see a professional also. While I don't deny that things have been rough for me, I'm coming out of the depression I've spent the last year living in. I'm not all the way there, I still have my issues, but at least I'm trying. Sara seems to be pulled further down every day. It scares me, but I can't force her to do anything about it.

"Archer, push!" Emmy calls out from in front of the swing. She tries to heft herself up, grunting as she struggles to get her knee on the rubber strip of the swing. I chuckle and jump up to help.

"Hold on, tiny tot. I'm coming."

The next couple days fly by. Between working at the docks and taking care of the kids, I barely have time to think. Sara retreats inside herself more and more. She won't talk about the divorce or finding a lawyer. I come home from work to find the house a mess, the kids staring at the TV, and her buried under blankets on her bed.

I want to help her, but I have no idea how. By the time Saturday rolls around, I get the idea to ask Kian how she's been at work. We've been texting all week, mostly at night after I get the kids to bed. We have very different schedules, so we haven't seen each other, but with Sunday and Monday being his off days, I'm hoping to rectify that.

"Hello," he answers on the first ring.

"Hey."

"It's my favorite fisherman. How are you?"

"I'm fine. Just got the kids up and ready."

"You sound like such a housewife," he teases.

"I feel like one lately. That's kind of why I'm calling."

"What's up? Need to borrow my feather duster?"

"Maybe, but that's not why I called." I fix my third cup of coffee for the day and go outside where I can watch the kids play in the backyard. Sara is still sleeping. She's always sleeping.

"Go on."

"It's Sara. She's been a little sad lately and I was wondering how she's been at work."

"I'm taking it she isn't a ray of sunshine for you either?"

"I'm worried about her." I admit.

"Want me to talk to her? I don't know her well, so maybe she'll respond better to me saying something."

"If you do, don't tell her I told you to. God knows she doesn't need more reasons to yell at me." I scratch my fingers through my beard.

"No problem. I'm an expert at forcing conversations."

"I've noticed that about you." I chuckle.

"What else have you noticed about me?" His voice turns flirty.

"Why don't we get together this weekend and I'll show you in person?"

"It's my ass, huh? It's always my ass."

"It is pretty perky."

"What does perky mean?" Emmy appears at my side.

"Oops." Kian laughs in my ear.

"I'd better go," I say.

"Okay. Text me later. Let me know what you want to do this weekend… in detail."

"You got it."

Later that afternoon, Sara finally leaves her room. She's still in pajamas and her hair is a rat nest on her head. She goes right into the kitchen without saying anything to anyone.

I get up and follow her in. I watch as she reaches in the cabinet above the fridge and pulls out a bottle of vodka. She hasn't seen me. She pours half a glass full of the liquor and then tops it with orange juice. It's when she's leaving the kitchen that she finally notices me.

"Spying on me?" she bites out.

"No, I'm checking on you. It's a little early for the hard stuff, isn't it? And don't you have to work tonight?"

"One drink won't get me drunk. Besides, by tonight, it'll have worn off." She brushes past me, heading straight for her room. I follow her in.

"The kids would probably like to spend some time with you today."

"Oh, I'm sorry. When you said you were coming to help me, I assumed you meant it." She takes a healthy swig of the booze. I haven't so much as seen Sara have a beer since I got here, so it's shocking.

"I have been helping you. I need you to start helping yourself."

"I am helping myself. I'm helping myself to a drink and a shower. Is that okay with you?"

"Fine. Do whatever you have to do, but you better not go to work drunk."

"Why? So you don't look bad in front of your new boyfriend?" The venom she's spitting at me takes me by surprise. We've never fought. And even when we do, we don't attack each other. This isn't my sister. This person is hurt, damaged, and taking it out on the wrong person.

"So you don't get fired," I say.

"It's just a dumb job. Anyone could do it. I'm not qualified for anything a monkey couldn't do. I left college to be with Chad. How stupid was that?"

"You left college?" I ask, shocked at this news.

"Yep. He said it was ridiculous for us to both collect college loans when I could be working and making money for us both. I put his ass through college and now look. He's got a degree and gainful employment while I'm here serving wine for tips."

"Sara, I sent you money every month to help pay for your schooling. What did you do with it?" My mind can't even keep up with the web of lies she fed me all those years ago.

"Graduate school was expensive. Chad promised after he graduated, I could go to school. It made sense at the time."

"For Christ's sake." I smack a palm to my forehead.

"Then he said I could go back after we got married. But I got pregnant. Then I got pregnant again and it was too hard to think about college with two babies at home."

"I can't even believe this."

"Do you see why I'm destroyed now? My whole life has been built around that man and now what?" Tears spill from her eyes.

"Now you pull yourself together and figure it out. What you did was stupid, but we can't change it."

"I can't. Everything is fucked." She collapses onto her bed.

"It is fucked, but we can fix it. You can get back on your feet."

"Please, can you just leave me alone?" she pleads.

"I have been leaving you alone, but it's not helping. You need to get yourself together. If not for yourself, for those kids out there."

"Please, Archer. Just go." She sobs into her pillow.

"I'll go but hear me when I say this isn't the end of this conversation. I won't lose you to this pity party you've got going on." I walk out, closing the door behind me.

I'm such a fraud coming down so hard on her when I was her for an entire year. Looking at it from this side, I can understand why Adler spent all those evenings yelling at me to snap out of it. When you're the one on the other end, things look so hopeless and bleak. But when you're the person on the other side, things are crystal clear.

I wish there were some way to show Sara that things will get better. If she had even an ounce of hope, she might not be lost to me right now.

FOURTEEN

Kian

I had a feeling I'd be receiving a phone call from Archer about his sister. I've watched everything about her deteriorate over the last couple weeks. Her appearance, her attitude, her work ethic. I've had to remind her about closing procedures and making sure her uniform is pressed.

But I'm in a precarious place. On one hand, she's the sister of the guy I'm into. On the other, this is my business and I haven't felt comfortable leaving it in Sara's hands over the last week. It's meant longer hours for me, choosing to stay at Focus to help out and supervise instead of going to Blur to do my paperwork.

I'd do a lot for a hard pounding, though, so if I need to spend my days in front of a laptop and my nights babysitting, it's a cross I'll bear.

"Hey, Sara," I greet as she walks in the door.

She brandishes a half-assed smile as she breezes past me. I get a slight whiff of booze.

Well, that changes things.

I'm prepared to overlook a lot, but not being drunk on the job. Still, I don't jump to conclusions and decide I'll keep an eye on her tonight. She clocks in and does her usual assessment of the tables. I try to get a read on her, but she doesn't sway when she starts serving and she isn't glassy-eyed or unfocused. Maybe I was wrong.

"Can we talk a second?" I ask her after the tables are all taken care of.

"Um, sure."

"Things okay, honey? You've seemed a little out of sorts."

"I'm fine. I'm sorry I've been off my game. I just haven't been sleeping well." She yawns as if to prove her point, which I know is a lie. From the text messages Archer and I have shared, I know she's been doing her fair share of sleeping.

"It's all right. I just want you to know I'm here for you. If you want to vent, I mean. I'm a great listener."

"I'm okay. Just going through some stuff with the kids' father. It should be settled soon." Her fake smile is troubling.

"Is he giving you problems?" I don't let on that I know all about the kind of problems her lousy ex is giving her.

"Not really. Just the normal divorce stuff." It's clear she isn't going to spill. I wish I could pry it out of her so I could give Archer any reassurances.

"Okay. I'll let you get back to work."

She ducks around me and gets back to serving. It's clear she's not okay, but without anything concrete, I already know I won't say anything to Archer.

Jarrett and Fernando stop in for drinks and I lead them to a table where we can chat. Sara brings us wine, making me feel like a hypocrite. I often have a glass of wine while working. Why can't Sara do the same? I brush the whole situation off, choosing to gossip with my friends instead.

"So you two?" Jarrett shoves his pointer finger into his closed fist, making a crude gesture.

"Are we fourteen?" I sass.

"Bitch, sometimes it feels like we're teenage girls." He laughs out and I join him. It definitely does by how often we talk about boys and our bodies. "So? Did you?"

"Yes," I say dreamily. "And it was off the charts. He damn near broke my back."

"What I wouldn't give to be a fly on the wall. That man is yummy," Fernando says.

"He's even yummier naked." I sigh. "And his dick? It's art."

"You two agreed to be casual, though, right?" Jarrett's eyebrow quirks and I want to punch him in his face.

"Back off. He says it's casual, but he doesn't know what he wants yet. I'll lock him down."

Sunday morning, I wake with a start. I was up late again last night babysitting Blur and Focus, so I'm exhausted. But knowing Archer is coming over for dinner keeps my noon alarm from feeling too painful.

I'm making us dinner and I still need to shop, prep the food, and change my sheets. I'm expecting to end up in bed, so I want to make sure everything is perfect.

I buy some beautiful steaks and asparagus from the grocery store, then I stop at the fish market and pick up some lobster tails. I don't know if he's sick of the bugs since he spends all day catching them, but after he tastes what magic I can do to them, I'm certain he won't mind.

I've just pulled the steaks from the grill and wrapped them in foil to rest, when I hear the knock at the door. My ass clenches and I have to calm down. It's been a long time since I've had such a strong reaction to a guy. Not since Jax when everything we did was so new and exciting. Of course Archer has just as strong of a potential to hurt me, but the more we talk and text, the more certain I've become that if I allow things to go at his pace, we could have something special.

"Hey, handsome," I greet when I open the door. Archer stands in front of me wearing his usual T-shirt and beat-up jeans. His confidently casual appearance is a look I didn't know was such a turn-on for me.

"Hey. I brought wine." He holds up a bottle of cheap red.

"But now I'm realizing it was stupid to bring to a wine guy's house."

"No, it's great. I'll just let it breathe." I take the bottle from his hand and set it in the kitchen behind the two bottles I've already had breathing for tonight's meal. Maybe he'll forget what that shit bottle he brought looks like.

"It smells amazing in here." He takes a seat at the island.

"Thanks. I don't know if you know this, but I'm a mind-blowing cook."

"I figured you would be. I can hardly make rice, but I'm epic with pancakes." He smiles the smile that shows all his teeth and the sparkle in his eyes. My heart aches with the beauty of it.

"Maybe if I can talk you into staying the night, you can make me some in the morning."

"Maybe." He smirks.

We laugh and chat our way through dinner. I lit candles in the center of the table between us and turned the lights low, so the mood is painfully romantic. When I've finished my last bite, Archer takes my hand from his place across the table.

"We've kind of brushed on your coming out story and Jax, but I want to know more."

"Not much to tell. I fell in love with a boy who was so deep in the closet, not even losing me could pry him out. It was a huge blow to my teenage ego. I never forgave him. Even though I should. It was a long time ago."

"Some hurts cut too deep to forgive."

"True. But he's with Dante and I'm happy for him. It's not like if he showed up tonight and begged for me to come back to him I would. I guess it just feels like a slap in the face. Like I wasn't important enough to come out for." I admit sheepishly.

"It's probably best if he didn't show up tonight. I'd hate to get arrested for punching out the sheriff." The candlelight casts a warm glow on his features.

"You'd defend my honor, huh?"

"Of course. Besides, he had his chance."

"And now you're shooting your shot?" I tease.

"Maybe not shooting my shot, but definitely aiming. Someday perhaps I'll fire."

"Enough gun analogies. Tell me how you came out."

"I didn't really. There wasn't anyone to come out to. Except maybe Sara, but she always just knew," he says.

"You guys had it rough, huh?"

"Yeah." He lets go of my hand and leans back in his chair. "When I was in fifth grade, my mom had left with some loser and my dad was too depressed to get out of his recliner. Sara was having a read-a-thon in class and was supposed to wear pajamas, bring treats, a blanket, and a stuffed animal.

"I tried to get my dad up to do laundry and go to the store, but he kept telling me he would later. At some point, I knew it wasn't going to happen. I figured out the washer and then walked to the gas station down the road with a pocket full of change I'd been swiping whenever I saw it lying on the counters or in the couch. I bought Sara treats and made sure her pajamas were clean. That story describes my entire childhood, adolescence, and teenage years. I've never stopped looking after my sister."

His story is enough to make me cry, but the pride he exuded while telling it has me feeling nothing but respect. I never had a sibling, hell, I never had anyone but myself to look after. My parents, at seventy years old, even moved themselves into a home when they were having a hard time taking care of themselves.

"That's incredible. I see why you said you feel like her parent more than brother."

"Even to this day I do. I think that's what makes everything she's going through even harder. I want her to be happy and succeed. I know she still can. I just have to make her believe it." He sets his fork and knife on his plate, clearly done talking about this.

"Why don't I do the dishes and you can go hang out in the living room?" I offer.

"I have a better idea." He picks up our plates and sets them in the sink. "Why don't we worry about dishes later and you show me your bedroom?"

He walks over to my side of the table and helps me stand. "I like a man with a plan."

I lead him into my room and turn on the lamp on my nightstand, not wanting the harshness of the overhead light. I turn around and hold my arms out. "This is it."

"It's exactly like I imagined. Clean and minimalistic."

"What can I say? I'm a neat freak."

"How are you going to feel when I dirty you up?" His voice is husky and lust filled. It has my dick taking notice and hardening in preparation.

"I think I can handle that."

He stalks toward me and crushes my lips to his. His brand of fucking is rough and unforgiving. It makes me feel like I'm the sexiest man he's ever laid eyes on when he manhandles me, like he can't possibly wait another second to bury himself inside me.

"Clothes need to go." He rips my button-up open, sending buttons pinging from the walls and my dresser. Fuck, that was hot. I don't even mention this was my favorite shirt. It seems irrelevant. He pops the button of my pants and I shimmy them down, exposing myself fully. "I like that you don't wear underwear. It's sexy as fuck."

"I like that you do. You in a pair of boxer briefs is the hottest thing I've ever seen."

He starts to strip and I bite my lower lip, watching as his layers are pulled from his body. With the soft lighting only bright enough to highlight the dips and valleys of his pecs and abs, he looks artful. When he's down to his boxer briefs that are straining to contain his hard dick, he makes eye contact with me and holds it while he lowers them to the ground.

"On the bed." He commands and I scurry to obey. His balls hang heavy and low as he pumps his dick with long and languid strokes, walking toward me. He eats me up with his intense gaze. "You gave me your mouth last time, now it's my turn."

He climbs over my body and lowers his face to my groin. Taking me in his hand, his lips wrap around my cock and my hips buck off the bed uncontrollably. *Lord, give me the strength to not shoot off in three seconds.* I count backward from a hundred, allowing myself to feel it, but not too much.

He moans from around me and the vibrations feel otherworldly. He palms my balls and rolls them around his hand, tugging ever so slightly. He takes me clear to the back of his throat and swallows, leaving me out of my mind. Not even counting is going to stave off this orgasm.

He lets go of my balls and brings his fingers to my lips. I suck them in my mouth, knowing what he wants. I wet them the best I can with a dry mouth. He uses the lubricated digits to probe at my asshole, working them in slowly but deliberately.

I try to think of anything to keep from coming. The dirty dishes in the sink, the bills I need to pay, the receipts I need to organize for my accountant, anything to stop my traitorous dick from spurting. But I'm too weak and it feels too incredible. I slap his shoulder in the international sign for *I'm coming*. Instead of backing off, he doubles his efforts, hooking his fingers forward to bump against my prostate and sucking my soul out of my cock.

I come so hard, my vision goes dark. My lips move and I hear sounds, but I'm almost certain I'm not making sense. He drinks me down, taking everything I give him. Just the knowledge that he would swallow increases my pleasure. *I'm going to marry this man.* Thankfully, even with the blinding orgasm, I don't say that thought out loud.

He swirls his tongue over my tip, making sure not to miss even a drop before setting my limp dick down and crawling the rest of the way up my body.

"I don't know what you expect from me after that, but I think my bones are gone," I whine.

He laughs, the sound hearty and low. "You don't have to do a thing. Just lie there and take it."

"Spoken like a true man."

"Damn straight. Where do you keep your supplies?"

"Top drawer. Nightstand," I mumble.

I hear the tear of the wrapper and the squirt of the lube. Then he's back, wedging a pillow under my hips to prop my ass up and spreading my legs wide.

"You have the sexist little asshole. I can't wait to fuck it again." And then he does just that. He takes his time but gives it to me just as hard as when I was pressed up against the window in my office.

Every thrust is purposeful and deep. Our eyes lock and my heart stops at what I see. The emotion and intensity are something I wasn't prepared for. Face-to-face with Archer in this moment has me on the brink of ecstasy.

It has nothing to do with an orgasm because my body is spent. It has everything to do with the sparks flying between us and the dazzling swirls of two people connecting on a deeper level.

By the time he comes, I'm clinging to the cheeks of his firm ass and encouraging him to go harder. This man does things to me no other has before. What used to be a race to get myself off before my partner could is now an entire experience I never want to end.

"Fuck," he grinds out through gritted teeth before slumping on top of me, careful not to crush my smaller frame from under his much larger one.

"I need you to do that again." I stroke the top of his head.

"Right now?" he asks through pants.

"At least one more time tonight. Will you stay?"

"I wouldn't want to be anywhere else."

FIFTEEN

Archer

I don't know how life can be so perfect and so wrong all at the same time. Kian and I are vibing so well together. He respects my boundaries and doesn't pressure me for a commitment. We see each other every Sunday night for marathon fucking, a couple times a week we meet at Fran's for coffee on my break, I've been to the club multiple times, and we text daily.

But while things are going so well for Kian and me, things with Sara continue on a downward spiral.

She's drinking more, which she excuses off with her stress level. She's short-tempered, not only with me but with her kids. They're feeling it, too. They beg for me not to go to work every day, claiming their mom stays in bed and gets mad at them for being noisy. They're too young to be watching over themselves and I see a familiar pattern beginning with Lou becoming protective over Emmy. The only difference between when Sara and I were kids is my niece and nephew have me.

So I make sure the nights I see Kian, I wait until after bedtime. I come home for lunch instead of eating with the guys at the dock. I do everything I can to be around as much as possible.

I try to talk to Sara, but she shuts down immediately at the mention of her divorce. Part of me is angry at her for treating her kids the way she is, but another part of me understands that she needs to go through the loss of a life she thought she was going to have. I can't blame her. A year ago I wasn't getting out of bed either. She just needs time and with more effort on my part, I can make sure she gets it.

Which is why I take a random Friday off work to take the kids hiking in the Beacon Island National Forest. It'll give Sara a day to herself and wear the kids out so I can sneak off to meet Kian at the club later. One of the guys I work with has a teenage daughter who comes to babysit now and then. The kids love her and she seems to enjoy them just as much. It makes sneaking away easier.

We drive out to the forest and park. I pack Emmy up in some kind of hiking backpack I bought online and make sure we have snacks and bottles of water. We find the trail head for the beginner hike and start our walk through the lush trees and brush. Sun beams break through the dense forest keeping the temperature just warm enough to not need a sweatshirt.

"Watch this, Archer." Lou climbs on top of a two-foot-tall rock and jumps off. He lands with a *hmph* and looks up at me like he did something epic. I hold my hand out and give him a high-five.

After a while, Emmy grows tired of being cooped up and makes me set her down. She giggles and chases Lou down the path, keeping me entertained. I'm sad Sara is missing seeing her kids with beaming smiles, finding slugs and spiders to inspect, picking out the perfect walking stick, and talking about the most random things.

Just give her a little more time. She'll snap out of it.

"My feet are sleepy," Emmy whines. I find a clearing for us to sit and have a snack. They happily chomp on crackers and cheese sticks while I pull out my phone.

Kian: You still coming out later?
Me: Definitely.
Kian: What are you doing right now?

I snap a selfie with the kids and send it to him.

Kian: Uncle Archer's on duty, I see.

Me: Sara needed some time.

Kian: Have you told her about the therapist yet?

Last week Kian had given me a card for a therapist he knows. He's mentioned a few times that she seems to be falling more and more depressed. I know he means well, but every time he brings it up, it feels like a personal attack.

Me: No, but I will when the timing is right.

Kian: I think she would benefit from talking to someone.

Me: She talks to me.

Kian: A professional someone.

Me: Kids are done snacking, we're off to finish our hike. See you later.

I tuck my phone away. Sara won't even talk about signing the divorce papers. I can't imagine her being receptive about a therapist. The official documents haven't left her nightstand. I read through them more thoroughly one time while she was at work. She was right, he gave her sole custody, only writing in minimal child support payments. Such a piece of shit.

I get the kids squared away with the sitter and tell her I'll be back by two. Thankfully, she drives, so I don't have to worry about having a few drinks. I walk to the club, deciding small towns are my favorites. No need for designated drivers or Ubers because the bar is a few blocks away.

The bouncer, Steve, knows me by name now and I walk through the heavy curtains without paying a cover charge. I make my way through the throngs, although that's a bit dramatic since a gay club in Brigs Ferry Bay isn't all that crowded. There are enough people I don't spot Kian right away, though.

I stop by the bar and order a drink. I wave to a couple

people I've been introduced to over the last couple times I've been here. It's strangely calming to know people and connect with a community. When I'd first moved here, I didn't think I'd stay for longer than Sara needed, but I'm changing my mind day by day. And not just because Sara will most likely need me for a long time to come.

I walk the perimeter of the club, still not seeing Kian. I'm starting to think he's in his office, when I see him on the dance floor.

Fernando stands behind him, one of his legs between Kian's and his hands on his hips. The diner owner is ridiculously sexy and I've often wondered if he and Kian had a previous relationship, or at least something casual. I've noticed the way Fernando touches Kian when they talk, their inside jokes they don't bother to explain, and I know he and Jarrett stop into Focus most every night.

Maybe they're just close friends. I haven't asked, telling myself it's none of my business. But seeing them dancing together, the flare of jealousy has me questioning how much I consider Kian and me to be nothing more than friends with benefits anymore.

I find an empty bistro table and stand next to it, watching the scene and trying to make sense of my feelings. It shouldn't matter who he dances with or who he fucks. That's what we agreed on. Seeing him on the dance floor laughing and moving with Fernando, though, I wonder if it's me keeping us as just friends or him.

Kian turns around so he's facing toward me now. He pops his ass out into Fernando's groin. I scrub my fingers through my beard. My insides twist up and I fight the urge to rush over and put distance between them. I'm not some twenty-something barbarian, pushing people around to get what I want, but that doesn't mean I don't want to.

Kian's gaze locks on mine and he beams over at me. Within seconds, he's abandoned Fernando and is in front of me, swinging his arms around my neck. I breathe him in, his sweet and spicy scent hitting my nostrils. I grab his ass and press him tightly against me so he can feel the instant hard-on having him close gives me. He leans his head back, his brows meeting his hairline.

"Someone's happy to see me."

"I'd be even happier if we were in your office with you bent over the arm of your sofa, your ass bare to me." I squeeze a cheek to punctuate my suggestion. Maybe the caveman part of me is stronger than I thought because the only thing I can think of to make my head right is to claim him.

"Come on." He leads me toward the stairs, not even bothering to say goodbye to Fernando. My chest puffs and my fears calm.

I've barely shut and locked the door when Kian is all over me like a spider monkey, tugging off my shirt and unbuttoning my pants. The first time we were together, he had a perpetual look of shock on his face. He was timid and allowed me to take control fully. The more we fuck, though, the more his power bottom energy comes out.

Being a switch, I like the top and bottom dynamics. With Kian, I'm the only one who penetrates, but he fucks me from the bottom just as often as I fuck him from the top. It proves we're even more compatible than I initially thought.

"I guess I'm not the only one feeling needy." I laugh, watching him struggle to yank my shoes off. "Want some help?"

He jumps to his feet, blowing his floppy brown hair out of his eyes. "Please."

"Did dancing with Fernando work you up?" I toe my shoes off and shove my pants off the rest of the way.

"What?" he asks as his head pops free from his own shirt being removed.

"You seemed into him out there." *Shut up. Shut up. You're going to ruin the moment.*

"Oh. No, we were just goofing off." Kian presses his lips to mine, his tongue demanding immediate entry.

"It looked like more than that," I say against his mouth.

His lips freeze and he rears back, his eyes narrowing in question.

"I mean, it's none of my business," I add.

"It's not, but I wouldn't lie about it." He crosses his arms over his smooth, flat chest.

"So you aren't fucking him?" *Fuck. Why can't I drop this?*

"I have in the past, but I put a stop to it before you and I even started hooking up."

I nod, but then more questions pop into my head and I can't shove them back down. This isn't the time or place. I'm standing here naked, for chrissakes, and his pants are undone, his cock desperate trying to get free. I should shut up and do what I came up here to do.

"Are you sleeping with anyone other than me?" *I'm an idiot.*

"Why do you care?" Annoyance drips from his tone.

"I think if we're having sex regularly, we should know who the other person is fucking. To be safe, you know?" I swallow the lump in my throat.

"We are safe. We use a condom every time."

"But condoms break."

"What is this about?"

"Just what I said."

"Is it? Because until tonight, you never even asked how many partners I've had. Or if I've been safe or tested." He flops down on the couch exaggeratedly.

"How many? Have you been safe?" Since my pants are still around my ankles, I pull them back up.

"Yes, Archer," he says my name like a curse. "I may live in a tiny town, but I'm not an idiot."

"It's not a ridiculous question."

"It's not, it's just ridiculous timing and I don't think it's what you're really worked up over."

"If you know me so well, what I am worked up over?" At this point, I don't even know what I'm upset about.

He stands up and struts my way. He oozes sexuality with everything he does. The way he walks, the glint in his eye when he's talking, his fluid gestures, and how he never tries to hide who he is. His confidence is an aphrodisiac.

"I think you're jealous."

"I'm not."

"You are. You want me all to yourself." He's inches from me now.

"I always want you." I admit.

"It's not just that." He wiggles his arms around my waist. "It's scary. I know. You suffered a big loss. But you're still here. It doesn't mean you love him less to continue living your life."

All the air leaves my lungs. I'm jealous and I want to be the only man to fuck the maddening man in front of me. I hadn't realized it went that deep. He's right. It feels disrespectful despite knowing it's not.

"I wish he'd send me a sign. Let me know it's okay. I'm navigating… whatever this is between us blindly."

"I know. The only advice I can give you is to go slow. If it starts feeling bad, we can slow down." He rests his head on my chest, fitting just under my chin. I accept the comfort he offers and hug him to me. "Let's start by admitting we want to be the only person the other sleeps with. It's what we've been doing anyway, so it doesn't require any more effort. You just have to say it."

He's right. This whole time I haven't even thought of seeing anyone else and deep down, I knew he wasn't considering anyone else either. We've spent every second of free time we have together. I'm a fool to pretend we aren't dating.

"You're the only person I want to fuck." I kiss the top of his head. Peace fills me and it's all the confirmation I need that I'm making the right choice.

"You're the only one I want fucking me."

He peers up at me through his eyelashes. I lean down and take his mouth. His lips are soft, but his kiss is hard. His hand skims down my torso and he cups my still rigid dick. He rubs up and down, teasing me. I reach under the waistband of his pants and take a handful of his fleshy, naked ass. Something about knowing there's nothing underneath his pants turns me on. We'll be at Fran's, having a normal conversation, and I'll remember he's free balling. Then I spend our entire twenty minutes together trying to regain control of my hard-on.

"You're so hard already," he groans. "How about you bend me over that couch like you promised?"

In one fluid motion, I yank down his pants and lead him to the sofa. I push him face first over the arm, propping his ass up. I kick his legs apart and get down on my knees. I spread his cheeks open, his tight hole coming into view. Using my tongue, I lick from his balls up the place I want to be sheathed in. He whimpers, egging me on to do it again and again.

I gather spit in my mouth and dribble it down his crack. Using my middle finger, I rub it around his hole before pressing in, fixated on the way he so readily accepts the intrusion. I add another finger, scissoring him open, preparing him for me. When I feel he's ready, I swiftly gather the supplies and suit up.

The first thrust in is fucking magic. Ecstasy and pleasure have me wanting to spurt off right away, and also prolong this for a lifetime in equal measures. Using the cheeks of his ass as leverage, I pound into him. His hips rise and fall against the sofa, seeking friction.

"Such a tight fit, baby. You're strangling my cock," I say through a clenched jaw.

After the initial edge of my need is taken off, I home in on that spot inside him. I've never given anyone an orgasm through penetration alone, but if anyone's capable of it, it's

Kian. He's so reactive and he loses himself so completely when we fuck. I put all my effort into hitting his P-spot. I know when I've gotten it just right because his body shudders.

"Yes. There," he says breathily.

Sweat forms on my brow as I concentrate on milking his prostate. I'm as hard as steel and it takes active effort not to come, but I've taken on the challenge and I can't quit. He mewls from underneath me and his breath hitches. He quakes and calls out my name. I don't stop until he's clawing at the sofa and squirming to get away. I pull out, knowing he's probably sensitive.

"I just—" He sounds shocked. A quick look at the side of the sofa and seeing the product of his release tells me yes, he did. He spins around, the look of glee coloring his cheeks. He sinks to his knees and rips the rubber off. "You're about to get the best blow job of your life."

He swallows my dick whole, rolling my balls in his hand, and pressing a finger down on my perineum.

"Oh fuck." I gasp.

He pumps my shaft in time with his sucking, making me lose control. I slam a hand onto the wall at my side, my knees suddenly feeling weak. He pulls off me and sticks out his tongue, resting the tip of my dick on it while he jacks my cock. My balls tighten and an orgasm rips through my body uncontrollably. I don't know what flies out of my mouth, but I hear my voice, so I know I'm moaning something.

I watch as my cum paints his tongue. When every last drop has been milked from me, he meets my eyes and swallows.

Goddamn.

SIXTEEN

Kian

I float on cloud nine for a solid week. Archer has me smitten. Not only by the magic he performs with my body, but also with how he's opening up to me. I thought it would take much longer to get him to admit he wants to be exclusive with me.

What can I say? I'm just that fucking powerful.

Now that Archer and I aren't pretending to be friends, our coffee dates at Fran's have us holding hands and discussing more permanent plans. Like someday taking a vacation together and things we can look forward to doing when summer arrives, and we need to beat the heat.

The only damper on my elevated mood is Sara. I keep it to myself, though, because Archer thinks I'm criticizing her when I mention her downward spiral. She's been late more than on time lately, she spends more of her shift staring out the window than serving customers, I've smelled alcohol on her numerous times, and she refuses to talk to me about it. But what do I do? I can't fire her. That will undoubtedly cause Archer to rethink our relationship.

I'm stuck.

So I ignore it. I let Sara know I'm here for her. I keep an eye on her. I make sure she isn't driving home when I'm certain she's had a glass of wine or two during her shift. I listen without judgement when Archer shares what's going on at home. And I'm supportive of all the time he spends with his niece and nephew. I know those kids are the ones suffering the most. No relationship is without challenges, right?

That's what's going on in my head on a Wednesday night as I'm tucked into my office at Blur, paying bills and my cell rings from the corner of my desk. I smile, thinking it's my nightly call from Archer. After he gets the kids tucked in, he calls, and we catch up on how our days were. Not that we don't constantly text anyway.

I lift the phone up and see it's not Archer, but Duke, my cook at Focus. He never calls me, choosing to communicate anything Focus needs while I'm there early on in the night. My lips turn downward as I click the accept call button.

"Kian, you gotta get over here," Duke rushes out. "She's drunk."

"Who?" I ask.

"Sara. She's stumbling around. She spilled wine on a customer. She's tanked, dude."

"Shit. Okay. Be there in a second."

I end the call and slam my laptop shut. I thought I'd have more time to get on solid footing with Archer before things got this bad. Dread fills my gut, knowing this is the last straw. I like Archer. More than I've liked anyone in a long time. But this is my business. My baby I birthed from an empty warehouse. There are not many things I will protect at all costs, but this place is one of them.

I rush through the front door of Focus and all eyes land on me. The customers look uncomfortable and weary. I plaster a fake as hell smile on my face, showing confidence I don't feel. Neither Sara nor Duke are anywhere in sight. I walk into the kitchen and spot them. Sara is kneeling over a garbage can, sobbing and spitting. Duke is pacing behind her, the grumpy man looking uncomfortable.

"I'm sorry I had to call. I didn't know what to do. I mean,

she's been having a drink or two during her shift, but you have wine while you work, so I didn't think it was an issue," he blubbers.

I hold a hand out to silence him. "It's fine. Thank you for calling. Can you tell everyone the bar is shutting down for the night and whatever tabs they have open will be comped?"

"Sure." He leaves us, no doubt cursing me at having to deal with customers. He keeps his life private for a reason. He absolutely hates people.

I crouch down next to the mess of a girl on the ground. I brush her hair back, taking in her red, swollen eyes and tiny chunks of puke clinging to her lips.

"Hey, honey. Bad night?"

"I'm sorry, Kian. I tried. I'm just so sad." She rests her head on her arms that are draped over the trash and cries loudly. It's the most pitiful thing I've ever seen. My heart clenches tightly and if I could, I'd remove the pain from her life.

"I know. It's okay. I need to call Archer, okay? Hang tight."

She jerks to sitting, her eyes pleading with me. "No. Don't call him. He's going to be so disappointed and I can't take that on top of everything else."

"I'm sorry, I have no choice. You need to go home."

"I'll walk home. Just don't call him. Give me a cup of coffee and a half hour. That's all I need. Please. It was probably food poisoning anyway," she slurs.

"Sara, you're drunk." The alcohol and puke stench coming off her leaves no room to argue.

"I only had a glass of wine. Maybe it's because I haven't eaten today. I'll be okay. Just don't call him." She repeats.

Her explanations plant doubts in my mind, or maybe it's me letting them live there because I don't want to call him either. She's right. He'll be disappointed in her, but he'll blame me for not telling him she's been drinking on the job.

I'm an idiot for even contemplating not telling him. This

has gone on too long. She needs help. Professional help. I can't put my own happiness above hers. It's not right.

Sara lies down on the tile floor, curling herself around the trashcan. Her eyes close instantly and I know she's passed out. The sound of her soft snores echoes through the otherwise silent kitchen. I dig my phone out of my pocket and click on Archer's contact button.

"Hey, you. Perfect timing, I just got Emmy to sleep." He's happy, chipper, excited to talk to me and I'm about to ruin that.

"Archer." It's the only word I can force out of my mouth.

"What's up?" he chirps. "I was thinking, Sunday night we can—"

"Archer," I say again, only this time with more edge.

"What?" I hear his face fall. In my mind, I watch it happen. It guts me.

"It's Sara. I'm bringing her home, but I didn't want you to be surprised when we show up because she isn't well."

"What do you mean? She's sick? She seemed fine when she left."

"She's not sick. Not like you think, anyway. Babe, she's drunk."

"Drunk?"

"I'll explain it to you when I get there, just meet us outside," I say.

"Yeah. Okay."

I hang up and give myself a second to process. I need to think about what to say and how to say it. This has been going on for months, first with her sadness and now the drinking. If Archer doesn't pull his head out of his ass and realize how serious this situation is, it's only going to get worse.

Duke comes back into the kitchen and plants his hands on his hips. He reminds me of a biker dude from that popular TV show. He's massive and has a handlebar mustache.

He's gruff and honest to a fault. He's also been with me since day one and his support is a huge reason why my business has been so successful.

"What do I do?" I ask him. He knows about Archer and me. He's witnessed the few times he's stopped in to see me and acted annoyed whenever I come into the kitchen with hearts in my eyes, reciting some story about Archer's and my time together.

"With her? Take her home and toss her in the shower." He suggests.

"I mean about Archer. I have to fire Sara. I can't trust her."

"If he doesn't understand that, then you two were doomed anyway. This place is your life."

"You're right." I sigh loudly. "Help me get her to my—shit. I forgot I didn't drive."

"I can take you two. Then I'll come back here and close up."

"Thank you."

We maneuver her out the back door and into his minivan. Honestly, I never understood why he has a mom mobile. I've made fun of him a few times for it, because what does a single guy need with three rows of seats? But right now, I'm thankful we can lay her down on the long middle bench seat.

Minutes later, we pull up to her house and Archer rushes outside. We don't speak as we get her out of the van and into her bed. She doesn't respond much, other than a painful whimper. It's not physical, though, and that's so much worse because there's no end date to emotional torture.

Duke leaves and I sit down on the couch while Archer settles his sister. Minutes later, he reappears, his fingers combing through his beard. He sits down on an upright chair across from me.

"Is this the first time she's been like this?" he asks barely above a whisper.

"This bad? Yes. But not the first time she's been drunk."

"You let her drive home every night knowing she's been drinking?" He accuses.

"No. I walk most nights, so I make an excuse as to why I should drive her home and then I walk the rest of the way. I don't know why I bothered to beat around the bush. We both knew why I was doing it."

"I wish you'd said something."

"I tried. A few times. But you get so defensive and take it out on me. You told me over and over that you know what's best for her and that she'll snap out of it." I can't help my self-justifying tone.

"I would've listened to this." He points in the direction of Sara's room.

"Would you?"

"Yes. Of course. I mean, I know she's been down—"

"It's more than down, Archer. She's depressed. Not in the *my favorite TV show has been cancelled* way. In the *she needs to be on medication and see a psychologist, maybe even psychiatrist* way."

"I know. Okay? I know." He jumps out of his chair and paces. "I gave her that card. I told her to call. I've begged her to. But she's a goddamn adult."

"It's going to be okay. She'll get through this. I'm sure it was a wake-up call."

"I don't know if she will. She still hasn't called a lawyer. Those divorce papers are still on her nightstand. Yesterday, she got a letter saying if she doesn't respond, the judge will issue a default judgement siding with Chad on everything. He wants them to sell the house and split the profits. The only house those kids have known. She doesn't have the money to buy him out." He spills everything he's been holding in. I'm sure he didn't talk to me about it before now thinking I'd butt in. And before now, I might have done just that. But it's not what he needs right now, so I listen to everything he says. Eventually he sits down on the couch next to me, leaning forward with his head in his hands.

"I'm sorry you've been going through this alone. But there's one more thing I need to talk to you about." I rub his back, hoping to give him comfort when my next words will do anything but that.

"What?" He turns his head in my direction. His eyes are glassy and his face lax, like he's had all he can have tonight. I hate that I need to bring this up.

"I have to fire her," I blurt out and he's up on his feet again.

"Please don't do that. Not right now."

"Archer, it's my business and she was drunk. If she'd hurt herself or someone else? She's a liability."

"But she's so fragile right now and if she doesn't have a job, she'll for sure lose this house."

My heart breaks for the boy who spent his life protecting his sister. He can't help himself.

"I'm sorry. I'll hold her job. I'll find someone who can work temporarily. But I can't keep her on." My voice is quiet, unsure. I don't know if I'm making the right choice.

"She doesn't need another rejection." His voice rises and I feel the frustration coming off him in waves.

"It's not fair for you to ask this of me. If her employer were anyone else, you wouldn't be." I try to make him see reason.

"But it's not anyone else. It's my boyfriend."

Ouch.

"I didn't think the first time I heard you call me your boyfriend would be when you want something." A lump forms in my throat. "That's not fair."

"I may not have said it before, but we both know that's what this was." He's grasping at straws and with every justification, a knife digs further into my heart.

"Did you know? Because I didn't. I knew we were working toward that and I was fully prepared to wait. Even if it took years."

"I'm sorry, okay? You're right. That was a dick move. She's just lost so much. If she doesn't have a way to pay her bills or have a reason to get out of bed, I don't know what will happen," he argues.

"That's the problem, Archer. Her kids, her brother, her life, all of that should be enough to get her out of bed. But right now, it's not and until it is, she's just going to sink further and further down into this hole." I stand up and move to the door. This isn't going anywhere and I don't want either of us to say something we don't mean.

"This is just perfect. I'm glad I'm seeing you fail me now instead of later when things get tough."

"You know, I knew you weren't ready. Jarrett warned me, Fernando warned, hell, I warned myself. But I saw something in you. Our connection? That doesn't happen with every guy you meet. I'm just bummed you want to throw it away because you're blinded by your reality."

"Again, you're right. And now I have to help my sister find a new job when she's already at her lowest, so thank you for that."

"I'm not the enemy, Archer. That is business, what we have is personal. The two are very separate."

"That's the difference here. To you my sister is business, to me, she's personal. Just go. I don't need someone else in my life who's going to end up failing me." He waves me on like he's dismissing me. It makes my blood boil even more.

I walk out and shut the door behind me. With each step, the reality of what just happened hits me harder and harder until I can't go any further. I pull out my phone. I need a friend. I need alcohol. And I think I need to cry. Just the thought has my vision blurring and tears bulging on my water line.

"Jarrett?"

"What's wrong?"

"Can I come over?" My voice squeaks.

"Sure, bitch. Come on over."

SEVENTEEN

Archer

God fucking damn it. I stew all night, pacing the floors of this house that suddenly isn't roomy enough. I'm pissed at Sara, I'm pissed at Kian, but most of all, I'm pissed at myself. It was wrong of me to ask him not to fire her, but what choice did I have? Sara won't be asking for her job back. I'm the only one fighting for her life and it aggravates me.

By morning, I've had enough coffee to make an elephant's heart explode. Which is helpful, because I'll need the caffeine to keep me awake at work. I don't have days off I can take yet and since I'm the only one with a job right now, I can't afford to call in anyway.

After I'm showered and dressed, I barge into Sara's room, opening the blinds and letting the morning sun stream through the window. The light shines right onto her face like a spotlight highlighting the person of the hour.

"Wake up," I rasp out.

Sara stirs, one eye opens and she groans, throwing a pillow over her face. I can't let her get away with this shit anymore. No more being nice and understanding. It's gotten me nowhere so far.

"Sara!" I yell. "You have to get up. I have work."

"Then go!" she groans, but it's muffled under the pillow.

I rip it off her face and throw it across the room. "Do you even remember what happened last night? Do you even care that Kian fired you?"

"He fired me?"

"Yes! What do you expect? You got drunk and puked while on the job."

"I didn't have anything to eat yesterday and I had a glass of wine. It went straight to my head. It's not a big deal. I'll explain it to him."

"It's already done. There's no explaining."

"I'm sorry, okay? I'm sorry I'm a shitty mom. I'm sorry I'm a shitty sister. I'm sorry I was a shitty wife. I get it. I'm a shitty human being who doesn't deserve to live." Her face contorts in pain. It's not even tears spilling down her face, it's a waterfall. Her life has been a series of letdowns and misfortunes I tried to shield her from, but I can't do it anymore. It doesn't work.

"Sara." I sit down on the edge of her bed. "You aren't a shitty anything. If you asked those kids out there, they'd say their mother is awesome. They'd say she's sad and tired, but they'd also say she's the best mom ever. And you're not a shitty sister. I couldn't live without you in my life."

"Then why does everything feel impossible and painful?" She gasps for breath. "It shouldn't be this hard. I'm pretending like all this happened when Chad left, but it didn't. Not really. I haven't been happy in a long time."

"Then it's time to figure out why. You need therapy, maybe medication, I don't fucking know. But you have to do something."

"I will, okay? Just not today. I'm tired."

"Sara," I warn. "You need to take care of the kids."

"Can you call the neighbor? See if she can take them. Just for today," she pleads.

I war with myself on whether I should do it. But when I think about the kids sitting in front of the TV all day while she stays in here and cries, the decision is made. They don't deserve that.

"Fine."

"Thank you." She sniffles and settles back into bed.

This is above my life skills. I don't know what to do. She's not a child anymore. I can't order her to do things like I did when we were kids. And I just insulted and hurt my only friend in the world, so I have no one to ask for advice.

I call the neighbor who is elderly but loves spending time with the kids. She happily agrees to take them for the day. I rush to get them up and fed before dropping them off and hurrying to work. Even still, I'm five minutes late.

"The lobstah are going to be gone by the time we get out there," Oliver grumbles.

"I'm sorry. I had a tough night." I toss my backpack in the cabin and get to work, baiting the traps.

"I heard." Oliver steers the boat away from the dock and out into the open ocean.

"What did you hear?"

"Not much. Something about your sistah being hammered at work," he states matter-of-factly.

"Fucking small towns."

"You wanna talk about it?" He pins me with his no nonsense stare. We've been working together for almost two months and the most talking we've done is an ongoing argument about whether crabbing or lobstering is more difficult.

"You have any experience with a depressed sister or pissing your boyfriend off?" I ask.

"Can't say I do."

"Didn't think so."

"I can listen, though." It's the first caring thing out of his mouth and whether from desperation or insanity, I take him up on it. I tell him the whole thing, starting with Sara's and my childhood all the way to what happened last night, all while tossing out traps despite my overwhelming exhaustion.

I'm done shutting people out. It took me forty years to realize I need people. I need friends. I need family. I can't navigate life like this. Mason was the first person I let my guard down for and when I lost him, I told myself that's what I get for allowing someone to get close. But what it should've told me was I needed to let more people in so when bad things happen, I'm not alone.

"Well, fuck, man. I don't know what to say." Oliver yanks his knit cap off his head and tucks it in his back pocket. "You've been dealt some shit."

"Tell me something I don't know."

"I don't have any experience in any of that, but can I tell you my opinion?" he asks, steering us to the dock for lunch.

"Sure," I say hesitantly.

"I think you fucked up. I mean, what would you do if your employee showed up drunk after spending weeks doing a bad job? You'd fire them. You put that boy in a tough position and you better start groveling." He parks and grabs his thermos and lunchbox. "And your sister is a ticking time bomb. This kind of behavior isn't a normal response to a divorce. Sure, she'd be sad and cry. But drinking enough to get fired and not taking care of her kids? She needs help, man. I don't know how you'll talk her into it, but you need to."

He doesn't wait for my reaction. He simply leaves me there. But his words remain with me, resonating down to my soul. I want to be angry and tell him he's wrong, but I know he's not.

Now to figure out what to do about it.

I return home after a long day, bone weary. I pick up the kids and we grab a pizza before heading home. I'm assuming Sara'll still be tucked away in bed when we get there, but she's not. She's at the kitchen table, documents laid out in front of her.

"Hi, my babies!" She opens her arms and the kids run

into them. She looks better now that she's showered and dressed. It's weird, considering everything. I should be happy she's making an effort, but I'm suspicious.

"What are you doing?" I ask, setting the pizza down on the island and grabbing paper plates.

"You were right. I need to get everything in order. I called a lawyer. He agreed to look at the divorce papers. I have an appointment tomorrow. So now, I'm getting everything together for him."

"That's great. I'm glad."

"I thought you would be."

"Are you hungry?" I put a slice on a plate and hand it to her, expecting her to turn it down.

"Starving. Thank you."

What the fuck.

We eat dinner as a family and Sara participates in the conversation, asking her kids silly questions and laughing at their answers. I start to relax, thinking maybe she hit rock bottom and it was enough to snap her out of it.

She gives the kids baths and puts them to bed. I don't remember the last time she did that. When I first got here, I guess. Nothing is amiss, so why does my gut tell me something is off? I wish I could call or text Kian and talk to him about it. He'd know what was going on and explain it to me. He's perceptive with human behavior.

But before I can do that, I need to apologize, and I need to make it something special. That'll require much more planning on my part and I'm too tired tonight. I'll get a good night's sleep and deal with it tomorrow. I only hope I didn't do more damage than what's repairable.

I grab a beer and sit down on the couch, hoping to have a conversation with Sara before I pass out. She returns a few minutes later, pouring herself a glass of wine. I raise my brows at her when she walks into the living room and sits across from me. I know I tossed all the liquor in the kitchen last night. She must be hiding it in her room.

"I can have a glass of wine, Archer. I'm fine."

"Okay, I'm not judging," I say, even though I am.

"Listen, I'm sorry." Immediately, her eyes well with tears. "I appreciate everything you've done for me. I love how well you get on with the kids. It puts me at ease."

"I raised you, didn't I?"

"You did. I wish we had a different childhood. I would've given anything to have normal parents. But that wasn't in the cards for us, so I'm glad I at least had you. I hope you know I love you and I'm so grateful I had you to take care of me. It makes me happy to know you'll always be there for my kids, too." She sniffles and wipes her nose with the sleeve of her cardigan.

"Why does this sound so ominous?" Dread churns in my gut. She's done a complete one-eighty and something about it doesn't feel right. At all.

"It's not. It's good. I promise. I feel better than I have in a long time. I have a plan in place. Everything's going to be fine." She's still crying, but she smiles through the tears. It gives me hope.

"I'm glad. Do you need anything from me before I go to bed?"

"Nope. I'll enjoy this glass of wine and go to bed myself. I want to make sure I'm up with the kids tomorrow."

I stand, and to my surprise Sara does too. She wraps her frail arms around my middle and squeezes me tight. I hug her back, wanting to make sure she knows I'm here for her. With her. The Warren siblings against the world.

EIGHTEEN

Kian

"You want to tell me what last night was about now?" Jarrett asks, pouring water over two tea bags.

I don't remember much of what happened after I got to his condo, which is only down the hallway from my own. But I woke up tangled up in a blanket on his couch. It's an antique rolled arm, bowed back, traditional style with deep button tufts in a herring bone fabric. It's also the most uncomfortable thing I've ever sat on, let alone slept on.

"What do you mean?" I clear the sleep from my eyes. My mouth feels the way a cat's tongue looks, dry and scratchy. My head is throbbing and I have enough acid swimming in my belly to strip the finish off of one of Jarrett's metal plant stands.

"You came over, went right to my kitchen, grabbed my expensive bottle of gin, and bawled your eyes out. Nothing you said made sense, so I just nodded and waited for you to pass out." Jarrett walks into the living room.

"Jesus, Mary, and Joseph, you could at least put on pants when you have a guest." I cover my eyes, shielding myself from his lower half that's barely covered by super short hot pink flamingo trunks. At least he had the decency to wear a T-shirt and a knee-length silk robe.

"You showed up on my doorstep, a hot mess, drinking my booze, and I get the lecture?" He hands me a cup of tea.

I huff an annoyed breath. "Anyway, I had to fire Sara last night. She's been drinking on the job and last night she got so hammered, she puked and passed out on the kitchen floor."

"No, really?" His concern is fake as fuck.

"You already knew, didn't you?"

"I may have gotten a phone call or two from a few of your customers." He takes a seat in an equally uncomfortable looking medieval wooden chair. Jarrett is a forty-five-year-old man with the style of an eighty-year-old. He thinks because an antique is expensive, it's worth displaying. We all have those friends. The ones who grew up poor and when they finally got some money, they began associating expensive with worthy. Newsflash, this furniture is not worthy of my ass.

"Anyway, I took her home and at first, everything was fine. I listened to Archer vent and we had a real moment. Then I told him I had to fire Sara for the safety of my business and he lost his mind. He called me his boyfriend—"

"The audacity!"

I roll my eyes. "Can we save the dramatics? He only called me his boyfriend because he was trying to guilt me into not firing his sister. It was a low blow."

Recalling everything from last night hits me hard. I didn't want to fire her and I worried I'd regret it today, but even with a hangover from hell, I stand by what I did.

"I'm sorry, you're right. That's awful and uncalled for." He sets his tea down on a side table and crosses his legs, resting an arm on his knee. "But if I play the devil's advocate, I might say he was out of his mind with stress and maybe said something out of desperation that he didn't mean."

I think about that for a minute. Jarrett's probably right. I'm sure he's right. I just don't know if that makes it any better. My head hurts too bad to think this hard.

"Maybe. Though I don't know where that leaves us."

"I think you're going to have to let him come to you. It's one thing to understand his position, but it's a whole other thing if he doesn't come back groveling." He runs a hand through his dark, voluminous hair that's long on top and short on the sides. Despite the graying at his temples, the curl that always falls over his forehead makes him appear youthful and flirty.

"You know that's hard for me. I want to call him right now and hash it out."

"You never were one to let people be in their feelings before trying to resolve issues."

"Thank you."

"That wasn't a compliment."

I open my mouth and then close it back up. Is that a bad thing? I've always thought stewing in your own juices causes you to rot. I never considered marinating to be healthy. This is why I don't do relationships. Or why relationships don't do me.

"Ugh. You're making me doubt myself. I don't like it."

"Sorry, sweetie. I'm your friend, not your mommy. Don't come crying at my door unless you want the tea." He picks up his tea and takes a sip, looking way too kermit the froggy for me. "Listen, run home. Take a shower. Put on something cute. And then let's go shopping."

"There's an estate sale, isn't there?" I groan.

"Yep. Mrs. Pickett kicked the bucket last week and I've heard she had quite a furniture collection."

"Really? Mrs. Pickett? That's so sad."

"Is it? Because the last time I saw her, she was holding her rosary up at me like she was trying not to catch the gay." He stands up, thankfully closing and tying his robe.

"Fine. I'll be back in an hour."

Two hours later, because I required a face mask and cucumbers to sit on my eyes for half that time in order to look presentable, Jarrett and I are at Mrs. Pickett's house, going through each room.

"Kian?" I hear my name come from a voice I never want to hear. I look up to see Dean Bell, mayor of Brigs Ferry Bay, and Jax's dad. Fuck my life.

"Mayor, nice to see you," I greet in my most smarmy tone.

"Such a tragic thing to lose Mrs. Pickett, but I'm glad we ran into each other."

"I'm not," I say under my breath and Jarrett elbows me.

"I heard what happened at your little wine bar last night." The condescension drips from his words like greasy cheese on a pizza. "I think you need a reminder that it's a code violation to have employees drinking while on the job. I'd hate to have to send the sheriff—"

"You mean your son, my best friend our entire childhoods?"

With one eyebrow quirked, he says, "I guess I forgot you two used to be friends."

Yeah fucking right.

"Anyway," he continues. "I'd hate to have to shut you down. I'm sure there are plenty of other businesses just waiting for the chance to acquire your prime location on Main Street, but again, I'd hate to see that happen."

"I'm sure you would, but don't worry. The employee made a mistake and I let her go because of it. I run my business by the book."

"Let's make sure you do." He walks away and like the child I am, I mockingly mouth his last words.

"You shouldn't piss him off like that. There's a clear and growing divide in this town. You don't want the negative forces against you," Jarrett chides.

"He can eat me."

"Classy."

"I'm sorry, okay? I'm hungover and grouchy. Can we please get out of here and go get some food?"

"There're only a few more rooms."

We walk through two more bedrooms and a formal sitting room. Jarrett pays for his treasurers that he'll no doubt take back to his shop, paint outrageous colors, and sell for three times what he just bought them for. His store is hugely popular around here and the hippie makes a killing.

We eat lunch at Comida's. Fernando's younger brother, Ricky, greets us as we enter. And I use that term loosely because the seventeen-year-old is a psychopath in the making. He exudes angry vibes and I can't imagine why. But whatever. *Teenagers.*

Luckily, the lunch rush is over, so Fernando is free to sit and eat with us. I order the largest plate of huevos rancheros they sell and large iced tea.

"You eating for two?" Fernando jokes.

"Eating away a hangover." I clarify.

"I heard what happened with Sara. That's sad."

I look over at Jarrett, who's staring at the ugly drop ceiling. After an uncomfortable amount of time passes, he finally makes eye contact. "What? You took two hours to get ready."

"So you called everyone we know to tell them?"

"Not everyone, just him." He motions to our friend.

"I should've just gone right to Paul and had him print the whole story, that way everyone would all know at the same time."

"Eew. Don't even joke. Besides, that homophobe wouldn't run anything if it's attached to one of us," Jarrett says.

"True that." I gulp down my tea, hoping it'll give me the energy to get through the night.

"Did you hear Dante moved in with Jax?" Fernando asks nonchalantly, like he didn't just drop a bomb.

"Seriously?" My jaw drops and my eyes roll.

"I overheard them talking about it while having lunch a week or two ago. I guess things must be growing serious between them." Fernando jumps up. "Be right back. I'll go grab our food."

"You okay, sweetie? You're not blinking. It's a little weird." Jarrett rests a hand on my forearm. He's sixteen years my senior, so he wasn't around when I was going through shit with Jax, but I've told him about the whole ordeal.

"Fine," I mutter.

"It's not like you're still into him, anyway."

My shoulders slump. "It's nothing like that. I don't want him, I just have these residual feelings of not being enough. I gave my tender teenage heart to him and he stomped on it over his family. And oh my God, it's happening all over again."

"What's happening all over again?"

"Jax put his family's welfare over mine and now Archer's doing the same damn thing. Why does no one consider my feelings? Why am I not enough for someone to put me first?"

"I mean, it is his sister who is clearly battling mental illness. You can't expect him to turn his back on her."

"No, of course not. That's not what I mean. What I mean is, he asked me to put my future at risk for his sister's. Why didn't he consider me before asking that of me? And with Jax, he didn't even try to make things work."

"You're right. But you realize it has nothing to do with you, right?"

"Doesn't it, though? If you were in Archer's situation, would you ask me to not fire her?"

He thinks about that for a minute and his face falls. "No."

"See? And you're a friend, I didn't even give you my ass."

"This conversation took a turn," Fernando says, placing plates in front of us. Suddenly, I'm not so hungry. I'm sad.

We eat lunch in relative silence, Fernando and Jarrett trying to cheer me up and make me feel better, but I've already been sucked into the deep emotions. The rehashing of old insecurities that spill into your life years after you thought you were over them.

I'm a whole ass adult still fretting over pain from my adolescence. Ain't that some shit.

I say goodbye to my friends and walk across the street to Focus, where Keith is waiting for me. I asked him to meet me here so we could talk about him working at Focus temporarily. He was the one who I'd bumped over to Blur when Sara came to work for me, so he was the obvious choice.

"Thanks for coming in early," I say, unlocking the door.

"No problem. Everything okay?" He drags a hand through his shaggy, blond hair. Keith is my only straight, male employee.

"Let's sit." I gesture to a table.

"That sounds ominous."

"I don't know if you heard what happened with Sara, but she won't be coming back for a little while. She has some personal stuff to take care of."

"I heard about last night."

"Figured you did. Anyway, that opens the position up here and I'm hoping you'll come back."

"It wouldn't be my first choice. My tips doubled when I moved over to Blur," he says.

I was surprised when he applied to work for me, but it all made sense when I saw how my customers reacted to his all-American, boy next door, mixed with California surfer good looks.

"How about I give you five dollars more an hour? I know it won't make up for it, but it might help."

"I guess I could go for that. Give the other bartenders at Blur a chance to make some money for a change." He flashes me a blinding smile, his blue eyes twinkling with mirth.

"Thank you."

"It's not a problem. It'll be nice not to have my junk pawed at for a while."

"I'm pretending I didn't hear that so I don't have to hire security."

"Probably best. Our tips would go way down."

"I didn't hear that, either."

Keith motions like he's zipping his lips and throwing away the key.

This is my life. Ignoring the safety of my staff because my head is too full of personal shit. How did things get so complicated?

Oh yeah. Archer Warren.

NINETEEN

Archer

I expected Sara's sudden reemergence into the land of the living to be short-lived, that I would find her in bed when I woke up, buried under blankets and a pile of tissues next to her pillow. That's not what I find when I enter the kitchen groggy-eyed and in need of coffee.

Sara's in front of the griddle, flipping chocolate chip pancakes, humming a song I don't recognize. After months of her being a shell of a human, it's almost bizarre. It's like watching her rise from the dead, but not in a good way. In a scary movie way where zombies claw their way up from the grave. It's fake and makes me uneasy.

I can't say that, though. She does truly look different. She's calm. At ease. I don't want to bring anything up that will set her back.

"Good morning," I say. "Kind of early for pancakes."

"I'm getting a head start. I have a bunch of errands to run today, so I'm making breakfast before I shower and wake the kids."

"What errands?"

"I'm meeting with that lawyer at nine this morning. Which reminds me, do you think I could stop at the docks and have you sign some things for me during your lunch?"

"Sure. What kind of things?" I pour myself a cup of coffee and take a seat at the island.

"The lawyer suggested making a will after signing the divorce papers so the kids won't get stuck with Chad should anything happen to me." She sets a plate of pancakes in front of me.

"Why do you need my signature?"

"Because I'm leaving the kids to you. And everything I own. Which I realize isn't much."

I choke on my bite of pancake. "You don't think they should go to their dad?"

She slams the spatula down on the counter. "He's giving up parental rights. He wants nothing to do with me or them and you think they'd be better off with him?"

The sudden change in mood reminds me she's still teetering. I need to talk to her about the therapist Kian mentioned. More and more, I'm thinking there was a whole lot more going on with Chad than she's told me. Not that he hasn't done enough. I just can't imagine the affair, the one instance of abuse I know about, and him abandoning his kids happened overnight. She's hiding a lot. If she doesn't want to talk to me, she needs to talk to someone.

"No, I guess not." I glance at the oven, noticing the time. I have twenty minutes to get to work. "It's fine. I'll sign. It's not like you're going anywhere."

Something unreadable flashes across her features. "Nope. Just want to make sure everything's in order."

"I usually am at the dock around twelve-thirty, but I only have a half hour before we leave to pick up the traps."

"Okay. I'll see you then."

While Oliver drives us out to sea, I pull my phone from my pocket and open my text messages. I scroll through the many conversations Kian and I had.

Me: This one is kind of cute.

I attached a selfie of me holding up a red lobster, its claw stretched toward my face, centimeters from pinching my nose.

Kian: Not as cute as the man holding it.

Me: How dare you.

I sent another selfie, only this time of just the lobster. Its claws straight up in the air, looking affronted.

Kian: Stop playing with your food.

Me: What are you doing? You sound short.

Kian: If you must know, I was jerking off to images of this guy I'm seeing. Then that same guy sent me pictures of a bug and it killed my hard-on.

Me: Fuck. Really?

Kian: Yes. Now go away so I can try and finish myself off. I don't feel like having blue balls for the rest of the day and you're working tomorrow so I can't even convince you to stay up late and meet me at my house.

Me: Tell me what you were fantasizing about. In detail.

Kian: Last weekend when you fucked me with my knees pressed into my chest. You hit just right from that angle.

Me: Are you touching yourself right now?

Kian: Yes. Why?

Me: Goddamn. Now I'm hard. On a boat with Oliver.

Kian: Oliver's kind of hot in a grandpa sort of way. Maybe he could help you with that.

Me: He's only ten years older than me.

Kian: I forgot you're so old. Can I call you daddy next time we have sex?

Me: No.

Kian: Fine, but right now, while my hand is on my dick and I'm imagining you here with me, I'm calling you daddy.

Me: All right, but if it slips while I'm balls deep in your tight little hole, you're in trouble.

Kian: Would you spank me, daddy?

Me: Kian.
Kian: Go away, you're ruining this for me.
Me: Send me a picture of the mess you make.
Kian: You want a picture of my jizz?
Me: Very much.
Kian: That almost made me come.
Me: That was the plan. Don't forget about that picture.

Then there's an image of Kian on his back, a serene look on his smiling face, and a puddle of cum on his abdomen. Fuck, he's so sexy.

I'm a special kind of stupid to fuck things up with him. I went an entire year resigned to spend the rest of my life alone. I couldn't imagine finding anyone who could make me feel again. For as hard as I tried to not let him in, it was a lost cause.

Even from the first moment we met, cleaning up diarrhea, of all things, I felt like I knew him. Like he saw me. He saw I was hurting. Most strangers run from that. Not Kian. He ran into the inferno, not knowing how badly I was burning on the inside and while the flames aren't extinguished, he became a barrier. Blocking the most painful licks of the flames.

I must get him back. I was a fucking idiot. I wasn't thinking clearly. Surely, he'll understand.

I shoot off a text asking him to call me later. I don't wait for a response before tucking my phone away and getting back to work.

After our morning traps are thrown, we return to the dock. I find Sara perched on a picnic bench, the kids running circles.

"Hey, troublemakers," I say.

"Archer!" the kids cheer, attacking my legs with hugs.

"How'd the lawyer go?" I ask, taking a seat on the aluminum bench seat.

"Kids, why don't you go see how many fish you can count? Just don't climb on the railing." Sara points to the dock and they run over, sticking their heads through the wooden slats and pointing sea life out to each other. "It went well. I had him write one thing into the divorce and then signed. It's been faxed to Chad's lawyer. I'd imagine he'll sign later today and file."

"You didn't contest anything? Sara, he wants to take away your house."

"I know, but I don't have it in me to fight."

"I'll look into seeing what it'll take to buy him out. I'll take the mortgage out myself. I still have money saved and with this job, it shouldn't be an issue."

"We'll see. That's not why I came. Here are the documents I wanted you to sign." She pulls a stack of documents out of a manila folder, multicolored tabs marking where I need to sign. I flip through them, not understanding ninety percent of the legal jargon.

"What does all this mean?"

"This one makes you the executor of my will." She points to a line and I scribble my signature. "This one makes you the guardian of Emmy and Lou in the event of my passing. This was the only thing I had written into the divorce. Even though Chad gave up custody, the kids would still go to him. So he'll sign off on you having guardianship and then we'll be divorced."

I sign on the line, expelling a heavy breath. "Why the sudden need for a will?"

"It wasn't my idea. It was my lawyer's when he saw Chad's terms. In all his years, he's never seen a father sign over all rights. He thought I should protect them from Chad should anything happen. And I agree."

"Makes sense. Is that it?"

"That's it." She stacks the papers neatly and tucks them

back into the folder. "I brought you lunch since I knew you wouldn't have time to run home or grab something after this."

"That was nice."

She opens a large brown paper bag and pulls out containers of fried chicken, potato salad, and green beans. She calls the kids over and we have a picnic lunch. It's nice to feel like I have my sister back.

I feel bad I've been absent through her whole adult life. I didn't mean for it to happen. I planned to bring Mason here a few times to meet Sara and for me to meet my niece and nephew, but our schedules never seemed to align. One year turned in two turned into too many to count.

The reason I'm here is shitty, but I'm glad I get this time to reconnect with family. They're every bit as responsible for me feeling more like myself as Kian is. I now have the chance to make up for lost time.

Maybe we'll be okay, after all.

My phone rings at two-thirty in the morning. I'd tried to stay awake after texting Kian and asking him to call me after work, but I must've dozed.

"Hello," I answer.

"Did I wake you?" His timbre is low and flat. He doesn't sound like himself at all.

"I meant to stay awake."

"We can talk tomorrow instead. It's late."

"No, don't go. Please. I miss you." I shoot for humility, hoping I can win him back.

"I miss you too. How's Sara? I've been worried."

"She's good. I think it was a real wake-up call for her. She actually saw a lawyer about her divorce today." I flip on the lamp on my nightstand and sit up, my back pressed to the wall. I've yet to do anything in this tiny bedroom to make it my own.

Just a queen-sized bed with a metal frame, an oak nightstand, and matching dresser. All of which Sara already had in here. My bedding is plain black and there's nothing on the walls.

It's a contrast to the small house Mason and I shared where he'd decorated with poster-sized paintings of all the things we loved. The ocean, wildlife, and even one rainbow-colored king crab that matched the logo for our business. The furniture was oversized and comfortable, our bed a king. I got rid of it all after he died, though, and moved into a five-hundred-square-foot apartment that wasn't any more decorated than this room.

"I'm glad. Maybe a break from life is what she needs right now." I hear what he's trying to say. That him firing her was ideal for her mental health. He's probably not wrong.

"Agreed." It's silent for a moment, which is stupid because there's so much to say. But I don't know how to start.

"Was there a reason you wanted to talk? I mean, I'm really glad to hear about Sara, but if there isn't anything else—"

"There is." I throw out to stop him from trying to get off the phone. "I need to apologize. There's no excuse for the position I put you in."

"There wasn't." I agree. "You know I had the mayor threatening to take away my business license earlier for having a drunk employee?"

Well, that makes shit real. I knew rumors would most likely spread. God knows they do about everything else. I didn't think about who they might spread to.

"Fuck. I'm so sorry about that."

"It's not your fault, but I had to tell you so you could understand how things work around here. There are people in charge of this town who don't like the gay population. They're homophobic and feel threatened when we do well or own any significant stake in the businesses. Not to mention the big business who keep trying to move in and take over. One tiny mistake and everything I own could be gone. I wasn't firing

Sara as a personal attack and I wasn't being overly dramatic when I told you what she did put me at risk." His voice rises with growing irritation and rightfully so. I had no idea.

"I don't know what to say, other than I was being an idiot. I was only thinking about my sister and that was wrong. Really wrong. You know how we grew up, it's a knee-jerk reaction to stick up for her. I should've tried to understand you."

"Agreed. I should apologize too, though."

"Why do you need to apologize? You did nothing wrong. It was all me."

"No, it wasn't. You told me over and over that you weren't in a place for a relationship. That you wanted to just be friends and I didn't listen. I pushed, knowing you were still fragile. I'm sorry. It was wrong. I should've been a friend. Maybe things would've gone differently."

"Kian, that's not it at all. It was a fight. A disagreement. I don't want to break up." No, no, no. This isn't how this conversation was supposed to go. This is all wrong.

"We were never together, remember? Not really. That was the goal and maybe we could've gotten there if we'd had more time before things got real."

"Don't do this. We can work it out."

"Maybe in the future, but all of this brought back some bad memories I need to sort through. Shit with Jax I don't think I ever dealt with. I need to take a break, let myself heal a little, and then we'll see." The sound of his small sniffle kills me. The most positive person in the world is hurting and I can't do anything to fix it.

"Okay. But know I'm here. I'm waiting for you because you came along when I would've rather spent the rest of my life alone than let someone else in. You helped me heal and made me realize I still have living to do."

"I can't make promises." He repeats the words I said to him numerous times.

"Mark my words, Kian. This isn't over."

"Goodbye, Archer." His voice cracks on my name and the line goes dead.

I toss my phone on the nightstand and throw an arm over my eyes. I can't believe I fucked up so epically. If I had just shut my mouth. Let things play out. Had a conversation instead of trying to manipulate him.

He'll see, though. I'll win him back. It'll take a long time and I'm not sure how I'll do it, but life is fragile. What you have in this moment can be gone in the next. I learned this lesson in the most horrific way and let it destroy my hopes and dreams. But Kian was right when he told me I'm still here. I lost a lot, but I didn't lose myself. There's still happiness out there for me and I plan on living every moment of it.

I throw off my covers, feeling parched. I need a beer, except I threw out all of the alcohol after Sara was brought home drunk, determined to make it hard for her to reach that level of intoxication again. Water will have to do.

I pad down the hallway, grab a glass from the cupboard, and fill it under the tap. I gulp it all in one go. I refill it and head back toward my room, but something in my gut stops me outside of Sara's room.

I'm panicked and uneasy. I want to both throw open the door and never open the door. Intuition tells me what I'll find, and bile rises in my throat as I turn the knob.

Even knowing something's wrong, I'm not prepared to see my sister on her bed with a bottle of pills next to her and unconscious. I sprint to her side and notice there's a froth around her mouth and nose. I press two fingers to her pulse point on her neck, feeling a faint heartbeat. Thank fuck. I run to my bedroom to find my cell and call nine-one-one.

The operator answers and I tell her what I know. She has me check to see if she's breathing. She's not. Adrenaline like I've never felt pumps through my body as the operator has me clear her mouth of the weird white foam and begin CPR. I don't process what I'm doing, I just do it.

She stays on the line, telling me someone will be there soon. In Brigs Ferry Bay, there is no ambulance service waiting for calls. Apparently, they have to get someone out of bed.

"The sheriff lives only around the corner, so he'll most likely be the first to arrive."

In my traumatized brain, all I can think is that it's ironic. The same person who broke the man I care about is coming to save my sister. It's not important in this moment, not even a little. Yet it's what I'm thinking about as I blow breaths into her lungs. Shock, I think is what it's called. The same thing happened after Mason. The only thing I could latch onto in the moment was that Adler and I still had traps to pick up.

Irrelevant.

I don't have a lot to be thankful for tonight, but if I can find anything, it's that the three and five-year-old sleeping down the hall don't wake up. They stay asleep as Jax rushes into the house, assessing Sara and radioing the hospital to be prepared. They stay asleep as the ambulance arrives and places her on a gurney. And they're still asleep as the ambulance speeds away carrying their mother.

I call Mrs. Porter next door to ask her to come sit with the kids, explaining what happened. Luckily, she answers and shows up on my porch in a robe with her hair in curlers. She pushes me out the door and tells me not to worry. But that's all I can do as I speed to the hospital.

Sara can't die. Those kids don't deserve that kind of pain. I slam my hand on my steering wheel, over and over. She had me sign papers. She knew what she was going to do. I ignored every single sign, even when my gut told me something was off. I ignored Kian when he told me I wasn't taking her depression seriously enough. If she dies, this is on me.

And I'll never forgive myself.

TWENTY

Kian

I turned my phone off and didn't set an alarm before going to bed last night. I planned to sleep my entire Saturday away and not wake until right before I had to be at Focus to open the doors. But I'm jolted awake by pounding on my door when the sun has barely risen, judging by my dimly lit bedroom.

I turn my phone on and see multiple missed calls from Jax, of all people. I go on high alert. I scramble from bed, throwing on last night's pants, and rush to the door. Peeking through the peephole, I see Jax on the other side, his head down and his fist poised to knock again.

"What's wrong?" I ask as I swing open the door.

"A lot, actually. Can I come in?" He doesn't wait for me to answer before he's pushing past me and walking inside my condo. "You need to take a seat."

"I don't need to do anything because this is my place." I fold my arms across my chest. I'm still half asleep and in no mood to deal with whatever this is.

Then he lifts his head and my breath leaves my lungs in a giant whoosh, as if I've been kicked in the chest. His features are dark even on the brightest of days, but whatever's wrong, along with the twilight, has his brown eyes near black and his worry lines even more shadowed.

"Seriously, Kian. Sit down." His commanding tone has

me obeying. I slink down onto my couch, my eyes widening as he paces back and forth. "I have something to tell you."

"If you're here to tell me you're still in love with me, you can just leave now."

"What?" His brows knit together in confusion. "No. God, no. I'm with Dante. We're living together."

"Then what is it?"

He sits down next to me and takes my hand in his. If he's not here to admit his undying love, then what the ever-loving fuck is this?

"It's about Archer. Well, his sister," he says so low, his words are barely heard. I go from absolute confusion to complete clarity. Before he says the words, I know. "She overdosed."

"Is she—"

"She's alive, but barely."

"Oh my God. I need to go." Panic like I've never felt before consumes me. I pull my hand free and stand up, looking around for things I need.

Keys, phone, shoes. What else? Fuck, I can't think.

"A shirt." Jax instructs and I look down at my bare chest.

"Okay." I slip into my room and yank on a black Focus tee. I toe on a pair of sneakers and then I'm back in my living room, still searching for my goddamn keys. Jax dangles them from a finger.

"You can have these, but I'm driving you."

"What? No. That's stupid." I snag the keys from him.

"Kian, you're in shock. I can see it on your face. You can't be behind a wheel."

"Fine. But you better not go the speed limit and I want lights and sirens."

Once out my door, I jog to the stairwell and take them two at a time, thankful Jax is right behind me. He opens the passenger side of his Tahoe that's parked illegally in front of the condos. My mind races. Chasing circles around a million thoughts at once.

I knew she was severely depressed.

Why didn't Archer listen to me when I said she needed help?

He must be broken into a thousand pieces.

Oh my God. Emmy and Lou.

It's that final thought that brings tears to my eyes. If she dies, he'll be the one who has to tell them. He hadn't even recovered from his last trauma with Mason. My breaths come faster and my vision narrows, my chest constricting.

"Breathe. Lean over and put your head between your legs." Jax presses between my shoulders, forcing me to do what he said. But a feather could knock me over right now, so it doesn't take much to get me into position. "Just breathe."

I focus on inflating and deflating my lungs until the woozy feeling passes. By the time I sit up, we're already at the hospital.

"He's here?"

"Yes. When I left his place, he was calling the neighbor to come sit with the kids." Jax pulls into the emergency lane and puts the car in park.

"Will she live?" I ask, knowing I can't ask Archer this question, but needing to know.

"I don't know. She had an empty bottle of Vicodin next to her. I guess it was prescribed to her after her C-section. Archer didn't find her until it had already gotten into her system. It suppresses the respiratory system in high doses, and she wasn't breathing. Archer performed CPR until I got there and could take over. She had a weak heartbeat and wasn't breathing on her own when the paramedics took her."

I take in everything he says, frozen in place. I want to rush to Archer, be there for him. Especially since I know he has no one else. But I can't. The second I see him, this will be real. I'll have to set aside my own feelings to be what he needs and I don't know how to do that.

"What do I say to him?" I ask in a small voice, peering over at my once best friend and boyfriend.

He blows out a breath. "I don't know. I don't think words are what he needs right now. You know?"

"Yeah." I steel my spine and step out of the car, but lean back in to say thank you.

"No problem. If you need anything, you know how to reach me."

I nod and shut the door after me.

I walk into the waiting room of the small emergency room. I scan the space until I see one lone figure in the corner. Bent over, head in his hands, is Archer. For such an enormous man, he appears small, collapsed in on himself.

Nerves give way to my immediate need to comfort him and I rush over. "Archer?"

He looks up, his cheeks tear-stained and his eyes swollen and puffy. The second our eyes meet, his chest heaves and he wails in pain. Not the kind of pain you can see or hear, but the kind that stems from your soul. From the most locked away parts of you that you don't know exists until something so bad happens, you're forced to feel just how deep your emotions run.

I bend over and crush him to me, kissing the top of his head and running my hands up and down his back, through his hair, along his shoulders, everywhere I can touch to remind him he still belongs to this world. He buries his face in my chest and sobs. No words are needed. Not for a long time. Not until someone clears their throat.

"Mr. Warren?" a tall, handsome man in a white lab coat asks.

"That's me." Archer wipes the tears from his face and stands up. I do the same, clutching his hand in support.

"I'm Dr. Miller. I've been taking care of your sister since she arrived."

"How is she?"

"She's alive, but she's in a coma. She still isn't breathing on her own, but she's a fighter."

"What does that mean? Is she going to live?"

"She's stable. I'm optimistic. We've done all we can. Now it's up to her and God. She's on a breathing machine and we're running tests. An EEG is being administered right now to see how badly the lack of oxygen has damaged her brain."

"Brain damage?" Archer asks, his words slow and labored. I grip his hand tighter.

"There are two types of brain injuries, hypoxic and anoxic. Hypoxic is when the brain doesn't get enough oxygen and anoxic is when the brain doesn't get any. Your sister suffered an anoxic brain injury. When you found her, she wasn't breathing at all and the longer the brain is left without oxygen, the more severe the injury. The EEG will measure brain activity and that will give us a better idea of what we're dealing with." He places a hand on Archer's shoulder. "She's made it this far, let's not lose hope."

Archer clears the emotion from his throat. "Can I see her?"

"I think so. Just prepare yourself. She's hooked up to machines and there's a tube down her throat. It looks scary, but it's needed to keep her alive." He looks from Archer to me and down to our joined hands. "But only one of you should come back at a time."

"I'm her brother, Kian is… a friend." Archer drops my hand and turns to me. "I'll call you later."

"Go. Don't worry about me. I'll wait here for you."

"I don't know how long I'll be."

"When you're ready, go to the nurse's station. They'll tell

you where to go and I'll stop in after a while." Dr. Miller holds out his hand. Archer shakes it and thanks him.

"I can wait for however long. I don't want you to be alone after you've seen her."

"I'll be okay. You don't need to waste your whole day in the waiting room."

"Archer, I'm not some stranger. It's me. I want to be here for you." I insist.

He scratches his chin through his beard the way he does whenever he's stressed. "Um, do you think you could go by the house? Check on Emmy and Lou? They were still asleep when I left and I'm worried they'll be scared waking up with Mrs. Porter."

"Of course. Can I take over babysitting and send Mrs. Porter home?"

"That'd be great."

"Call me when you know more."

"I will." He promises.

Before he has a chance to walk away, I wrap my arms around his middle and rest my cheek on his chest so I can hear his heartbeat. He hugs me back, but only for a second.

"I gotta go," he says, walking backward. "I'll call you."

I watch until he disappears through the swinging doors that'll lead him to his sister. I want to do more. I want to reach inside him, take his worry, and give it to myself. It's not fair for someone who has already lost so much, to be on the verge of losing more. I fear what it'll do to him and if he'd be able to recover.

It's not until I step outside that I remember I don't have a car. I debate calling Jarrett or Fernando, but ultimately decide to walk. It's only two miles to Archer and Sara's house and I use the time to process my life right now.

Just a couple months ago, my life was predictable. I was happy, but I was stagnant. I had my bar and club, my friends, my cute condo, and peace. Then Archer came and nothing's been the same. Even with all the pain from the last two days, I can't regret us. He made me feel big emotions, made me excited about life, and recently, made me deal with emotions I didn't know I was harboring.

It's no wonder I never pursued anything deeper with anyone. If I hadn't met Archer, I don't know when I would've realized I'd been holding myself back. But he was never a choice for me. My attraction to him was instantaneous, with his rock-hard body and sad eyes. Then after he opened up to me, it was all over. I fell for him recklessly and without a shred of self-preservation.

There's a wrong time even for the most right of couples, and Archer and I managed to find each other before either of us had any business trying to merge our lives. It's time to backtrack. Do that friends thing we talked so much about but failed so horribly at.

***

I walk through the front door of Sara's house a half hour later with a clear head. I don't know what I'll tell these kids, but I'm hoping I'll figure it out in the moment.

Mrs. Porter pops her head around the corner and smiles sadly when she sees me. "How is she?"

"She's okay. Hanging on, but not in the clear." I don't divulge too much. It doesn't feel right. "Archer sent me to relieve you."

"Okay, let me finish washing these dishes and I'll leave you to it. The kids are still sleeping and I got bored, so I started cleaning."

I follow her back into the squeaky-clean kitchen. I must look as shitty as I feel because she sets a mug out for me without being asked. I pour a cup of coffee, drowning it in cream. The black sludge is a necessity, but I don't like the taste. Mrs.

Porter finishes loading the dishwasher and hugs me before leaving. She's someone I've known my whole life and part of the woke elderly in this town.

I take my coffee and explore. I've never been past the living room and combined kitchen. I find Sara's room first. Her bed is disheveled, the room is a mess, and there's a sad, dark vibe emanating from the space. I set my cup down and make her bed, pick up her laundry, and close all her half open drawers. When, and I mean when, she comes home, it should be to a more serene space.

Then I find Archer's room. Or at least I think it is. I wouldn't know because there's absolutely no personality in here. No pictures, no decorations, even the bedding is boring. It's no wonder he never feels settled. He's not. Whenever we spent time together, it was always at my place. I thought maybe it was because his family lives here, and maybe that's true to some extent, but I'll bet it's also because this doesn't feel like home.

I make his bed, feeling like a creeper when I pick up his pillow and breathe in his manly scent. It's woodsy and masculine. Sexy.

"Kian?" a small voice asks. I drop the pillow and spin around to find Lou there in only a pair of little boy boxer briefs and I decide right then and there, I've never seen anything more adorable.

"Hey, buddy. Just waking up?"

"Yeah. Where's Archer and my mom?" He tips his head to the side like a little puppy.

I kneel down to his level. "Your mom got sick overnight and Archer took her to the doctor."

"Did she barf?"

"I don't think so, but she wasn't feeling well. The doctor is looking at her right now and he's going to make her all better." I pray I'm not lying to him.

"When will they be home?"

"I'm not sure. But I'll stay with you until they are. Sound okay?"

"Are you going to make pancakes?" This feels like an important question. Like my answer will depend on how upset he is about having me here. I answer wisely.

"Of course I am. Is there any other way to eat breakfast?"

"Nope. Come on. I'll show you how." He grabs my hand and leads me to the kitchen.

Emmy wakes up not long after and we make an obscene amount of pancakes, which we eat with a disgusting amount of syrup. They may not know how close they are to losing their mother, but I still give them everything they ask for because even if Sara makes it, it's going to be a long recovery and who knows what kind of mom will walk back through that door.

TWENTY-ONE

Archer

"Come on, Sara. Open your eyes," I plead, her hand in mine.

I broke down when I first saw her. Every inch of her has some type of tube, chord, or patch connected. Her head's tipped back with a tube down her throat. Her skin's an odd gray color and she's pale and clammy. I wouldn't think she was alive if it weren't for the constant beeping of the machine next to her.

Nurses flitter in and out, taking vitals and giving me sympathetic looks I don't want. I don't know how she ended up in this place, how things got so bad right under my nose, but she's not weak. I don't need the pity. As soon as she wakes up, I'll make sure she gets the help she needs and she'll be better than ever. If I don't kill her for trying to leave this world.

I text Kian every hour to make sure he and the kids are doing okay. He insists they're fine and not to worry. I have no reason to doubt his capabilities. He's always been amazing with them. So I tell him I'm not and I'll check back in a while.

Dr. Miller pops in every so often, checks her chart, tells me to be patient, and leaves again. Sara remains unmoving. I doze off in the uncomfortable chair once or twice, but mostly I stare at her, willing her to wake up. It doesn't work.

I check my phone and notice it's 8:00 p.m. and I freak out. Kian had a bar to open. *Fuck*. I kiss Sara on the forehead and tell her I'll be back in the morning. Then I find the nurse's station and tell them to call me if there's any change and that I'll be back tomorrow.

I speed home, hoping he's not pissed at me, or worse, took the kids to the bar. I wouldn't put it past him. I rush through the front door and am struck by an amazing smell. Onion, garlic, and tomato assault my nostrils and my stomach growls, reminding me I haven't eaten since… fuck, I don't remember when.

Emmy and Lou are at the kitchen island, slurping spaghetti noodles, happy as little clams. Kian's on the opposite side of the island, plating up a portion of noodles.

"Hey, guys," I say as cheerily as I can muster.

"Archer!" they yell back. Two sets of eyes look behind me and then turn sad.

"Where's Mommy?" Emmy asks, red sauce all over her face.

"The doctor is keeping her overnight, but she'll be home before you know it." *If she decides to wake up at all.* These kids will never trust me again if I'm lying to them.

"Can we call her on your phone?" Lou forks noodles into his mouth.

"Not tonight, buddy. She was already asleep when I left." I ruffle his hair.

"Want some spaghetti?" Kian asks.

"Yes, please. I'm starving." I walk into the kitchen and stand next to the stove while Kian makes me a plate. "I'm sorry I'm so late. I forgot you had to open Focus at six."

"It's not a problem. I asked one of my Blur bartenders, Keith, to fill in. He worked Focus before Sara did, so he knows how things work."

"If you need to get over there, you can go now."

"I don't. I took the night off."

"Thank you, Kian. I don't know what I would've done without you."

"Don't even worry. We had fun." A crooked smile creeps onto his lips.

"Even so—"

"How is she?" he asks in a hushed tone, changing the subject.

"The same," I say through an exhalation.

"The doctors don't know any more?"

"No. They keep saying she'll wake up when she's ready. They mentioned taking the breathing tube out tomorrow or the next day to see if she can breathe on her own now that the drugs have worked their way through her system."

"I'll bet you didn't eat all day. You need to take care of yourself in order to take care of her."

"Honestly, the day flew by. I didn't realize how late it had gotten."

"Parmesan?"

"Please."

He grates fresh cheese over the top of my noodles. I look around and see a garden salad and bread. I shouldn't be surprised because he's an amazing cook, but I'm almost certain none of these ingredients were in the fridge.

"Did you take them grocery shopping?"

"Yep. We had an adventure." He turns to the kids. "Didn't we?"

"Kian bought us cookies," Emmy says.

"Why don't you guys go wash your hands and faces? When you're done, I'll turn on a show for you." Kian suggests.

The kids cheer and jump down to wash up. Kian clicks on Netflix in the living room, while I clear their plates and sit down to eat my own dinner. Seconds later, Kian's back to make his own plate before sitting next to me at the island.

"I hope they weren't too much of a hassle."

"Are you kidding? Sara's taught them right. They're angels."

I shovel another bite in my mouth, savoring the slow cooked flavors. "This is delicious."

"Thanks. I usually don't cook much because it's just me or sometimes Jarrett if I talk him into coming over for dinner, so it was nice to have a group to feed. Even if the circumstances are terrible."

"Did the kids ask much about Sara?"

"They did at first. I told them she had a tummy ache and you took her to the doctor. They seemed to accept that explanation." He sets his fork down and pins me with a look. "How are you holding on?"

"I don't know. I think I'm confused more than anything."

"What all happened last night? Was she upset? It wasn't too long after we got off the phone that Jax showed up to tell me."

"No, it was the opposite. She was happy. She'd just been to see the lawyer. She had one stipulation added to the divorce papers and had a will drawn. Looking back, I can see she was preparing. She spent time with the kids and handled her affairs. It's so obvious to me now. I'm a fucking idiot."

Kian rubs circles on my back. "Hindsight and all that."

"You warned me she was in a bad place. I'm sorry I ignored you and dismissed your opinion every time you offered it. I didn't want to believe she could do something like this."

"Don't apologize. Who would ever want to think their family member is capable of suicide?" He stands up and takes his dishes to the sink. "I better get going. What time do you want me here in the morning?"

"You don't need to—"

"Archer, it's been a long day and I'm tired. Can we skip the argument we're about to have? You can't do everything on your own. You can't be at the hospital and with the kids. It's impossible. Can we please just get to the part where you say, 'if you're sure.'" He deepens his voice to mock me. "And I'll say it's no problem and then you'll tell me what time to be here tomorrow."

My head lulls forward as I shake it, knowing he's right. "Fine. Is ten okay?"

"Yep and if anything changes overnight, call me." He pats my back and brushes past me, heading for the front door.

"Why are you helping me?" I ask without turning around.

"Because we're friends."

Sunday morning, I'm back at the hospital. I didn't sleep worth a shit last night and the kids were impossible after they woke up, not accepting my vague answers about their mommy's whereabouts. I was happy when Kian showed up with a full day planned to keep them busy. He rushed me out the door, telling me I was hovering when I asked what he was going to do with them.

I run into Dr. Miller leaving Sara's room as I'm walking in. He's not in the same lab coat and dress shirt like he was yesterday. Today he's casual and I can't stop my perusal. The doctor is fit. His biceps stretch across the sleeves of his T-shirt to accommodate them and his jeans showcase his thick thighs.

"Archer, I'm glad I ran into you. Why don't we step inside Sara's room so I can go over everything with you?" He holds the door open and motions me in.

Sara's in the same position, looking small in the cumbersome bed. Her eyes are still closed and the tube lodged in her mouth. Her color has changed, though, and she looks very much alive. I sit next to her and take her hand.

"Her vitals are improving and her EEG showed brain activity. Those are all good signs that she's going to make it through this," Dr. Miller explains.

"Okay, so when will she wake up?"

"If she pulls through, and I have every hope she will, it'll be when she's ready. Her body went through a huge trauma and she needs this time to rest. I'm off today, but since we have a limited staff, I'll be keeping in constant contact with the nurses and I'll rush over the second there's any change."

"You're going to leave her here like this?" I panic and wonder if I should move her to a bigger city where there are more equipped hospitals.

Miller chuckles. "I assure you, she's in better hands with my nurses than with me alone."

"Okay, I guess. Have fun golfing. I'll be here with my comatose sister," I lash out.

He scowls at me, making his handsome face contort into something ugly. "I'm not the enemy, Archer. I know you're scared, but my patients are my priority. I wouldn't be leaving if I thought it was detrimental to Sara's health."

"I'm sorry." I run a hand through my hair. "You're right, but I'm scared. She has two little kids at home. Did you know that?"

"I did. Even if she didn't, I would make sure she was given the best care."

"Thank you."

"Here's my card. It has my personal cell on the back. Call me if you have any concerns the nurses can't help you with."

I accept the card, making sure the number is legible. "Thanks, doc."

"Lance. You can call me Lance."

I nod and he leaves. I tuck the card away in my wallet and spend the day talking to my sister, telling her all the things I wish I'd said before she tried to take her own life.

"Do you remember the time I botched our mac and cheese? I think you were eight or nine. Mom had left with some guy named Axel or something. Dad was too depressed to quit drinking and go to work. Yeah, I know. One of the many times. Anyway, we were so hungry and all we had was mac and cheese in the cupboard. I misread the directions and put the milk, butter, and cheese packet in with the water so when I drained it, we were left with plain noodles." I chuckle at the memory. "You didn't want me to feel bad, so you ate them anyway and said you liked them better that way. I knew you were lying, but I remember being proud of myself anyway.

"I always wanted to take care of you. I felt like it was my duty. But I've failed you for many years now. I thought when you went off to college that I was done, that you were an adult. I never considered you still needing me. I got caught up with Mason and then caught up in grief. I'm sorry about that."

She doesn't respond, but still I reminisce for hours, only stopping when the nurses come in to take her vitals. I pray to a God I don't know exists. I will her awake. I scold her and yell at her. I guilt her about her kids being sad without her. Nothing works. By 10:00 p.m. she still lies there and here I am, leaving her here yet again. All alone.

I stop in, reminding the nurses to call me no matter the time. They're annoyed with me, I see it in their eyes, but they agree and tell me to get some rest. I wish I could. I really do. I'm exhausted. But I know it won't happen until Sara opens her goddamn eyes.

I drive home, wondering what I'll do. I need to work, but I also can't imagine not being next to Sara's side. Plus, there are the kids. I'll have to find a babysitter. Maybe Mrs. Porter can help, at least for a while.

As I pull into the driveway, I've already decided to call in sick tomorrow. I'll work out what to do for the rest of the week later. I can't fish when I haven't been sleeping. It's not safe for Oliver or me.

Inside the house is silent, other than the TV in the living room on a low volume. I find Kian sprawled out on the sofa, dead asleep. One arm hangs off the cushion and the other is draped over his eyes. His pouty mouth hangs open and he's snoring softly.

"Kian." I rub a hand on the center of his chest. It's an intimate touch, but I don't want to startle him. A week ago, I would've woken him with a kiss. But we're back to friends only mode, so I ignore the pull.

"What?" He groans, stirring.

"I'm home."

"Okay." He turns on his side and is instantly asleep again.

"Kian. Don't you want to get home?"

I'm met with more sleep sounds, so I grab a blanket from the back of the couch and spread it over him. I flip the TV off and turn out the lights. If he wakes up sometime in the night, he can leave, but he's so peaceful, I can't press him to get up.

I find a change of clothes and take a quick shower, wanting to wash away the antiseptic smell of Sara's hospital room. Clean and warm, clad only in my boxers, I fall face first into bed.

It's strangely comforting to have Kian under the same roof. His presence alone lifts the pressure and burden off me. It's because of him I'm able to fall asleep.

Just friends or more, I'm glad I have him.

TWENTY-TWO

Kian

I startle awake with a crick in my neck like I've never felt before. My eyes slowly focus and I realize I'm not in my room, on my comfortable memory foam mattress. Nope. I'm on an old sofa in Archer's living room, my head bent back behind a sofa cushion and an arm's asleep from dangling over the edge.

I slowly sit up, giving my body time to readjust. I find my phone tucked in-between two cushions and see it's three in the morning. I'm too tired to go home, but I'm also too much of a princess to finish my night on the couch.

I think about taking over Sara's bed, but it feels wrong. So instead, I find myself padding down the hall to Archer's room. His door is open a crack and I look in to make sure he's not naked or in some other type of private situation. He's not, but he does look like he literally fell into bed and hasn't moved a muscle. He's on top of the blankets and sheets, in a pair of plaid boxers, with his arms tucked under his pillow.

For all of his brooding and tough guy masculine energy, he looks like a child when he's asleep.

I return to the couch and grab the blanket he must've given me when he got home and cover him up with it. I dig through the top drawer of his dresser, happy to find his underwear drawer. I know we aren't dating or anything right now, but I need these tight jeans off my body and for once, the whole no underwear thing is biting me in the ass. I figure

Archer will be quicker to forgive me for borrowing a pair of boxer briefs than he would if I climbed into bed naked next to him.

I lie down on the opposite side of the bed and pull half the blanket to my side. He stirs and turns onto his side, facing me. I hold my breath, praying he doesn't wake up. His eyes blink a few times, then close. Then open again, only wider this time.

"Kian?" he whispers.

"Shh, just go with it. I can't drive home. It's too late and that couch is the worst thing I've ever tried to sleep on."

"It's fine." He yawns and his eyes flutter shut. Seconds later his breathing slows and he's back off to dreamland.

Phew. I snuggle into my pillow. An overwhelming feeling of comfort spreads through my body and I stretch long before curling onto my side. My eyes feel heavy and sleep finds me within minutes.

The next time I wake up, sunshine is pouring through the curtains and I have a bear wrapped around me. An Archer shaped bear. He's taken up the big spoon position, I'm the little spoon with his arm around my middle, and his breaths blowing across the back of my neck.

This is bad. I try to extricate myself slowly, but his arm tightens around me. *This is not friendly behavior, Archer.* I wait until he relaxes and roll off the side of the bed, landing on my ass.

"Ouch." I moan.

Archer's head appears over the edge of the bed. "What are you doing on the floor?"

"Isn't this how everyone gets out of bed?" I joke and stand up.

"Are you wearing my underwear?"

The boxer briefs are two sizes too large and have slid dangerously low on my hips. I yank them back up. "It was either that or sleep naked."

A sly grin appears on Archer's lips.

"No." I point at him. "No. No. You aren't allowed to smile at me like that."

"Why?" He chuckles.

"It's flirty and we're not doing flirty. Or snuggly. We're friends who are figuring out our lives before jumping into another anti-relationship with each other."

"All right. I'm sorry."

I grab my clothes and stomp to the bathroom. After I've done my business and dressed, I return to Archer's room to find Lou next to him in bed. He has giant tears falling down his cheeks and it breaks my heart. No, not accurate. It eviscerates my heart.

"Buddy, she's fine. I promise. But she has to sleep lots and lots so she can get better." Archer wipes the tears from his squishy cheeks. "She misses you so much and is trying so hard to get better."

"Can I go see her?"

Archer shoots me a broken and sad smile before answering. "Not yet. The doctor wants her to get a little stronger first."

"Hey, Lou. Remember how we made chocolate chips pancakes yesterday? I was thinking we could try Oreo today." I intervene.

"Really?" He jumps off the bed and takes my hand, dragging me out of the room. Archer mouths *thank you* and I nod.

All day long, I keep the kids busy. We go to the park, we have lunch at Comida's, we even stop by the boardwalk to play some carnival games, and still these kids are not worn out. By the time we get home to make dinner, I'm dragging ass. I don't know how parents do it. Children are exhausting.

Archer texted me earlier to tell me Sara squeezed his hand. The nurses warned him it was probably a reflex, but he felt her with him briefly. Hope is a fickle bitch that can sometimes be mistaken as truth. I don't tell him that, though. I celebrated with him because no matter if it's a lie, you need hope to get through the bad times.

Bedtime for Emmy and Lou is 8:00 p.m. and you better believe they were both tucked in by one minute after the hour. All I want to do is watch TV and be a potato, but the paperwork of owning your own business never stops. So I work on my laptop until I hear the front door open.

"Hey. How are you?" I ask as Archer walks into the living room. His eyes are wide and glassy. I can feel the nervous energy coming off of him in waves. Fearful apprehension lands in my gut like a boulder. I push my laptop onto the couch next to me and jump to my feet. "What happened?"

"She woke up." He smiles and drops of happiness spring from his eyes.

"She did?" I screech and then flinch, hoping I didn't wake up the kids. "Really?" I whisper this time.

"Really."

I run over to him and we embrace for a long time. Archer's cheek rests on my head and we sway. His body trembles and I hold him to me harder. It doesn't feel real. It's only been a few days since Sara harmed herself, but it's felt like a lifetime. I'm certain it's felt even longer to him.

"Tell me everything." I pull him to the sofa and move my laptop to the coffee table.

"About two hours ago, she squeezed my hand again and I had that same feeling. Like she was in her body again. Then her eyes opened. She panicked and I called the nurse. They ran a couple tests and decided they could remove the breathing tube. We didn't get a chance to talk. Dr. Miller warned me her throat would be sore and she'd be exhausted after they took it out. By the time they let me back in the room, she was asleep. I thought maybe she'd gone back into a coma, but he assured me she was just resting." He scratches his fingers through his beard. "They told me I should go home for the night because she'd more likely be out of it for a while."

"That's incredible. I'm so happy."

"Me too. When I saw her eyes, it was the best feeling in the world."

His excitement is palpable and I get caught up in it. Unable to stop myself, I give him another hug, which he happily returns.

"So what now?" I ask.

"Dr. Miller said tomorrow they'll run some kind of brain test so he can see if the lack of oxygen gave her any lasting damage. But other than that, I don't know. I was so worried about her waking up, now that she did, I don't know what to do. I mean, she tried to kill herself."

"How long will they keep her in the hospital?"

"At least a few more days, depending on the test results."

"That's reassuring. It'll give you time to talk to her and figure out what's best."

"What if she refuses to get help? What if she tries again?" His leg bounces and he worries his lip, like I've seen happen so often the last few days. I take his hand in mine, turn it over, and rub comforting circles on his wrist.

"Let's not jump to conclusions. Maybe this will be the wakeup call she needs."

"I can't go through this again."

"You'll make her understand. I know you will. Now that you know just how depressed she's been, you know how hard to fight. I'll help any way you need."

"Thank you, Kian. I honestly don't know what I would've done without you."

"I do make an awesome babysitter." I boast.

"It's not just that. I didn't feel alone in this. You supported me and gave me an outlet to vent to. I don't deserve you, but I'm glad you're my friend." He stutters on the word friend, but I don't read into it.

"You're welcome. On that note, I better go. I'll be back tomorrow morning. I do have to go into Focus tomorrow by six, but I can ask Mrs. Porter to sit with them, or we can call Oliver's daughter."

"Are you sure you can do another day with them?"

"Of course. You can assume for the next little while that I'll be here every day. Doing whatever you need." I assure him.

"I think you should stay," he blurts.

"Huh?"

"I mean, in Sara's room. At least for a few days until we know what's going to happen. You've been staying so late and have to wake up so early to be here when I leave for the hospital. I think it makes sense. You can sleep in until the kids wake up. Especially since you have to work late at night."

"I guess I can." I want to argue, but after tonight, I'll be arriving home at two in the morning and then waking up at six to be here for Archer to go to the hospital. At least if I were here, I could sleep until eight when the kids get up.

"I'm glad. Do you want to go pack a few things up and I'll get the bedding changed on Sara's bed?"

"Oh, you mean tonight?"

"Not if you don't want to." He rubs at the back of his neck, looking sheepish. It's a hard expression to pull off when you're built like a lumberjack, but he manages.

"No, I do. It's a smart idea." I grab my keys. "I guess I'll be back in a half hour or so?"

"Perfect."

I calmly leave and get into my tiny Smart car. Then I proceed to freak out and call Jarrett.

He answers on the fourth ring. "Bitch, it's ten p.m. and I'm in bed."

"Where you'll stay awake for two more hours watching *Gossip Girl*. You forget I know you."

"You're right. What's up?"

"Archer just asked me to move in with him."

"Into his sister's house? Aren't you two taking a break?"

"Technically he asked me to move into his sister's room to make it easier to babysit."

"That makes sense since you're the manny now," he says in a bored tone.

"Exactly. So why am I freaking out? It's a logical decision."

"Because you like the guy and want to be sleeping in his bed where he can dick you down every night."

"Not every night. My ass couldn't take it." I clench just thinking about it. I mean, I could try and see, but—

"Told you that's why you're having a panic attack."

"We decided to be friends for a reason. I have unresolved teenage angst I haven't had a chance to deal with and he's still neck deep in sister troubles." Logic returns like a hammer to the face. I have no business romanticizing practicality.

"Kian, Kian, Kian. I'm only going to say this once, so listen up." I hear him adjust in his bed, getting comfortable. "You don't have 'teenage angst' issues or whatever you want to call it. You have trust issues like ninety percent of all people out there. It's scary to fall for someone. It gives them power over you. You were hurt once, sure. But who actually ends up marrying their high school sweetheart? None of us. It's been eleven years. Let that shit go. Archer isn't Jax. He's still a man, so he's going to fuck up, but he's not Jax. If you don't suture the wound he left, it's going to keep bleeding on everyone else you try to have a relationship with."

Realization hits me. He's right. Jax and I probably would've broken up over something else if it hadn't been his complete inability to show anyone but me his true self. Who knows? Maybe I would've been the one to break it off. We were kids. I need to let it go.

"Wow. That was actually sound advice."

"I know," he says and I hear the smug grin in his tone. "Thank you."

"You're welcome. Now, more importantly, how's Sara?"

"She woke up," I say.

"She did?" He gasps. "That should've been the headline of this phone call. Next time lead with the breaking news and not this fake news bullshit you were spewing."

"Archer hasn't talked to her or anything. She fell asleep after they took out her breathing tube. But at least she's awake."

"Thank God."

"It'll be interesting to see what happens from here."

"Hopefully she'll want to get help." He gasps loudly, startling me. "You know what she should do? She should take up yoga. It does wonders for your mental health."

"I'll mention it to Archer." I won't. Personally, I don't see how twisting yourself into a pretzel can make you not depressed. "Listen, I better go. I need to pack a bag and get back to Archer's."

"Okay, honey. Fernando and I will stop by for wine tomorrow."

"See you then."

As I put together an overnight bag with my essentials, I think about what Jarrett said. The more I churn the conversation around in my mind, the more it all becomes clear, and even though Archer still isn't in the place to pick back up on us, I am. I always was. But I was scared and chose to blame my insecurities on my past instead of just talking them out with the other person in the relationship.

I'll wait for this to be all over, but once it is and things are settled, I'm getting my man back.

TWENTY-THREE

Archer

It was a spontaneous decision to ask Kian to stay here while I figure things out with Sara. I'd been feeling so alone and to wake up with him in my bed this morning was a balm to my soul. Combine that with seeing my sister's eyes open and I guess I got caught up.

I change the bedding in Sara's room. I doubt she'll mind given all that Kian has done for us the last few days. Assuming she cares about anything anymore. A pain stabs through my heart. What the hell was she thinking? I want to storm to the hospital and demand answers from her.

After the bed is squared away, I hurry and take a quick shower. I change into a pair of navy sweats and a T-shirt, then return to the living room to wait. Or maybe I shouldn't wait. He knows his way around the house. He doesn't need me to tuck him in. Dirty, filthy images spring to mind when I think about all the things Kian and I have gotten up to in a bed. And in his office. And on his dining table.

Fuck.

I'm not going to wait. It's weird. Right as I stand up, I hear the front door open. Kian pops into the room, a duffle bag slung over his shoulder. He looks as awkward as I feel. Good. We're on an even playing field.

"You going to bed?" he asks.

"Just heading that way." I scratch my fingers through my beard.

"I'll bet you're exhausted." He looks from one corner of the room to the other.

"You need anything?"

"No. I can get myself settled. Mind if I shower?"

Goddamn. The shower. We haven't ever done anything naughty in the shower.

"Go ahead. It's all yours."

"Okay. I guess I won't see you tomorrow if you get home after I've left for work," he says.

"Guess not. Unless, I could wait up for you."

"Don't do that. But will you call me tomorrow? You know, to let me know how Sara is and all that?"

"Sure. I'll want to check on the kids and make sure the babysitter shows up and all that." This conversation is awkward. If I were feeling more stable on my feet, I'd say fuck it and drag his ass to my bed. That's a bad idea right now, though.

"Okay. Good night, then." He brushes past me, heading to Sara's room. Our arms touch and a static, electric spark prickles my skin. The same sensation I get every time we touch.

"Good night."

I don't usually close my bedroom door to make it easier for the kids if they wake up in the middle of the night, but tonight, I shut it. It feels more absolute. As if simply turning a knob is what'll stop me from sneaking down the hallway.

I share a wall with the bathroom, so I hear when the water turns on. A minute goes by and I hear the shower hooks slide open across the rod and then shut. He's naked in there. I picture his smooth skin and lean body dripping with water. He's hairless *everywhere*, making his long, cut dick look even more massive. And his ass. Goddamn. His ass. Perfect round pillows hiding the tightest hole I've ever been inside.

My cock hardens and I squeeze it through my boxers to get some relief, but it doesn't work. Instead I groan from the almost painful touch. I want to march in there, climb in behind him, hook his leg over my elbow to spread him open, and then drill into him. I want to hear his breaths catch, feel my balls slap against him, and watch him come apart for me.

Before I realize what I'm doing, I'm reaching inside the top drawer of my nightstand and squirting slick on my palm. My boxers come down past my ass and I grip my aching dick. I jerk myself with a vice-like grip, making it feel as tight as Kian's hole does.

I lose myself to the fantasy, tasting his skin, though my mouth is dry. I reach over and grab the pillow he'd been sleeping on and press it to my nose. Thank fuck his pine sweet smell is still there. It makes it seem that much more real. Before I know it, I'm coming all over my abs and chest, muttering a curse under my breath.

It didn't feel half as satisfying as it does when I'm with him, but for now, it'll do. When I hear the water turn off, I briefly wonder if he was doing the same thing. Seems like such a waste for us to be together in our minds, but physically apart.

The next morning, I'm at the hospital bright and early. I need answers that only Sara can give me. I can only pray her brain tests come back in the clear so I can get them.

"Mr. Warren. It's nice to see you," Dr. Miller greets as I walk into the hospital room. He has his tablet open and is tapping the screen with a stylus. There's a woman sitting in the corner, dressed professionally and with a hospital nametag in a lanyard around her neck.

Sara is propped up on pillows, staring blankly at the stark white wall. She doesn't acknowledge me, even though she knows I'm here. I notice her hands are now bound to either side of her hospital bed by padded cuffs. I glare at Dr. Miller.

"Is that necessary?" I bite out.

"It's procedure."

I'll handle him later. I walk around the side of her bed and sit down. I cover her hand with mine to get her attention, but her eyes remain fixed.

"Hi," I say gently.

"I was just talking to Sara about how she's feeling. Her EEG came back and it's right where we want her. We'll need to do more tests in the coming days, but after what her body has been through, it can wait." He flips the tablet closed. "Would you like to go get a cup of coffee with me?"

I stare at the man dumbly. Sure, he's hot as hell, but this is hardly the time or place for him to hit on me.

"I'd like to update you more about Sara's condition," he clarifies.

"Right. Sure." I lean over and kiss Sara on the head. "I'll be right back."

We walk out and he leads me down the hall to the small cafeteria that's more the size of a break room. He orders us a couple of black coffees and swipes his card to pay. He hands me one and we take a seat at a small, round table next to a window.

"Your sister is in a fragile state," he says.

"Of course she is, she just tried to kill herself."

"There's that, but when someone who wants to die, fails, it makes their headspace much more delicate. The woman you saw in the room is a social worker who will work with Sara to put together a game plan. Until they can talk more, I think it might be best if you came back this afternoon."

"Dr. Miller—"

"Lance." He interrupts. "You can call me Lance."

"Lance, you only know my sister through a chart and medical history. I've known her since she was born. I'm certain she'll want me around to support her through this."

"She's the one who asked me to tell you to come back."

I frown. "That's not her talking. I've been the only person who's ever taken care of her."

"She's embarrassed and disappointed about her choices. Especially because she failed. In her mind, her pain was over when she took those pills. Only she didn't die and now that pain she was trying to escape is worse. I'm sure your sister loves you a lot, but she needs to focus on getting better and when there's family involved, it makes things more… complicated."

"No offense, but fuck you. And fuck her, too. She has two babies at home who have been crying every single day to see their mama. I don't know why she thought it would be better to leave them to me than to raise them on her own, but I deserve those answers. She's the only family I have left other than those kids." My eyes well and my breath catches. "She needs to look me in the eyes and explain herself to me."

"I completely understand. I'd feel the same way. But I think it's important to remember the end goal here. We want Sara to get better so she can come back to her kids and give you those answers. I think if you were to ask her in the fragile state she's in, though, you might push her the opposite way. Make her feel backed into a corner." Lance's ice blue eyes pierce into me. He's kind, but also firm. I have no doubt if I were to push the matter, he would have me escorted out. "That's not what you want, right?"

"Of course not." I back down. "I just want her safe and healthy."

"We're on the same page then." His icy eyes melt and turn into cool, crystal blue. "Take the day off. I'll call you later, let you know what Sara and the social worker decide."

"What are the options?"

"It's up to her. She could refuse any help and return home, she could opt for outpatient intensive therapy, or she might decide on an inpatient option. The social worker will bring in a therapist to assess her mental state and they'll decide as a team."

"Inpatient?" I croak.

A million things are running through my mind. Babysitting, my job, bills, the stress of it all feels like a weight on my chest.

"It's a decent option. She can focus on working through her problems while not having outside stressors." He takes a sip of his coffee and winces. "I've only been at this hospital for a week and I'm ready to petition for them to change the coffee."

"You're new to town?" I ask, realizing out of all the gossiping Kian does, he's never mentioned the doctor.

"Yep. Just moved from here from Florida."

"Why?" My brows furrow. Brigs Ferry Bay has grown on me, but it's not a place I would've intentionally chosen.

"Divorce. My wife and I"—he searches for the right words—"we didn't work out and I needed a change. A friend of mine told me his dad was retiring from this hospital and they were looking for a new resident. It kind of just happened."

"Sorry, didn't mean to pry."

"No, it's okay. I'm not hiding skeletons or anything." He laughs nervously, telling me that's exactly what he's doing.

I stand up. "I guess I'll go. Make sure you call me later. Do you have my number?"

"The nurses do and I'll be sure to check in this afternoon."

"Thanks, Dr. Miller."

"Lance." He corrects.

"Right. Lance."

I walk into the lobby and out the door, unsure of what to do now. I've called into work for this whole week. Depending on what the social worker and Sara want to do, I'll either be preparing for her to come home or preparing for her to be gone for an unknown amount of time.

I hate this up-in-the-air feeling. I want a definite plan where I know what to expect. Doesn't seem like that's possible, so I do the next best thing. I head home to where Kian is. He makes lists and schedules in his sleep. He'll know what to do.

TWENTY-FOUR

Kian

I've just finished making a ham and scramble for Emmy and Lou when I hear the front door open. Archer comes strolling around the corner, his brows knitted and his plump lips turned down. My stomach flip-flops, wondering what's wrong.

"Archer!" The kids jump down and hug their uncle around his legs.

"Hey, guys. Breakfast time?"

"Yup. Kian said no more pancakes, so he made green eggs and ham. Like in the book," Lou says animatedly.

I tilt a plate, showing him the eggs I colored with food dye and the bite-sized pieces of ham mixed in.

"Looks interesting. Why don't you guys go eat before it gets cold."

Archer jerks his head toward the living room and I nod. I set the plates in front of the kids and give them utensils and napkins, then follow Archer into the other room. I find him looking out the giant picture window in the living room, his tree trunk arms folded across his chest.

"What happened?" I rest a gentle hand on his forearm.

"Absolutely nothing. She won't talk to me and the doctor sent me home."

"Why?"

"He said she's fragile." He air quotes the last word. "Then

he said she might decide to go to an inpatient treatment facility for depression or some shit."

"And that leaves you in a pickle." I sigh.

"I don't know what to do. I have to go back to work. I can't afford daycare now that I have mortgage and utilities to pay for. I have some savings, but it won't last forever." His entire body is tense, like in those videos of people who wrap a million rubber bands around a watermelon. The top and bottom swell to almost bursting right before they add that final rubber band and then boom! It explodes into a million pieces. If one more thing happens to this man, he's going to explode.

"Archer, you know I don't mind babysitting. I'm fine to be here for as long as you need." I rub up and down his arms, trying to release some pressure.

"It's too much to ask a friend to do." He studies me, looking for any sign of hesitation.

"It's not. We've been having fun. I'll never have my own kids and I don't have siblings. This is giving me the full gunkle experience." I don't mention how exhausting they are. I'm not about to be the final rubber band. Plus, I can tough it out. It's temporary. "Why don't you not worry about it yet. Wait and see what they decide and then we'll make a plan. My dad always used to say, don't count your chickens before the eggs hatch."

"Everything feels so out of control. I mean, what do I tell Emmy and Lou? What if she goes to some facility and doesn't want her kids to visit? Or—"

"You're counting those chickens and one of those eggs might not hatch."

"I think you're using that idiom in the wrong context," he mumbles.

"Same difference. It works."

"I'm glad you're here." The muscles in his jaw relax and it makes my chest puff up in pride. I did that. I calmed him.

"Me too. Now, let's go eat some green eggs." I tug him by the hand to the kitchen and the four of us laugh through breakfast. For the first time in days, Archer smiles a real smile.

I did that.

The calm is short-lived, though. Because after a walk through town and a stop for coffee and Italian sodas, Archer gets a phone call. He steps away and I find a grassy area with some shade to sit and wait. I watch as he paces, jutting his chin out and scratching through his beard. I can't tell what's being said because his only response is a series of "okay" and "I understand" and "whatever it takes."

A minute later, he's tucking the phone back in his pocket and making his way toward us. His mouth is in a firm line, giving nothing away.

"Was it the hospital?" I ask.

"Let's get the kids home and I'll tell you what they said."

"Mommy come home now?" Emmy peers up at him, hope sparkling in her eyes.

"Not quite yet. But he said Mommy is doing so much better and she can't wait to see you." Archer tugs on one of the pigtails I wrangled in her hair. Up until today, I'd only brushed it after she woke up, but this morning she asked for piggy tails like her mom does. I know how much these little squirts miss their mommy, so of course I pulled up a tutorial and figured it out. Not half bad, in my opinion.

Her face falls and she reaches out to hold my hand. "Okay."

The walk home is quiet with the kids sad about Sara and Archer lost in his thoughts. This whole family has had a storm cloud over them for as long as I've known them and from what Archer has told me, it's been even longer than that. I want to chase the dark and gloomy away, leave them with enough sunshine and rainbows to last a lifetime.

I get the kids set up playing Legos in Lou's room and then

seek out Archer. I find him in one of the outdoor chairs in the backyard, staring off into the distance.

"How are you?" I sit in the chair next to him.

"Just thinking. Thank you for settling them."

"No worries. What are you thinking about?"

He turns to face me. "I guess she's going to the inpatient treatment facility. There's one in Camden. It's expensive, but they're applying for some kind of grant or something. I think I'll still have to pay some."

"Is that what has you worried?" I reach over and smooth the lines of worry between his brows. He leans into the touch. I want to kiss him, make him forget his troubles, but I know he needs a friend more than anything right now.

"Not really. I'd do whatever it takes, you know?"

"Then what is it?"

"She doesn't want to see me before she goes. Or the kids. They'll shuttle her up there and she'll be gone at least a few weeks."

"Your feelings are hurt?" I ask.

"Yeah, my feelings are hurt. I don't even understand what's going on and why things got this bad. I think if she could talk to me, explain it, I'd be able to accept it a lot easier. You know?"

"I'd feel the same way. I guess all you can do is be patient."

He leans back in the chair, extending his long legs in front of him, resting his arms on his head. A sliver of his abdomen and happy trail are left on display. It's not the time or place to have thoughts of all the times I'd licked my way down his body, but I can't help it. He's the sexiest man I've ever met.

"I guess."

We sit there for a long time in comfortable silence. Him worrying his lower lip between his teeth and me reminiscing of all the times he was mine and wondering if he ever will be again. It seems inevitable, but I don't know how much of all this is breaking him and if he'll ever be able to focus on his own happiness again.

After a few days, we get into a routine. Archer goes back to work and is home just in time to take over kid duty, then I go to work and am home only hours before he has to leave for work. It's hard and I feel lonelier than I ever have before. Sometimes I take the kids to Comida's or Jarrett's just to talk to my friends.

Before all of this, my time was spent with my friends, meeting Cato for lunch or helping Jarrett paint or stain whatever trash he's found to turn it into treasure. But with two little ones in tow, it's been complicated. They get bored easily and somehow always need a snack. Most days, I don't even bother going out because it's more hassle than it's worth.

When I'm at work, I'm so bogged down with paperwork I can't complete during the day, I spend my hours at Focus and Blur tucked away in my office. I miss my old life, as selfish as that sounds.

By Thursday, I'm having a pity party for one. Archer and I trade off kid duties and I leave for work, dreading the long night ahead. I unlock the front door of Focus for Duke and me, then get started on opening duties.

"Wassup, bitches!" Jarrett calls from the front door. I don't have any customers yet, so I smile instead of scolding him.

"Hey." I try to match his cheer, but I fall short.

His head tilts to the side. "What crawled up your ass and died? I read an article about a guy who slept nude and a fly had crawled its way up his asshole and laid eggs. Dude was shitting maggots for a month. It's nothing like that, right?"

I narrow my eyes at him. "Your mind is a dangerous place."

"I know, right?" He sits down on a barstool and props his head in his hands. "What's up, buttercup?"

"I don't know exactly. I mean, I'm really tired. Like *really tired*. Kids are exhausting. Three out of ten recommend and

I'm only rating it that high because Emmy tells me how pretty I am every day." I pull out two wine glasses, set one down in front of each of us, and pour.

"I can't imagine. I get tired of dealing with Frankie and I leave him in the shop at night," he says, referring to his shop kitty Cato talked him into adopting. Frankie is old as fuck. He has patches of fur missing, one eye, his meow is more of a gravelly hack, and only three legs. If that cat hasn't burned through eight of his nine lives, I don't know who has.

"Take him and multiply by a million. And all my free time is gone. I haven't had time for a facial, I haven't online shopped in over a week, and for lunch I had three half-eaten chicken nuggets and a scoop of cold mac and cheese. I haven't even masturbated in a week. I'm worried my dick is going to forget how to get hard." I sulk.

"That's bad." Jarrett's face scrunches in disgust.

"I just don't feel like myself."

"Any news on Sara?"

"Not yet. Next week Archer is going to Camden to sit in on a family therapy session. I guess he'll get more information then." I shrug and chug half my glass of wine.

"Sweetie," he drawls, his expression turning serious. "I've never seen you like this and we've been friends for a long time."

"It's fine. It's temporary, right?"

"I'm worried. I think you need a break."

I laugh without humor. "And what will Archer do? He can't afford childcare. He's already stressed about money because even after the grant Sara got, he has to fork out a few thousand dollars for this facility she's at."

"This is going to sound harsh, but I think you need to hear this." He rests his hand over mine. "It's not your problem. You and Archer aren't even together. You aren't family. I know you want to help, but when it's affecting your own mental health, it's gone too far."

"You don't understand."

"I think I do. It's you who doesn't understand. What do you get in all of this? Because from here, it looks like you're carrying all this weight for Archer and then what? Sara comes home and you both walk away? I think he's using you."

"He's not using me," I snap, my hackles rising at him even saying something like that.

"Okay, so what do you get out of this? Because he's getting a lot. He's saving money by having a free live-in nanny and housekeeper."

"This isn't easy for him." I defend.

"I don't think it is. He's in a difficult position. But it's *his* family. It's *his* responsibility. You have no stake in this game. No cock in this fight. Literally and figuratively." He arches a brow pointedly.

"Maybe I just want to help someone in need. Maybe I get the satisfaction of doing the right thing."

"Oh my God, you love him." He gasps.

"I do not."

"You do. I didn't see it before, but I do now." He throws his hands up. "It's even worse than I thought."

"What do you mean?"

"You're going to get hurt. You think Sara will come home and miraculously everything will be puppies and whipped cream?"

"Puppies and whipped cream? That's not a thing."

"No one is unhappy when there are puppies and whipped cream around. Fight me." He pushes his empty wine glass toward me for a refill. "The point is, you're an amazing person and not many people would step up the way you have, but he's taking advantage of you and you deserve to know what's going to happen between you two after this is all over. Does he plan on keeping you friend zoned? Will you pick up where you left off? What?"

I don't have an answer for him. I don't want to think he's right because even if Archer had only ever been a friend, I'd like to think I'd do exactly what I've been doing. But this small voice in the back of my head knows I'm hoping for more. Somewhere in all this craziness, I've caught feelings and it might not be love... yet. But it's something.

I feel this constant tug toward a man with more emotional baggage than I have space for. But I desperately want to make room for him.

TWENTY-FIVE

Archer

I drive south, leaving Brigs Ferry Bay for Camden. I'm nervous as fuck about this therapy appointment. I'm worried this therapist will blame all of Sara's problems on me, on the way I took care of her when our parents were unable, or maybe on the way I abandoned her when she went to college. As hard as I tried to make up for Mom and Dad's failures, I doubt it was enough.

I pull into the parking lot of Seasons of Maine with a rock in my gut. I'm excited to see Sara and I came with my phone full of pictures from the last couple weeks, but I'm also nervous. I don't know what to expect or even how she's doing.

I check in at the front desk and am led to a spacious room, decorated in coastal colors with floor-to-ceiling windows overlooking the ocean. If she had to be in a place like this, I'm glad it's somewhere so beautiful.

I take a seat on an oversized leather sofa. My knee bounces frantically, my palms are sweating, and I might throw up. I don't wait long, though, because not two minutes later, Sara and an older woman with kind eyes walk in. Sara has a smile on her face and tears in her eyes when she sees me. She rushes over and hugs me tight.

"I missed you," she whispers.

"Me too," I reply.

"Hi, Archer. I'm Colleen, a therapist here at Seasons. Would you like to take a seat?"

"Sure."

Sara and I sit side by side, but she doesn't look over or say anything else as we wait for Colleen to settle in a chair across from us. I rub my palms down my jeans, feeling uncomfortable and anxious.

"So, Archer. The reason why we asked for you to be here was to discuss Sara's progress, but also because she has done some amazing work and is ready to share some things with you," Colleen says. "Sara, would you like to start?"

Sara nods and turns to me. "First, I want to thank you for taking care of everything while I've been… away. Next, I want to apologize. I haven't been honest about everything and it wasn't fair. It also wasn't right for me to dump everything on you."

"It's okay. I just want to know what's going on and how we can fix it."

"It's important for Sara to take accountability for her actions," Colleen interjects and I want to shove her from the room so my sister and I can have a real conversation.

"With the help of the therapists here, I've learned a lot about myself and while I still feel like I have a long way to go, I also feel like I can tell you the truth about the last few years." Sara's shoulders hunch and she scratches her forehead while her eyes wander.

"Take your time, Sara," Colleen says and turns to me. "Because of the lack of oxygen to her brain when she overdosed, she's experiencing a few challenges. One of them is gathering thoughts. Her balance has also been a little off. She's been doing some occupational therapy for these things, but she might always experience some degree of difficulty."

"That's a lot better than it could've been." I watch Sara patiently until she's ready to finish.

"I told you I dropped out of college to pay for Chad to go, but what I didn't tell you was that he was very controlling and abusive. He basically forced me to quit. He told me I could go back later, but I think it was just something he said to stop me from asking. I think he wanted to keep me reliant on him in all ways. For instance, I was on birth control both times I got pregnant. He never admitted it, but I think he was swapping my birth control with something else. He wouldn't let me get a job or have my own money. He would take my cell phone during the day and only let me call you when he was around."

"You've got to be kidding me." I stand up, the anger building inside me needing to escape. "You could've used someone else's phone, something to get help. You know I would've been here so quick."

"I think part of me liked it, if I'm honest. He was all about me. With the way we grew up, completely neglected by Mom and Dad, it was nice being the center of someone's world. At least, at first. But after I had Emmy, I started growing depressed. Really depressed. Chad was spending less time on me and I knew he was cheating. I could feel him distancing. And as much as I hated not having freedom, the thought of him being with someone else, giving someone else his attention, it drove me deeper into depression." Tears stain her cheeks and Colleen passes her a box of tissues.

"Why didn't you tell me all of this?" I ask and sit back down.

"A couple reasons. You spent so much of your life taking care of me, I didn't want you to give up more. Then, after what happened with Mason, you were going through too much on your own."

"That wouldn't have mattered. I'll always put you first."

She picks apart the tissues in her hand, gathering her thoughts. "You shouldn't have to. I'm a grown woman. I should be able to handle my own life. But I couldn't."

"What happened next?"

"He started becoming more abusive. Calling me names, telling me I was lazy because I was so sad I couldn't get out of bed some days. He was coming home less and less. One day he told me it was over and he was coming home to move out.

"I panicked. He was all I had other than my babies. I'd given him my whole life and he wanted to abandon us. I didn't see it as a blessing he'd found someone else to fixate on. I saw it as yet another failure. That's when I called you. It was the smartest thing I could've done and as soon as you were on your way here, I felt relief. I thought things would change."

"But they didn't?" I take her ice-cold hand in mine.

"T-they did at first. I got a job. I thought I was doing better. But slowly, the depression came back. Then when I got the divorce papers and I saw C-Chad was not only throwing me away, but our babies, that failure intensified. I'd somehow managed to create the thing I never wanted for my kids, a broken household."

"It's not the same as our parents, Sara. Emmy and Lou have you. We didn't have anyone but each other."

I hate that she feels like she'd done the same thing to her kids that our parents did to us. Our parents were so wrapped up in each other and their own drama, they completely forgot they had kids. Sara's not that kind of parent. Maybe Chad is, but Sara isn't.

"But it felt the same to me. The d-depression"—she swallows thickly—"it was like a crushing weight on my chest. I was drowning and I didn't see a way out. I tried to fight it, but it felt impossible. I'd lie awake at n-night thinking my kids would be so much better off without me. You would be better off, too. You were so good with them and they took an instant liking to you. In my sick brain, I knew you'd be a much better parent to them. After all, you were an incredible parent to me."

"Obviously not if this is where we are now." I motion to the room around us.

"Archer, Sara's brain doesn't work the same as a healthy person's brain does. Some of her thought processes are greatly skewed by chemical imbalances and childhood trauma. None of that has anything to do with you. Even if you had done every single thing perfectly, she might still feel and think the same way. From what Sara has told me, you did a wonderful job given you were only two years older than her." Colleen smiles and although she's complimenting me, this feels too personal for a stranger to be intervening.

"Anyway, I'd been drinking a lot. I was g-good at hiding it. Until I wasn't. The night at Focus was my breaking point, once I had sobered enough to remember what happened. That night I got it in my head that I needed to end my life. I came up with a plan. I was excited. I was finally doing something right. I was putting my kids' needs ahead of mine and I just knew it was for the best." Her eyes plead with me to understand, but I don't. How could she think I'd be better off without her?

"I knew something was off. You went from so sad to almost giddy. I feel dumb now because it was so obvious. Even Kian told me I should be worried, but I believed things were taking a turn, so I ignored him."

"I know. And I'm sorry about that, too."

"Well, I think that's enough serious for now." Colleen clicks her pen shut and closes her notebook she's been jotting down who knows what on. "I know you have a lot more to talk about, but this was a good start."

"So what's next? How much longer will she be here?" I ask.

"Sara?" Colleen refers to my sister.

"Not much l-longer. They're helping me get on some anti-depressants and if it's okay with you, I'd like to stay at least another week. I want to come back home when I'm stronger. I don't want this to happen again."

"Whatever you need. I don't want this to happen again either." I'll get a second job if I have to. Anything to keep seeing the light in her eyes get brighter.

"That's what I like to hear. I'll leave you two to visit, and hopefully you can come back next week for another session, Archer?" Colleen asks.

"Sure."

She exits the room, leaving Sara and me alone. I take her in. She looks strong. She's put on a little weight, her back is straighter, and the circles under her eyes are almost gone.

"You look so much healthier," I say.

"I feel better than I have in a long time, even though I miss the kids and I feel guilty for leaving them and you."

"I brought pictures." I pull out my phone, not wanting her to focus too much on the negative. I click on my camera reel and hand it over.

Her eyes brighten and her smile returns as she scrolls through the images. There are pictures of our hiking trip, picnics in the park, messy sherbet grins, and some art projects Kian had made with them.

"Aww, I m-miss them something fierce." She hugs the phone to her chest.

"They miss you, too. A lot."

"There's a lot in here with Kian," she notes.

"He's been watching them during the day. First, when you were in the hospital and now, while I'm at work. The kids love him and he's so damn cute with them."

"I think the kids aren't the only one smitten with him."

"Sara," I deadpan.

"What? Are you guys still hot and heavy?"

"No. After that night at Focus, he decided we were better off as friends." I frown remembering that argument. It seems like a lifetime ago.

"And w-what do you want?" She peers up at me.

"I want you to be healthy and happy. That's my focus right now."

"And I love you for it. But after I come home, I want you to find your own place and live your own life. You've spent too much time raising your baby sister. I need to stand on my own two feet and figure out what I want to do with my life."

"There's no rush. I don't think it's smart for me to leave you right away."

"I mean, maybe not the day I get home, but I've had time to think. I relied on you growing up, then I moved onto Chad the second you left. I want to discover who I am. What I want."

"How will you decide?"

"Being here helps. From sunup to sundown, I have therapy sessions. Group therapy, one-on-one therapy, art therapy, music therapy, you name it. It's been an entire week of working on myself. I feel something I h-haven't felt maybe ever." Her eyes glisten and she holds my hand. "I have hope. Thank you for always having my back."

"Always, Sara." I take her in my arms and hug her tight.

After a tour of where's she's been staying and being introduced to some of the friends she's made, I leave Seasons of Maine with peace in my soul. She's where she needs to be to get better. And maybe, just maybe, I can start thinking about what I want my life to look like.

TWENTY-SIX

Kian

I wake up Sunday feeling apprehensive. It's the first day we both have off since I moved in and I don't know how it's going to go. Do I leave and give him and the kids space? Do I stick around and hang out with them? Do I lock myself in Sara's room all day and hide?

A knock sounds on the door and I scramble to throw some clothes on. I tried to sleep with underwear on since I'm not at home, but I like things to breathe at night.

"Just a second." I yank a pair of running shorts on and open the door to find little, sweet Emmy standing there in her princess dress pajamas, her hair matted to the side of her head, and the most adorable smile on her face.

"I want toast. Help." She tugs on my arm, pulling me to the kitchen. I immediately regret not putting a shirt on when I find Archer, also shirtless, staring at bread on the kitchen counter with an egg in his hand. His physique is intimidating and since I've seen pictures of him and Mason, I know Archer must have a type. And that type isn't a skinny, out of shape noodle.

My thoughts are squashed when he notices me standing by the island. His lips part, his eyes go to half-mast, and the egg he was holding falls to the ground.

"Uh-oh," Emmy says.

"Damn it." Archer scrambles, grabbing a paper towel and

dropping to the ground. His gaze jumps from the mess to me and back again.

My cheeks heat and I look away, giving my attention back to Emmy.

"French toast, huh? Well, you came to the right person." I walk into the small kitchen and assess what ingredients they have out and what I still need to grab. "The trick to the best French toast is cinnamon and vanilla."

I open the spice cupboard and find what I need. I squish my way past Archer, who's moved to the side, making sure my ass brushes across his pelvis. I hear his sharp intake of breath, which has my normal confidence return. He wants me. He's into noodles.

"Okay, Miss Emmy, come here." I lift her onto the countertop and hand her an egg. "Crack this against the side of the bowl."

That little squirt hammers the egg into the bowl, dripping yolk and whites all over. Archer's right there with another paper towel that I use to wipe up the mess.

"Good job. Why don't I do the next couple and you can stir." I hand her a fork.

With Lou sitting at the island watching, I teach them all how to make French toast. Archer and I share stolen glances and secret smiles, while taking turns dipping the bread and sliding it onto the griddle.

I serve the kids at the island, but without a word spoken, Archer and I go into the formal dining room to eat, for some privacy.

"You're right," Archer says with a mouthful of toast.

"I'm always right, but what am I right about this time?" I tease.

"Vanilla and cinnamon are the key."

"You like it?"

"Very much." His gaze is heated and intense. Like he's

saying he likes more than my breakfast skills. "I hope Emmy didn't wake you up."

"No, I was awake. I just didn't know if you wanted me out here with you guys, so I was giving you space."

"I always want you around." He clears his throat. "I mean, the kids and I always want you around."

"What if the kids aren't around?" I want to keep pushing. I want him to admit he still has feelings for me, but he ends the conversation with his next words.

"I'm glad you're here. I'll leave it at that."

We eat in silence for a while after that, the only sound being our chewing and the giggling in the next room over.

"So, you're taking the kids to see Sara this week?" I ask, remembering our conversation after he got back from visiting her last week. He was a nervous ball of energy when he left, but when he came back, his whole vibe had changed. He was calm and happy. I was so grateful it went well.

"Yeah. On Thursday. I took the day off, figuring I'd take them for lunch and maybe tour Camden. I don't know."

"Do they know?"

"Not yet. As soon as they find out, they'll talk about it nonstop. I thought I'd save us both from that torture."

"Smart. Have you heard from her this week?"

"Yeah. She calls once a day to say good night to the kids. She sounds healthy. I can't wait for her to get home."

"I'll bet."

"You know, she wants me to move out after she gets settled."

"Oh yeah?"

"I guess I should start looking for a place on top of looking for a job for her." He takes his last bite, moaning in pleasure. I love feeding him. He makes the sexiest noises and loves food so much. It makes me proud that I make him happy with my cooking.

"I told you I'd hold Sara's job. Just say the word and it's hers."

"Thank you. I appreciate that and I'll mention it to her, but she said she'd like to find something during the day. She wants the kids to go to preschool or daycare, that way she won't be relying on me as much. She's all about gaining independence. Her therapist thinks it will empower her or some shit."

"What was she going to school for before she dropped out?" I ask, thinking of anyone I know who might have a position open.

"Business management is what she wanted to do, but she barely make it through one semester. Not enough to gain any real skills."

I think about the mountains of paperwork sitting on my desk and an idea pops into my head. "What if I hire her to help out with Blur and Focus? I've been thinking about finding a stock clerk and someone to help with payroll."

"Are you sure? I don't know. She doesn't have experience."

"I didn't either when I started, but I have a system now and it would be easy to teach her. She's smart and personable. I think she could help build relationships with my suppliers."

Jarrett's voice pops into my head about how much I interject myself into their lives for no reason at all, but I push it away. It feels right. Whether something happens with Archer or not, I'm connected to this family and I can't turn my back on them.

"And it would be a day job?" he asks, propping his elbows on the table and knitting his hands together.

"Yep. I usually do all of the purchasing stuff during the day and payroll and bill paying at night, but there's no reason she couldn't do all of that during the day. I can either put a second desk in my office, or she could even work from home. It doesn't matter."

I immediately regret offering a desk in my office. We've had some amazing times in that office and a second desk with pictures of his niece and nephew on it would most definitely stop that from happening.

"I'm sure working from home or even venturing to Fran's sometimes would be beneficial for her. But are you sure? You've done so much already. I feel as though you keep giving and giving and we've done nothing for you."

"I'm sure. Ask her about it on Thursday. I can't pay a ton, but it'll be more than she was making bar tendering."

"Thank you, Kian. You were put into my life for a reason. I've never been a spiritual person, especially after my childhood and then Mason. I thought I was put on this earth to suffer, that I would be shit on my whole life. But you came along like my very own good luck fucking charm."

"You would've figured it out on your own. I was just in the right place at the right time."

"It's more than that. Anyone else would've walked away the day I broke down over charcuterie. Or when my sister had a drunken breakdown at your bar. There were so many reasons for you to walk away and you didn't."

He reaches under the table and places a hand on my bare knee. My skin heats. Then his thumb rubs back and forth. *Fuck.* Arousal hits me fast and hard. I should've made more time to jerk off this week. I'm a ticking time bomb. He pins me with a look.

This is it. This is when he's going to tell me we should try again. I can feel it.

"You're the best friend I could ever ask for," he says, removing his hand and standing to clear our plates.

My dick deflates and my breakfast threatens to resurface. *Friendship.* I'm starting to hate that word.

We spend the day doing normal things. We go to the grocery store and out to lunch. To the outsider, I'm sure we look like a proper family. But after our talk at breakfast, I'm feeling like a third wheel. I'm just a man, who despite being friend zoned over and over, holds onto hope.

But that hope is dwindling and I'm starting to get the idea Archer will never come around. I'm an idiot. I should've been listening to Jarrett. And Fernando. And every other person who told me I was going to get hurt.

My mood progressively gets worse throughout the day. By the time we get home—correction, Sara and Archer's home—with a premade pizza to bake, I don't even want to be here. I'm so stupid. On a whim, I grab my car keys and head for the door.

"Where are you going?" Archer asks, brows raised.

"Out. You didn't have plans, right? You don't need me here?" My tone pitches despite trying to sound indifferent.

"No. I just thought you'd be here for the pizza party." He abandons the pizza he was putting on a baking sheet and approaches me. "Is everything okay?"

"Yeah, I'm great." I force a smile. "Jarrett called, asked me over for dinner at his place. I figured I'd give you guys some family time. I'll be back in time for you to go to work tomorrow, don't worry about that."

"Tomorrow? You won't come back tonight?"

"Probably not. Once we open a bottle of wine, somehow it turns into three, so I'll probably stay at my place tonight. You know how it is."

"Sure. Okay. Guess I'll see you tomorrow then." His words are slow and hesitant. He looks hurt, though I can't imagine why.

"Yep. Have a good night," I say as cheerfully as I can muster and walk out the door.

I don't go to Jarrett's condo. I don't even call him, or any of my other friends, for that matter. I go home. Feeling defeated and lonely, I open my front door. Everything is the same as how I left it, but it feels different now.

I pump myself up as I pick out an expensive bottle of wine. This is nice. I need some alone time. All that chaos and mess has been draining. A night to myself is exactly what I need.

I take the wine, sans glass, to my bathroom where I draw a bath and sprinkle in delicious smelling salts. Finding my e-reader, I'm grateful to have some down time. I haven't had a chance to finish my cowboy book and I'm dying to find out what happens between the cowboy and rancher.

I'll bet money on it not ending with the cowboy telling the rancher he's a good buddy.

Fuck cowboys.

As the tub fills, I scroll through the bookstore until I find a thriller. Blood, guts, people dying. That's more my mood tonight.

I pick out a sheet face mask and a deep conditioning treatment. With my face covered and my hair saturated, I lower into the warm water.

This. This is what I needed. No kids pounding on the door if I so much as try to pee alone. No TV blaring some movie with stupid songs I won't be able to get out of my head. No stupid man child giving me the eye and then pushing me away.

Nope. None of it. Just me and relaxation.

It's time I get back to myself. Archer did me a favor, really. I'll get Sara on her feet. Maybe I'll see Archer now and then. We can get a drink and talk about our lives. His will be busy and revolve around his family. Mine will be serene and revolve around doing what I want, when I want. I'm young. I don't need attachments.

That's what I want. Right?

TWENTY-SEVEN

Archer

I pack a bag with a change of clothes and snacks for the car ride to Camden replaying Sunday in my mind. For the millionth time.

I knew I fucked up when I told Kian I was happy I had him as a friend. His face fell and his shoulders slumped, making me wish I could take it back. I meant to say more, tell him we should start over with us and try and make it work, but the words didn't come.

He's been punishing me for it all week. First, by leaving for that night to do God knows what. He says he went to Jarrett's house, but it felt like a lie and I had no right to ask him about it. I tried not to let it bother me and continue with our fun pizza and movie night we'd planned, but I know I was a downer. The kids didn't even complain when I put them to bed. I think my messed-up emotions bled onto them.

Just another reason I'm an asshole.

Then yesterday, as he was leaving for work, he announced he was going home for the night since I had today off. He's putting so much space between us, I don't know if I'll ever be able to bring us together again. I should lay it all out on the table, tell him I need to get Sara settled before I can focus on us. But that sounds so incredibly selfish.

"Please, Kian, put your life on hold more than you already have on the off chance we can make a relationship work in the future."

Yeah, right. I'd sound like a giant asshole. No, I need to stay the course. Focus on what's important right now and then deal with the disaster I've made later. Assuming he'll still be open to trying by then. It'll be the biggest regret of my life if he's not.

"All right, kids. We've got to get going," I shout.

I opt to take Sara's car instead of the truck since we'll be going on the freeway and it's safer. It's crazy to think my entire life was based on risks not that long ago. In Alaska, on the fishing boats, everything was dangerous. Now, I'm all about five point harnesses and curtain airbags.

The drive is quiet, giving me time to beat myself to a pulp even more about Kian. I meant what I said when I told him he was my very own good luck charm. I think about how I would've handled everything without him there to lean on and it makes me sick.

The Warren siblings were broken disasters, then this bubbly, optimistic man showed up and everything was so much more bearable. I pray it's not too late. Just picturing seeing him around town holding someone else's hand makes me murderous. It wouldn't be hard for Fernando to step in, with his close shaved goatee, neck tattoo, and shaved head. The guy is fucking hot and knowing he's already slept with Kian, it's not a stretch.

Great, now I'm jealous over hypothetical situations.

I park the car at Seasons and unbuckle everyone from the car. I wish Kian were here for support. I almost asked him, but he seems intent on distancing himself and I have no right to even suggest it when I'm not giving him what he clearly needs.

We check in at the front desk and are led to the same room Sara and I were in last time. Except this time, there's coloring books and crayons on one of the tables by the window.

"My babies!" Sara rushes in and drops to her knees. The second the kids hear her voice, they turn and run to her.

It makes my nose sting and a lump form in my throat to see the three of them huddled together. It's been so hard on everyone, but in this moment, it feels like a corner is being turned.

Wiping her eyes, Sara stands up and takes each of them by the hand. "I set up some activities for us."

"You feel better, Mommy?" Lou asks.

"I f-feel a lot better," she stutters and I wince.

Although I understand her reasoning, I'm still angry she didn't come to me. That she felt her only option was dying when it wasn't. And now she's going to struggle physically on top of her mental health issues.

They sit down at the table and I stand back, wanting to give them their time. I pull out my phone for the millionth time today to see if Kian has messaged, but there's nothing there.

"What have you guys been doing?" Sara asks the kids.

"Lots of stuff. Kian taught us to make French toast and esketti," Emmy says.

"And he dressed up like a fairy princess and watched *Frozen*." Lou's nose scrunches.

"That sounds fun. Kian's been a good friend, huh?"

"Yeah, he's prolly my best friend," Emmy says nonchalantly.

"I'm so glad he was there when I couldn't be."

"I want you to come home now, Mommy." Lou pouts.

"Soon, baby. Maybe Monday or Tuesday."

"Monday would be perfect," he replies.

Sara giggles. "I'll see what I can do."

After a couple hours, filled with a walk to the beach where we gathered seashells and waded through the water, it was time to go. Emmy and Lou cried through the goodbyes. Sara tried to be strong, but I still saw the tears she refused to let fall.

"Thank you, Archer. For everything. I'll call you over the

w-weekend and tell you the plan." Sara gives me a departing hug.

"You look good, sis."

"I feel good. Maybe it's this place and things will look different when I get home, but I feel at peace and ready to get my life back."

"I'm glad. Talk soon."

With Emmy in my arms and holding Lou's hand, we leave Seasons. I'm so close to checking off the box in my head labeled, *Get Sara Settled*. Then I move on to the next box, *Figure Out My Life*.

I try to sleep after putting the kids to bed, but my mind won't shut down. Before I know it, it's 2:00 a.m. and I know Kian will be walking through the door any moment. He texted me earlier to make sure I knew he was still planning on hanging out with the kids Friday while I work. It'll be his last day here since Sara will most likely be coming home Monday.

Feeling thirsty, at least that's what I tell myself, I get up from bed and go to the kitchen. I dawdle. I fill and drink an entire glass of water, but Kian doesn't show up. I pour another glass and set it on the counter. I notice a few sticky fingerprints on the fridge and wet a paper towel to wipe them off. Still no Kian.

It's when I'm sweeping the floor I finally hear a car door slam from outside. I rush to put the broom away and pick up my glass of water, acting nonchalant. The front door opens and closes quietly. I have the glass to my mouth when he finally turns the corner to the kitchen.

"Shit. You scared me." He slaps his chest. He looks hot as hell. His dark gray, baggy slacks are rolled at the bottom and he's paired them with brightly-colored tennis shoes. On top, he's wearing a short-sleeved white button-up, the sleeves also rolled. But it's the suspenders that do it for me. Black, thin, and make him appear adorably fuckable. I fight the urge to grab those things and yank him to me. My dick chubs and I'm quick to change my thoughts because I'm in my boxers and I'm seconds from revealing my desires.

"Sorry. I didn't know you weren't in yet. I just needed some water." *Lies. Lies. Lies.*

"I'm just going to—" He hooks a thumb toward the hallway.

"It's your last night, huh?" I ask, wanting to keep him talking.

"Guess so. I'm glad Sara's doing so well and can come home. The kids must be so excited." He takes his crossbody bag off, sets it on the ground, and takes a seat on a stool at the island, while I stand on the other side. Only a slab of Corian and some wood separate us, but he feels miles away.

"They're beyond excited. They got a kick out of seeing her today."

"I'll bet. I'm sure they'll tell me all about it."

"How was work tonight?" I set the glass down and place my hands on the countertop, flexing my biceps and abs. It's a childish attempt to see the heat in his eyes I've missed so much, but I need it. I have to make sure he's still in it. That he isn't completely over me. His lips part and I watch his Adam's apple bob with a swallow. It tells me all I need to know.

"Busy," he says, an octave lower than seconds ago. "Thursdays are the new Friday."

"Busy is good."

"Did you talk to Sara about the job?"

"I did. She wants it. Though she's embarrassed and isn't looking forward to facing you."

"She shouldn't be."

"She hates that she put you out so much, but she's thankful you were here. I am, too, you know?"

"I know." He stands up and picks his bag up off the ground. "I'm wiped. Gonna head to bed."

"Okay. See you after work," I say and he gives me a tight-lipped smile before disappearing down the hallway.

I sigh. *One step at a time.*

I spend the weekend cleaning and organizing the house, stocking the fridge and cleaning Sara's room. Although she isn't an alcoholic, she was using alcohol to cope, so I empty the house of every drop, finding empty and half-empty bottles under her bed and in her bathroom. She'd been hiding more than I originally thought.

It's weird to spend a weekend without Kian and I've pulled my phone out to text or call him numerous times, only to stop myself and put it away. I don't know when I'll be able to shoot my shot again, but teasing him with something I'm not ready for won't win me points.

On Monday morning, I want to give myself a cookie for making it through the weekend. Emmy and Lou burst through the door at 7:00 a.m., as excited as they would be if we were at Disneyland.

"It's Mommy day!" Emmy cheers while bouncing up and down on my bed.

"When will she be here?" Lou asks.

"In a couple hours."

Seasons is bringing her home later this morning. I took the day off so I could be here when she is, but I've taken so much time off lately, today was the only day I was able to. I'm nervous about leaving her all alone tomorrow, but I trust the doctors when they say she'll be fine. She has a plan and a backup plan and a backup plan for the backup plan. She's strong, but most of all, she has a desire to be well and a cocktail of antidepressants and anxiety medication that seem to be working for her.

"Can we have cereal for breakfast?" Emmy cannonballs onto my chest and the air in my lungs expels with a whoosh.

"Oh, man. Em, I'm old. You can't jump on me like that." I barrel roll to the edge of the bed and get up. "Cereal it is."

After breakfast and a walk to the park, we come back home to wait for Sara. I think we're all nervous. I turn on a show and the kids quietly watch, piled on top of me. I hear the front door open and the kids freeze, staring at each other.

It doesn't last.

They jump up and run to the door. Sara comes in, holding her duffle of clothes and toiletries I dropped off at the hospital before she left for Seasons.

"Hey, guys. I'm home." Her eyes are bright and clear, her hair is down and in loose curls, and with the weight she's put on, her cheekbones aren't as prominent, and her eyes don't look sunken in. She looks like the old Sara. Like the sister I remember.

Peace fills me. I'm not dumb enough to think the road ahead will be easy, but I do think it'll be transparent and that's what has me sighing in relief.

TWENTY-EIGHT

Kian

Sunday afternoon, I find myself cleaning up and preparing food for the girls and gays night Cato decided I needed. Since *And Puppies!* isn't big enough for all of us, he assigned my house as the location for a sleepover. Jarrett, Fernando, Cato, and Jax's deputy, Brie, will be arriving in a few short hours.

I scrub down my dining room table since the charcuterie board won't be a board at all, it's going to cover the entire table. It's going to be a masterpiece. Then, I jump in the shower and put on a baby blue and white, tie-dye cotton onesie. I know Cato's going to show up with matching tiny undies for everyone, but I'm not feeling it tonight. Something tells me Brie will object, too.

My brain wanders as I methodically slice bread and roll prosciutto. It's strange how I was so quick to adjust to my new normal. I spent the last four years of my life having the same schedule, the same activities, the same people in my life. All it took was a couple months of being around the Warrens for me to be lonely without them.

I've gone back to my previous lifestyle, doing things for myself and hanging out with my friends, but I miss them. All of them. I even miss being bounced on by two tiny humans at 8:00 a.m. after only sleeping five hours. I miss spending Sundays with the family, doing family things. It's so unlike me, I never even did those things when Mom and Dad were around. I was too busy with friends, or later in high school, with Jax.

Yet here I am, wishing I was spending my Sunday at the boardwalk with sherbet in hand.

I've just finished spreading chocolate cherries and fresh blueberries in-between meats, cheeses, bread, pretzels, asparagus, and a hundred other bite-sized food, when there's a knock at my door.

"I've arrived, bitches," Cato yells from the entryway.

"In here."

"Holy fucksticks, babe. You went all out." Cato struts in and snags a chocolate covered strawberry.

I smack his hand. "That's for the party."

"Still cranky, I see." He backs away from the table, cradling his hand.

"I'm fine. Just, you know, off."

"This is when I tell you that I told you so. Because I told you so." He places a hand on his hip.

"You and everyone else."

"Has he called?"

"Nope." I sniffle, biting back emotion. "I didn't think he would. I mean, he has so much going on."

"Don't make excuses for his sorry ass. If he wanted to he would."

A knock sounds on the door, saving me from continuing this conversation. Cato runs for the door.

"It's busty Brie," he announces.

The beautiful blonde follows him in, a broad, white grin spread across her glossy lips.

"So this is how you guys party." She sets her bag down on the sofa and darts right to the table of goodness. "It's about time you idiots invite me to one of these."

"I figured you needed a little cheering up after what happened with Hank." Cato's lips curl back in disgust.

"It's fine. I've accepted I'll be alone forever." She swipes a pretzel and tosses it in her mouth.

"Why doesn't her hand get slapped?" Cato sasses.

"She's been through some shit. I'm commiserating."

"Yeah. We're sad and sad needs carbs to feel better." She wraps her arms around my middle.

"I wouldn't worry, Brie. You're young, hot, and have fantastic tits. You'll find someone."

"You still need to fill me in. Cato said things didn't work out with Archer, but he didn't say why because Jax was around."

"I doubt he'd even care. He's off in la-la land with Mr. Moneybags."

"Dante's not so bad. You'd like him."

"I know. I think I'm just jealous."

Brie side-eyes me. "You still have feelings for him?"

"God, no. But I'm the one who's been out and open since high school. I should be the one settled and happy. Not his closeted ass."

The door opens for the third time, Jarrett and Fernando entering this time.

"We're here, we're queer, and we brought wine." In each of their hands are two bottles of wine.

"It's going to be one of those nights, huh?" I mumble.

"Duh," says Fernando.

"First thing's first." Cato runs over to his glittery, gold duffel and pulls out four matching shiny blue undies and one shiny pink panty and bra set. "Let's get comfy."

The rest of us groan.

"Hell no, man. My dick won't fit in that." Fernando gripes.

"He's right, it won't." I agree.

"Wait, have you two battled swords?" Brie's eyes widen.

"It's not like there are many options in Brigs Ferry Bay." Fernando shrugs.

"Hey!" I point a finger at him. "You weren't complaining when you had your giant dick up my ass."

"Okay," Jarrett interrupts. "That's enough. Cato, we're not wearing that. Fernando, let's pop some bottles."

"Fine, but I am. I want to be comfortable. How about you, Brie?" He puts his hands into prayer position. "Pretty please?"

"Fine, but if you tell Jax about this, you're dead meat."

He grabs her hand and they trot to my bedroom, leaving me laughing. Maybe Cato was right and this was exactly what I needed to get things back to the way they were. I had a full life without Archer.

After everyone has wine, food, and are changed into comfy outfits, we gather in the living room. Cato and Brie nestle together on the love seat, a blanket wrapped around them since they're wearing next to nothing. Jarrett and Fernando are on either of my sides on the sofa.

"So spill. What happened with Archer?" Brie asks.

"Sara happened." Jarrett crosses his legs.

"I can't blame Sara. But Archer overreacted when I had to fire Sara. Which we could've worked out because the next day he was sorry. Then she tried to kill herself and everything kind of spiraled from there."

"Didn't you move in while she was away?" Cato asks, feeding Brie grapes.

"Yes. He didn't have anyone to watch the kids and I felt bad. We agreed it wasn't the time to work on us. It's for the better. He needs to focus on his family and not worry about a boyfriend."

"You are awfully needy," Fernando says.

I gape. "And you aren't, Mr. I-won't-date-someone-from-Brigs-Ferry-Bay?"

"It's incestuous. I've known you fools my entire adult life."

"Anyway, he wasn't ready for a relationship. He lost his

partner in a boating accident in Alaska and he has survivor's guilt."

"And you had 'I'm not good enough for anyone because my high school boyfriend wouldn't leave the closet for me' guilt," Jarrett adds.

"Wow. You two are quite the pair," Brie says.

"Pretty much."

"It'll be fine." Jarrett rubs my knee placatingly. "Give it some time. I did some meditating on it and set some intentions for you. It'd work better if you did it yourself, but someone's too superior for meditation."

"What about you, Jarrett? Any prospects on the horizon?" Cato waggles his brows.

"Who, me?" He rests a hand on his chest. "Unfortunately, I think I'm doomed to be a crazy cat gay for the rest of my life. The only thing I'm worried about right now are those bitches across the street trying to steal my business."

"Don't worry about them, Addison and Adeline are sweet. They don't mean any harm." Brie waves his concerns off.

"Any harm?" Jarrett brushes the curl that is perpetually falling on his forehead. "They set up a shop right across from mine. They're city girls. It's a direct attack."

"It's true." Fernando agrees. "It's not cool."

"Maybe you should go talk to them. You guys could help each other out." She shrugs.

"Actually, not a bad idea. Keep your enemies close and all that," I chime in.

"Maybe I will." Jarrett taps his chin with a pointed finger.

"Not what I meant."

Jarrett jumps up. "Fernando, help me move the coffee table."

"Why?" I ask.

"It's yoga time. We need to move to help with digestion."

"Maybe you can't find a boyfriend because you're always making people do yoga." I whine.

"Hush, you."

They push my coffee table to the side and Jarrett leads us in some yoga, because what can go wrong when you've been drinking wine and eating your weight in charcuterie?

A few minutes later, Jarrett has his legs twisted like a pretzel, Brie and Cato are flat on their backs giggling about how their undies keep creeping up their asses, Fernando's trying to get himself out of Lotus, and I'm chugging wine, laughing.

Hours pass. We continue to drink and talk. By one in the morning, everyone's yawning and figuring out sleeping arrangements. Brie and Cato take the spare bed, Fernando takes the couch, and Jarrett and I take my bed.

"You okay, honey?" Jarrett asks.

It's been an amazing night, really. In my crowded living room, I was feeling better than I have in a while. But here in the dark, with only my best friend and a belly full of wine, I'm back to my pity party mentality.

"Yeah. I'm glad you're here." I sigh.

"You know, you could always go after him."

"I know." I flip from my side to my back. "I guess I want to be chased for once. You know?"

"I guess with your past, it might feel important to have someone choose you over everything else."

"You don't think so?"

"I don't know. You're talking to a perpetual bachelor. Just seems like happiness is happiness, no matter how you get there."

I blow out a breath. "I always have a plan. I'm the person people run to when they need a plan of their own. I'm reliable. I know that, and usually it delivers a tranquil feeling of control I crave. But that's in my everyday life. Yeah, I could go over there and do it my way, with a calendar and asking him how long he needs, but I don't want that. Archer's full of passion and intensity. It's what drew me to him. I'm the ocean, calm and steady. But he's the waves, turbulent and unpredictable."

"Wow. That was beautiful."

I shove his shoulder. "I'm being serious, bitch."

"So am I. I'm the ocean, too. I think that's why we get along so well. Of course, I get there through holistic behaviors and you get there through wine, but still." He sighs this time. "I think I'd want the waves if I were looking for a relationship, too. Someone to keep me on my toes."

"How does this setting intentions work, anyway?"

"It's easy. You just have to state what you want and set it free into the world. You are what you think. It's about training your brain to stay focused on your true desires."

"So I just need to tell myself Archer and I will be together and we will be?"

"Not exactly. But you can say that you're open for love. In the long run, isn't that what you want? Even if it ends up not being with Archer?"

"I didn't even think I was ready for love until him."

"Well, then even if you don't end up together, he served an important purpose."

"Wow. That was beautiful." I repeat his earlier words.

"You're obnoxious." He shoves me this time. "But I love you and I'm glad we're friends."

"Me too, honey."

I fall asleep reciting that I'm open to love, over and over again. Hoping my message comes through like a neon sign in front of Archer's beautiful face.

TWENTY-NINE

Archer

"I'm fine," Sara complains over the line.

I've called her three times a day, every day, since she got home and I had to go back to work. Each time, she says she's doing fine. She's gone to therapy twice, leaving the kids with the neighbor, and found a pre-k for the kids to go to on Mondays, Wednesdays, and Fridays. She even called Kian and set up a meeting with him for today before Focus opens.

I haven't spoken to Kian, though. Still wanting to make sure everything goes smoothly at home.

"I know you are. Just humor your big brother, would you?"

"Fine. We're awesome. I'm dropping the kids off with Mrs. Porter and then I'll go to my meeting."

"Okay. Good luck."

"You should call him, you know."

"Who?"

"Don't play dumb. He asked about you when I spoke to him earlier this week."

"What did he say?" I ask way too anxiously.

"See! I knew you wanted to talk to him."

"Sara. What did he say?"

"You'll have to find out yourself. I'm not your telephone service."

I growl. "Whatever."

"If Kian agrees to give me this job, I want you to find your own place."

"I don't know why you're so stuck on me moving out."

"Because I want to stand on my own two feet. I want to prove to myself that I can do it without my older brother being around to save me every time I stumble."

"Can't we wait a bit and see how things go?" I ask. I want to tell her I'm not worried about her tripping over small problems, I'm worried about her falling over big ones, but I don't. I want her to know I believe in her.

"I know you're worried. I've given you every reason to. I just wish I could show you inside my head. I spent years feeling like a fog was all around me, but everything's clear now. And I promise I'd reach out if things got foggy again. I didn't understand any of it before, but I understand it now, and it's empowered me in ways I can't explain."

"Can we talk about this when I get home?"

"We can talk about it, yes. But it won't change my decision."

"Bye, Sara."

"Don't make me call Jax to serve you eviction papers." She giggles and I hang up on her. Maybe she's right, but she was in a coma three weeks ago. It feels way too soon.

I tuck my phone back in my pocket, step out from under the safety of the awning of the fish market, and head back to the boat. The beginnings of summer had just started to show themselves before a storm rolled in this morning. It's been miserable out all day.

I fight the wind as I make my way down the dock, wondering if Kian really did ask about me. I thought I'd kept Sara off my scent about missing him, but judging by her teasing comment, I don't think I succeeded. It doesn't help that Emmy and Lou are constantly asking about him and when they can see him next.

"Did you go to Nantucket for lunch, or what?" Oliver asks, already waiting for me. He unties the boat the second my feet hit the deck.

"Sorry. Had to call Sara."

"She doing okay?"

"Great, actually. Happier than I've ever seen her before and there's been reasons to not be so happy this week."

I think about the papers that arrived the day after she got home, finalizing her divorce and reiterating Chad's selfish desire to not be part of their lives anymore. I thought Sara would break down and all the progress would be lost. Sure, she was sad, even cried a few tears. But she called her therapist, got an emergency appointment, and by the time I got home from work, she was all Zen and shit.

I'm proud of her.

"That makes me happy to hear." He drives the boat past Blue Shark Islands and out to where we left our traps. The weather progressively worsens by the minute.

I pull the hood of my slicker down further to block the hard pellets of rain from falling into my eyes and tuck my hands in my pockets. I'd gotten lazy with the unseasonal warm weather, wearing T-shirts instead of my usual hoodie. A mistake I won't make again. I'm shivering and my fingers are numb.

"Let's start here," Oliver shouts over the wind.

I give him a salute and shuffle to the winch. I spot the buoy and hurl the metal hook attached to a rope at it. I've done it eight million or so times, so my aim is impeccable. It hooks right away and I press the button for the winch to haul the trap out.

Oliver steps up then and helps me maneuver the trap next to the table where we sort and the holding tank where the lobster will hang out until we get back to shore. One by one, we sex the lobsters, releasing any females with eggs on them back to the ocean, as well as any that don't measure big enough.

After that, Oliver takes us to the next drop point marked by the GPS. Each trap takes us longer and longer as the weather worsens. The wind has me leaning sideways just to stay upright. We're not pulling in nearly what we normally do, but that's to be expected. The real haul will come after the storm. Tomorrow will no doubt be profitable.

We're nearing the last of the pots when Oliver shouts, "I've got to take a leak. Hold on a sec."

I shove him toward the end of the boat. "I don't need the wind carrying your piss into my face."

"I thought all your people like golden showers," he jokes and I flip him off.

I chuck the hook at the buoy and miss. *Fucking wind.* I throw again and it catches. I use the winch to lift the pot from the ocean and although I should wait for Oliver to get back before trying to move it, I'm freezing to my bones and want to get home to a hot shower. I bend my knees to ground myself, positive I can handle it on my own.

I get a tight grip and turn the pot around to walk it over. The mechanical arm helps to move it in the right direction, but before I get set it down, the boat hits a wave. The trap swings forcefully, slamming me in the chest and hurling me into the icy water.

The air is sucked from my lungs from the sheer temperature and I take in a mouthful of salty ocean but catch myself before inhaling it. Instincts set in and I try to kick my way to the surface, but my boots are like cement bricks sinking me farther down. I reach down and push on the left one with all my strength. It takes a few tries, but I get it off. The world is pitch-black all around me and disorientation starts to kick in. I'll worry about that later. I fight with my second boot until that one is off, too.

A fisherman's uniform is sufficient at keeping you dry, but it's useless at keeping you afloat. Even with the weight off my feet, I still feel too heavy to swim. And even if I did swim, which direction do I go. Up is down and left is right, and I don't know where to go.

Panic has me forgetting everything I know about what to do in this situation. The salt stings my eyes as I look around, but there's nothing to see. I'm too deep and the sky is too dark to see any light coming from above. There's nothing but emptiness in all directions and I'm seconds from not being able to hold my breath.

I have two distinct thoughts before I lose consciousness.

Please, Kian, watch over my sister.

I hope Mason is waiting for me on the other side.

THIRTY

Kian

"Hi, honey!" I rush over to Sara as she opens the curtain to Blur for our meeting. She shakes the rain off her head and removes her coat.

"Wow. This place is beautiful. I can't believe I've never been in here." Her eyes travel the span of the club that I don't think is that beautiful with the lights on like they are. What looks dark and sexy in the dim lighting, looks scuffed up and used with the overheads on. We could paint once a week and there'd still be scratches from the bulldog leather harnesses some of these idiots think is the dress code for a gay club, or one of the other hundred ways people insist on ruining things.

"Aw, thank you. Follow me." I lead her up the stairs and into my roomy office. Enough time has passed that the first thing I see isn't Archer fucking me against the window anymore, although it's definitely still in my memory.

"So this is where you ran off to every time you left me at Focus."

"It is. Please, take a seat." I motion to the chair across from my desk and I walk around to sit on the other side. "I'm meeting you here because if you agree to take the job, you'll have to pop in and grab mail or other paperwork."

"Before we get to that, I want to apologize." Sara's eyes drop to her hands.

"Nope. No apologies. I know that person who was

working for me before wasn't the real you. I'm proud of you for facing me again. I know this must be hard."

"Thank you." She looks up with tears in her eyes. "I feel clear-headed and positive. I learned a lot while I was in treatment and I wouldn't be here if I didn't think I could handle it."

"I know. And I also know Archer wouldn't let you be here if you couldn't handle it." A twinge shoots through my heart at the sound of his name on my lips, but I push it away until later when I'm having my millionth pity party, followed by my millionth intention setting. That shit isn't working.

"You're right about that." She blinks the tears away and smiles.

"So, how about it? Will you be my office manager?"

"Yes. I'd love that."

"Excellent. When do you want to start?"

"I can start now, if you want. The kids are with Mrs. Porter for a few hours."

"Let's do it."

We go over salary, that I thought she would balk at, but didn't. Then I begin training her with the payroll program, the ordering system, and everything else I've been needing help with for a long time, but have been too stubborn to hire out.

Late afternoon comes fast. I didn't realize how much I'd been doing alone until it was time to teach it to someone else.

Sara's phone rings. "Sorry, I need to check that. It could be Mrs. Porter."

"No worries." I wave her off.

"Hello?" There's a long pause before Sara's hand flies over her mouth. "Is he okay? I'll be right there."

She jumps to her feet, grabs her purse, and fishes her keys out.

"What is it?" I ask.

"It's Archer. There's been an accident. I need to get to the hospital."

"Oh my God. I'll drive." I snag the keys from her hand since I walked to work. We run to her car. I don't even bother locking up. I don't know what happened, but I saw the look on her face. It's bad.

"What happened?" I ask once we're on the road. I flip the windshield wipers to high and still I have a hard time seeing through the downpour.

"He got knocked off the boat. I told him so many times that it's too dangerous of a job. After what happened to Mason, why would he not find a new profession?"

"Is he okay?" I need to know. I can't wait until I'm at the hospital to find out he died.

"Yes. He was under so long, he passed out, and got a lungful of water, but he's alive."

"Thank fuck." I breathe a sigh of relief.

"Pull up to the front." She points and I park, ignoring the signs warning me it's a no parking zone. I don't give a shit.

We stumble through the front door and I get a flash of déjà vu. It wasn't that long ago I was here for the other Warren sibling. I peer over at Sara, wanting to see how she's holding up. She's worried, it's clear by her drawn together eyebrows and shaky hands, but there's not even a hint of the blank expression she had the last time I saw her.

"My brother's here. Archer Warren," Sara barks at the registration desk.

"I'll let the doctor know you're here."

"Please, can I just go back and see him?"

"Dr. Miller gave me instructions to come get him when you arrived."

"Fine. Please hurry."

I wrap an arm around Sara's narrow waist and draw her to me. We stay locked in a hug until the door leading into the belly of the hospital opens. We break apart and see the handsome doctor approach.

"Sara, I wish we were meeting again under different circumstances."

"How is he?" Sara ignores the pleasantries.

"He's alive. Although he was near drowning when he was pulled from the water. It's a miracle, really. Usually in situations like this, it's a whole other conversation. Luckily, Oliver kept his head on straight and was able to find him floating near where Archer was knocked off the boat. He hooked him and pulled him up using the same equipment they use for the lobster pots. He immediately administered CPR and got him breathing. The coast guard met them and took over," Lance explains.

"Can I see him?"

"He's having some tests run, so give me a half hour. Then I'll have him taken to a room and you can come back."

"Okay."

"He's going to be fine, Sara. But are you sure you're okay?" he asks, knowing full well that she's in a fragile state.

"I am. I promise. Thank you, Dr. Miller. Not just for my brother, but for me, too."

"Just doing my job. Sit tight. I'll be back out soon."

I lead her to the waiting area and we sit side by side. I didn't notice as I walked in, but looking around, I spot Oliver. I don't know the burly old man well, but I recognize his face. He sees us and approaches.

"Are you Sara?" he asks and she nods. "I'm Oliver. I work with Archer on the same boat."

"You saved him." She stands and hugs the man tight. He looks uncomfortable with the display and after a few seconds, pushes out of her hold.

"It was my fault he fell. I had to"—he pauses, looking uncomfortable—"well, I had to pee. I should've known he'd try and bring the pot in by himself. He's pigheaded."

She lets out a sad laugh. "He is."

"Anyway, I'm sorry I let it happen on my watch."

"Not your fault. Like you said, he's pigheaded."

"The doc said he'll be okay, so I guess I'll go. But would you mind having him let me know how he's doing later so my wife doesn't kill me for taking off? Hospitals make me itch."

"I'll make sure he does."

Oliver's eyes travel to me next. "You're Kian, right?"

"Yes."

"Hm." He hums and walks away.

What did that mean? I want to chase him down and ask, but it's not the time or place.

Sara and I sit in silence until Dr. Miller comes back out.

"Okay, you can come back."

We follow him to a hallway of closed doors. He pushes the latch on one and we all walk in. There in the middle of the room, looking too sizeable for the hospital bed, is Archer. His eyes are closed and he has a large bruise on his forehead.

His eyelids flutter open at the click of the door closing behind us. My stomach threatens to empty itself at the sight of the man I care so much for looking so injured.

"Hey, you." Sara rushes over, sitting on the edge of the bed and lifting the hand without an IV needle poking into it. "How are you feeling?"

"Like I got tossed into the ocean and hit in the head with a hook," he croaks out and Sara looks over at Dr. Miller.

"Oliver missed hooking his legs the first time and accidentally hit him in the head," he explains.

"My leg isn't anywhere near my head. The old man didn't miss," Archer jokes, but it sends him into a coughing fit.

I stay huddled by the door, not knowing if I should be here. There wasn't even a question in my mind about coming back until I saw him. Then I remembered he's not mine anymore and I don't want to assume I belong.

"Don't try and crack jokes," Sara scolds.

"His tests came back mostly clear. We're going to keep him overnight because he has a concussion and some fluid in his airways. We're pumping him full of antibiotics so a bacterial infection doesn't form and we'll keep him on oxygen for a while," Lance explains. "He'll need to rest for a couple days, but then he'll be good as new."

"Thank you," Sara says.

"I'll be back before I head home to check on you." Lance pats Archer's leg and I want to smack his hand away. I don't know what his deal is, he's too new for me to know much, but I know I don't like him touching my man.

Except he isn't your man. I push that toxic thought right the fuck out of my head.

Archer's eyes follow Lance as he leaves the room. His gaze stops on me and he notices me for the first time. I take a couple steps into the room.

"Hey, you. Did you like the service here so much that you had to come back, only as a patient this time? I promise you the food isn't that great. I had my appendix out when I was thirteen and—"

"I'm so glad you're here," he says, his voice throaty and painful sounding.

"I am, too." I take a seat on the other side of his bed.

"Shit. It's five. I need to go get the kids from Mrs. Porter."

"I can go." I offer.

"No, Sara should go," Archer says. Sara's mouth opens, but no words come out. "The kids will worry if suddenly Kian's there and telling them I'm sick. They'll feel better if it comes from you."

"Great, so I'm the bad luck bear now?" I sulk.

"You're right. Kian, call me if anything happens." Sara instructs with a point of her finger.

"I will."

Sara leaves and it's just me, Archer, and a million things

left unsaid between us. I should open my mouth and tell him all the things I've been holding back. Make sure he knows that without him, I'd be as lost as he is without Mason. That I not only want him, but his family, too.

Behind his blue eyes, I see him warring with his own thoughts. I wonder if they align with mine.

"Do you need anything? Water? Food?" I ask when the silence has gone on too long.

"No, I'm fine. Just tired." He lets out a wet cough.

"Emotionally, are you okay? It must've been scary and then there's—"

"Mason," he says.

"Yeah. There's Mason."

"At first, I fought. I pushed my boots off, I struggled to find the surface. Then when it became too hard, I just… floated. I thought, if I can't be here with you, I might as well be up there, with him." He gestures to the sky. "Honestly, I didn't know which one I was rooting for."

"Oh." That's not the heartfelt speech I was hoping for. Even after everything, he'd still choose Mason. Maybe he always will.

"Wipe that kicked puppy dog look off your face, because in the end, I chose to live. I needed to be here for Sara and the kids."

"Right. Of course." Suddenly the strings on the threadbare blanket covering him become very interesting. I pull on one, separating the hem.

"Kian, shut up for a second and hear me out. I *needed* to be around for my family, but I *wanted* to be here for you. I didn't want to die without you knowing how I feel."

"And how do you feel?" I ask in a hushed tone.

His large hand covers both of mine, stopping me from ruining any more of the hospital's property.

"I'm not like you. I don't express myself or talk about feelings—"

"You don't say." I interrupt and he pins me with a look. "Sorry."

"Even from the first night we met, you weren't scared off by my bad attitude. There was no point in pushing you away, because you already knew who I was before I said a word. It was intimidating and scary, I didn't think that's what I wanted. I fought having you in my life. I forced you to have doubts of your own. I'm sorry for that." He brings my hands to his lap. "Then we got derailed with Sara and instead of running, you showed up again."

"I won't run away, Archer. The only way I'd turn my back on you is if you told me to."

"I didn't think that was true at first. After all, I'm kind of a lot to deal with." I open my mouth to agree, but he pushes a finger to my lips. "Nothing that happened was a test, but you passed anyway and I realized all this when I was underwater, way too close to death."

"You should know I'm falling in love with you," I blurt out.

"Me too." He smiles and even though I see the pain, I see the happiness, too. And not just from his injuries. There probably will always be some suffering along with joy where Archer is concerned. He thinks he's a flat liner, but he's actually the opposite. He feels things so deeply, but he's not comfortable expressing them.

"Really?" I squeak.

"Yeah, you grew on me."

"Like a fungus?"

"More like wildflowers that bloom on top of a rotten tree stump."

"In this scenario, I'm the wildflowers, right?"

He chuckles and then winces. "Don't make me laugh."

"I am the wildflowers. I know it." I puff my chest in pride.

"Yeah, yeah."

"Can I stay with you tonight?" I ask.

"That chair isn't comfortable. Trust me. I took many a nap on one just like it."

"I don't mind. As long as I can keep an eye on you."

"I have a better idea." He scoots over to the edge of the bed. He's a hulking man and the space he makes is hardly big enough for another man, but it's perfect for a noodle. I slide in, nestling my head in the crook of his shoulder.

"You know the nurse is probably going to kick me out of your bed, right?"

"She can try."

"Do you think Dr. Miller is hot?" I feather my fingers along his chest.

"He's okay."

"He thinks you're hot."

"How do you figure?"

"The way he patted your leg."

"I think that's a doctor thing. He was trying to comfort me or some shit."

"I don't think so. I think he's got a doctor boner for you." I lift my head and gaze into his ocean blue eyes.

"Jealous?"

"No." I protest a little too strongly and he pushes my head back to his shoulder.

"Sleep now."

"But it's seven o'clock."

"Babe, I have a concussion and almost drowned. It's quiet time."

"Fine."

I press my nose to his neck and inhale. He smells like saltwater and him. I could bathe in that scent and still not get enough.

"You need a shave." I scruff my fingers through his beard.

"That feels incredible."

"Is that why you do it all the time?"

"It doesn't feel like that when I do it. You have magical fingers." He moans.

"You're not the first to tell me that."

"Kian?"

"Huh?"

"Shh."

And so I shh. He immediately begins snoring softly and I bask in the vibrations of his breaths, while I repeat my mantra in my head.

I'm open to love.
I'm open to his love.
I'm open to loving him.

THIRTY-ONE

Archer

Things slow down after I get home from the hospital. I'm put on sorting duty at the dock until Oliver forgets I almost died. Apparently, it was more traumatic for him than it was for me. Sara and Kian were more than thrilled to have me on dry land for a while. I've explained how the accident was my fault. I know better than to try and maneuver those pots by myself, but they didn't seem to care.

Sara's got the kids over at a pre-k and is putting in about thirty hours a week working for my boyfriend. *My boyfriend.* First time I've thought about it that way, but it's what he is. We're taking it slow, easing into it, and staying away from the heavy.

I think we both could use a light load for a while.

That's why I've planned a date for us today. We're going to the remote Blue Shark Islands. You can get there by bridge, but I've borrowed a boat from my boss, Henry. I know Kian won't be thrilled, but hopefully the life jackets will make it okay.

I pull up to his condo and get out of the truck. Last time I picked him up, I shot him a text to get his ass outside, but that didn't go over well. I guess he's more traditional than I thought. I climb the steps to the second floor and knock on his door, like I found out he prefers.

He answers, wearing a bright blue T-shirt with *Sorry*

Girls, I Love Boys stenciled in black on the front. Of course, the short sleeves are rolled and he's paired it with black jeans that have gaping holes in the knees. It's a reminder of how much older I am than him, but it only serves to pump my ego full of pride. I bagged a sexy guy at forty years old.

"Hey, handsome." He lifts onto his toes and plants a kiss on my lips. He tries to pull away, but I wrap a strong arm around his middle and keep him pressed to me, deepening the kiss. He moans into my mouth and I reach down to take a handful of his juicy ass.

"Fuck, you're delicious." I release him and his knees go weak, but I steady him.

"I've been snacking on crackers and that fig jam you love." He licks his lips and it's all I can do not to back him into his bedroom and fuck him.

"You ready?"

"Yep. I packed a picnic lunch like you asked."

"Thanks for that. I thought about doing it myself, but you know how far my food prep skills go."

"I do. They send my stomach spiraling down the toilet." He sasses, bringing up the dinner I made and delivered to his work for him two nights ago.

"It wasn't that bad."

"The chicken was raw," he deadpans.

I have no defense because it was. So instead of arguing, I pick the basket up and we walk down to my truck.

"You ready to tell me where we're going?"

"You'll see." It's not a far drive since we're only going to the dock next to his house. I park and open my door to get out, but notice he doesn't move. "You coming?"

"Archer, is this a joke?"

"Do you trust me?"

"You know I do."

"Then come on."

We walk hand in hand to the boat launch where we meet Henry. He hands over the keys to his Searay SLX 280. It's a beautiful boat with U-shaped dinette and a bench seat on the back for having a few drinks while in the middle of the ocean.

"Thanks, Henry. I'll have her back in four or so hours. We're going to tool around Blue Shark Islands."

"No problem. It's a beautiful day for it. Have fun." He's right, the temperatures are warm enough that the sea breeze feels cooling on my skin and there's hardly a cloud in sight.

I jump in, set the picnic basket down, and turn back around to help Kian onto the boat.

"I'm warning you now, if either of us falls into the ocean, your ass is grass."

"Yeah, yeah. I got it."

After he's safely on, I pull out two ugly, orange life vests. "You're making me wear this, aren't you?"

He growls, but not in the sexy way I'm used to hearing. This one is feral and angry. *Message received.* I secure them around both of us and we pull away from the dock.

I speed toward the island, loving the freedom of being on the open ocean. No one's around, there's no speed limits, and the salty air smells like home. I take a quick look at Kian and smile to him lounging into the seat, sunglasses perched on his nose, and his head tipped back, soaking up the sun.

Twenty minutes later, I pull up to the beach. I drop my pants and love the way Kian's mouth drops open.

"What are you doing?"

"There's no dock and I didn't wear shorts. We need to jump in and walk to the beach."

"Archer, you know I don't wear underwear." He pouts and I waggle my brows. "You're incorrigible."

"I brought both of us swimsuits." I reach into my backpack and toss him his ultra-short trunks.

We rush to change and wade our way to the beach. It's not

miles of sand. Instead there are large boulders and rocks with sandy patches in between. I find the perfect spot, spread a large beach blanket, and we sprawl out.

"Not too shabby, huh?"

"Not at all. It's easy to feel a little claustrophobic living in a small town. It's nice to get away." Kian crawls toward me and sits between my legs, his back to my chest.

"Who would've thought this is where we'd end up, considering we met cleaning up shit."

He laughs, his legs curling to his chest. "Can we please come up with a better 'how we met' story?"

"I don't know. I kind of like it. It's unique."

"I guess."

I lean down and plant a wet kiss behind his ear. He rolls around and straddles my lap. My hands fall to his perfectly round ass. He rests his nose on mine and for a brief moment, we stay there, sharing a breath and gazing into each other's eyes.

But we never could be this close and keep our hands and lips off each other. I grip the back of his neck and bring him in for a kiss. Our tongues slide together and our lips move in practiced dance. He breaks away and kisses a trail to my ear. I groan when he sucks my earlobe into his mouth and flicks it with the tip of his tongue. My cock immediately stiffens between us.

"Fuck, babe," I breathe out.

"Feel nice?" He reaches down and strokes me over my trunks.

"Fucking amazing, but it'd feel better if those pouty lips were wrapped around my cock."

"Hell yes." He gets on his knees and elbows between my legs while I scramble to pull myself out.

He takes me in hand and squeezes me from base to tip until a bead of pre-cum appears. He laps it up like it's one of the sherbet cones he orders on the boardwalk.

"Suck me." I order, loving the way he rushes to do

everything I ask. He takes me as far as he can, swallowing around the head of my aching cock. "Fuuuuuuck."

I lean forward enough to push his swim shorts down to his thighs. His ass is propped up high, making it the perfect angle for me to get my fingers inside him. I gather some saliva in my mouth and use it to lube up my fingers before reaching around and rubbing them against his puckered hole. I press one finger in, pumping in and out.

"Mmm." He moans around a mouthful of dick. The vibrations have my hips lifting, frantic for more.

I add another finger, drilling into him until I find the spot inside that drives him crazy. I tap against it, making him squirm. He chokes around my length and I feel his saliva spill down my balls. I fucking love how dirty our sex is. I'll never get enough. Not ever.

"I need to fuck you. Please tell me you packed lube."

He pops off of me. "Yes, Archer. I packed the slick along with the bruschetta."

"Fuck."

"Wait a second." He digs through the basket and comes up with a container of oil. "I packed olive oil I planned on mixing with vinegar to dip crusty bread in. That'll work, right?"

"I have no idea."

"I'm sure it's fine." He tosses me the container and shimmies the rest of the way out of his shorts. His dick stands stiff and strong. I can't stop myself from pulling him closer to take a taste. I roll his balls in the palm of my hand while sucking him down. He's smooth like silk and hard as stone. "Archer, I won't last with you doing that."

"What if I do this instead?" I lick down the underside of him until I reach his balls. I suck them into my mouth and roll them around one by one.

"Especially if you do that," he whines.

I release him and flip him around. I rise to my knees and

press a hand on his lower back, forcing him to bend over. I spread his cheeks wide and eat his ass. His knees go weak, causing him to wobble, so I pull back and he drops down on all fours.

I pick up the olive oil, still feeling a little unsure, but not seeing any other option. I drizzle it down his crack and use my fingers to stretch him. It's slippery, just as slick as what we normally use. We haven't fucked since we got back together, but we've talked about it and decided we were done with condoms. It felt right after our declarations while I was laid up in the hospital.

I lube up my rigid length and slowly push my swollen head through his first ring of muscle, but he gets impatient and pushes back at a much quicker pace.

"Shit. Your ass is made for me. You know that, right? The perfect little hole for me to fuck," I grit out.

"Right there. Right there," he mumbles over and over.

"Jack yourself off. I want to feel the way you squeeze the life out of my cock when you come."

Using the top of his ass cheeks as leverage, I jackhammer into him, making sure to angle myself just right.

"I'm coming," he hollers and clenches down on me.

The air leaves my lungs from all the pleasure. My balls tingle, spreading up the base of my spine, and then like a firework, spreading throughout my body. I don't want to let go, knowing if I do, it'll all be over. But way too soon, I'm shooting off inside him with a roar, my thrusts becoming jerky and erratic.

I squeeze my eyes shut and little sparkles of light dance behind my eyelids. When every last drop has been wrung from me, I gently pull out. Kian's panting with his forehead resting on the blanket. He starts to move, but I hold him there. I spread him open and watch as my semen drips from his hole and down his balls.

"Fuck, that's a beautiful sight." And because I can't help myself, I scoop some of it up and push it back in.

"You're such a caveman."

"You can't see what I do."

"I can imagine and it's not as hot as you think it is."

"Oh trust me, it fucking is." I smack his ass and help him to standing. We trod down to the ocean and spend an hour splashing around in the waves and making out on the sand.

It's the happiest I can remember being in a long ass time. There's no weight on my shoulders, no pressure on my chest. It's just me and Kian.

"I'm starving. I'll set up lunch." He kisses my cheek and walks up to where our messed up blanket is.

"Toss me my shorts, would ya?" I call out and he throws them over. "Thanks."

I step into them, the waves tickling my ankles. I peer back at Kian and see he's busying himself by smoothing out the blanket and digging in the picnic basket. I unzip the tiny pocket in the waistband of my trunks and pull out a ring. I spin the gold band with a Koa wood inlay around my finger and stare out at the waves.

It's not the same ocean Mason died in, but he never did get to see the Atlantic. I think he'd approve. I kiss the ring and hurl it as far as I can throw it.

"Rest in peace, my love," I whisper.

Suddenly, I feel a sharp sting on my big toe. I look down. A rock crab scurries away.

He was such a nice person, the meanest thing he could think to do to me is make my big toe cold. Enough to make me uncomfortable, but not enough to hurt me.

The memory floods back to me, and tears fall from my eyes before I can bite them back. Maybe it's a coincidence, but it doesn't feel like it. It feels like goodbye.

"You okay?" Arms wrap around my middle and Kian's rests his chin in the center of my back.

"Yeah. Better than I have in a long time." I roughly wipe away my tears.

"Great. Because lunch is ready and last one there has to sit in my cum puddle on the blanket." He takes off in a sprint. I laugh and give chase.

I never would've given happiness a second chance if it weren't for this man and I'm so fucking grateful I became Kian's focus.

EPILOGUE

Kian

"**D**o you swear everyone's putting these on?" Archer asks, holding up tiny, shiny, rainbow-striped undies.

"I swear." I cross my heart. What he doesn't see is my other hand, twisted behind my back, fingers crossed. "See? I have a matching pair." I hold up my own undies.

"Fine, but I swear to God, if you're lying."

I almost second-guess my decision to pull this prank, but the end result will be so worth the punishment.

"Don't you trust me?"

"Why aren't you changing then?"

"I am. But I'll use the hall bathroom. You know what will happen if I see that big Mack truck. I'll have you parking it right in my little garage and then everyone will tease us for the rest of the night."

"I don't know what that means."

"I know, old man. Just go get changed. I'll meet you out there." I shove him toward my en suite.

He grumbles something unintelligible and stomps into the bathroom. The second the door is closed, I fold in half, stuffing my fist in my mouth to stifle my laugh. I take a composing breath and leave my bedroom, closing the door behind me.

In the living room is Brie, Cato, Jarrett, and Fernando. We've made our slumber parties a monthly thing, but this month, I was able to talk Archer into joining us.

"Did he fall for it?" Cato asks.

"Hook, line, and sinker."

Everyone's gathered around my dining room charcuterie, eating their weight in finger foods.

"I can't wait to see those thick thighs on display. Kian, is he big *all over*?" Cato asks and I growl. "Calm down. I'm not going after your man. I'm just curious, but you don't need to answer. All will be revealed in three, two, one."

Archer leaves the bedroom, damn near naked. The banana hammock hugs him in all the right places. My mouth waters and I have the sudden urge to kick everyone out of my condo.

"Kian!" Archer's eyes pop out of his head and his features look murderous. He spins around and storms back into my room. His backside looks just as yummy as the front. "Get your ass in here."

"Uh-oh. Someone's in trouble," Jarrett singsongs. "Can I watch?"

I roll my eyes, cross my arms over my chest, and follow him into my room like a petulant child. A roar of laughter sounds behind me and I shut my door to block it out.

"Why would you do that to me?" He peels the article of clothing, if you want to call it that, down his generous legs. His cock hangs heavy between his legs, causing my mouth to water.

"Hazing?" It comes out like a question and not an explanation.

"You're in so much trouble."

"I get that, but we have guests. Think we can wait until later?"

"You're asking for it."

"Right. Trouble. Punishment. Oh no, I'm so scared. I'll be shaking in my boots all night."

He stalks toward me, his chin lowered. For each step he

takes forward, I take one back, actually growing nervous. I've never seen all that anger directed at me. My back bumps up against my closet door. He closes the remaining distance between us and rests his hands on either side of my head.

"Little boy thinks he's funny, huh?"

"Me? No, not funny at all. I mean, maybe a little funny." I smirk. He presses his pelvis into me, his dick growing harder and harder by the second. "Well, that's certainly not comical."

"I want to tear your ass up," he says, low and menacing.

"I deserve it and I'll take it like a champ. But later." I lift onto my tiptoes, kiss his nose, and duck under his arm. I sprint out the door and slam it behind me.

The gang cackles from two feet in front of me, where they'd been attempting to listen in.

"You guys are such pervs." I push my way through and walk straight into the kitchen to pour a large glass of wine.

Hours later, things settle. We're all snuggled up in my living room. Jarrett and Fernando on either side of me on the couch, Archer sitting on the ground between my legs, with Cato and Brie on the love seat.

"So, Archer, you're all moved into your place?" Brie asks.

"I am."

"I thought for sure you'd end up moving in here," Fernando says.

"We thought about it, but we're taking it slow. He only signed a six-month lease, so we can reassess then," I explain.

"Plus, I'm only downstairs. It's not like I'm clear across town." Archer rubs my knee.

He ended up staying with Sara for a whole month after her suicide attempt. She was ready for him to leave by week two, but she also understood why he was hesitant. Plus, I kept him over at my house as much as I could to give her some space. She and I have become fast friends. We have absolutely nothing in common and are in completely different stages in life, but we share a bond formed in tragedy and heartbreak. She's the sister I never had.

"Was Sara excited for the move or was she nervous being on her own?" Brie lifts her glass of wine to her lips.

"She was excited. She's found herself some mom friends she met through the pre-k the kids go to and she has her job, she's ready to be on her own."

"What friends?" Jarrett's brows rise, ever curious about everyone in town.

"Eliza, for one," I say.

Everyone's eyes dart over to Brie. Eliza is Hank's ex-wife and Brie is Hank's ex-girlfriend and Hank is a homophobic psychopath.

"Oh, me and Eliza are cool. We've had lunch a few times to talk about what a piece of shit Hank is." Brie waves us off.

"You think you'll come to next month's sleepover?" Fernando claps Archer on the shoulder.

"Fuck no. You guys ruined your chances of being blessed with my company after that speedo incident. Girls and gays night will be down one gay."

"Aw, don't be like that." I rub his shoulders, working the muscles that strain every day while he's working.

"Matter of fact, I'm out. I have work tomorrow." He stands up and stretches.

"You can't go. It's a sleepover." I whine.

"You'll be fine without me." He bends down and kisses the top of my head, then turns to Jarrett. "Don't be snuggling too close to my man tonight."

"Oh, sweetie. He doesn't do it for me. Now you, on the other hand." He waggles a finger up and down Archer's body. I lean over and smack his arm. "Ow."

"Bye, guys." He waves on his way out the door.

"He's so swoony. Did you see the way he kissed Kian's head? I want that." Cato sighs dreamily.

"Your turn will come." I yawn. "I think I'm ready for bed."

"Me too," Fernando says.

"Good night. You all know where everything is."

Jarrett and I climb into my memory foam, king-sized bed and I flip off the lamp on my nightstand.

"I'm happy for you," Jarrett whispers.

"Things are much different than last month, huh?"

"Very different. Now we just need to find me a boy toy who likes middle-aged power bottoms."

"It'll happen. Have you been setting your intentions?"

"Every night." It's quiet for a moment and then he asks, "Do you love him?"

"I think so. For as much as I thought I loved Jax, my feelings for Archer are much stronger."

"That doesn't surprise me. You and Jax had puppy love, it just felt so intense because it was your first time for everything."

"I see that now. All I do is look at Archer and I want to cry because I'm so happy. He's not open with his emotions, he doesn't tell me how much he cares, or send me sweet text messages, but he does things in a quiet way. You know? Like he sets my kettle at night because he knows I like tea in the morning. Or he takes my car in to get the tires rotated and the oil changed. Things he knows I avoid doing." I smile, thinking about how he came unhinged when he found out I hadn't had my oil changed once since I bought the car. "And his dick is fire. He's forty, but I swear he'd go all night if I could."

"Then what are you doing in here with me?"

"Sleepover night."

"If I had someone to dick me down, I'm sorry, but I wouldn't be in bed with you."

"Rude."

"It's true."

"You wouldn't be upset?" I ask.

"Not even a little. Go get you some."

I flip on the lamp, jump from bed, and drop to my knees.

"What are you doing?" Jarrett asks.

"Found 'em." I hold up the undies. "Think he'll put these back on for me?"

"Hand to God, if you two ever make a sex tape, you better leak it my way."

"Bye, bitch." I wave.

"Bye."

I sneak out the front door, careful not to wake Fernando, who's snoozing on the couch. I take the stairs down a floor and use my spare key to unlock Archer's front door. I quietly close it behind me and am shocked to find Archer sitting on his couch, whiskey glass in hand.

"Jesus Christ, you scared me. What are you doing still up?"

"Waiting for you." He takes the last sip of whiskey and sets it down on the antique coffee table he got from Jarrett's shop.

"How did you know I'd show up?"

"I know you." He grabs my hand and pulls me toward his bedroom.

"Are you saying I'm predictable?"

He stops and turns around, taking me into his arms. "Kian, you are the biggest surprise of my life. I love you."

"I love you, too." My voice is shaky and full of emotion.

He leans down and kisses me sweetly. No tongue, just his soft lips moving against mine. It melts me to my core, turning my insides to mush.

"Now take off your clothes and lie flat on my bed with your head off the edge. I'll be fucking your throat for that stunt you pulled earlier," he says in a low, guttural tone. "And I don't want any of your topping from the bottom. I'm in control tonight."

"Yes, sir." I salute and he slaps my ass as I strut past him.

My insides melt for a whole new reason as I strip and get into position, but in my head, all I can think is, *words. He gave me words.*

He loves me.

If you enjoyed Kian's Focus and want to read more about the men of Brigs Ferry Bay, be sure to check out Sheriff's Secret by K Webster. You can also sign up for my newsletter to be alerted when more books in this series are released.

A NOTE TO THE READER

Thank you so much for reading Kian's Focus, the second book in K Webster and Misty Walker's charming, gay Brigs Ferry Bay world! If this is your first book by K Webster or Misty Walker, and you can't get enough, make sure you check out more of our work! We suggest you read K Webster's Hood River Rat and Misty Walker's Bohemian Mark.

We've been besties for years and our mutual love for gay romance is something we regularly gab about and connect over. It felt like serendipity when we decided to create our own world to write in, giving lots of gay couples their own stories in one unique small town. Check out the rest of the Brigs Ferry Bay series on Amazon.

Make sure to follow K Webster and Misty Walker on Amazon so you can be notified of all our new releases, and don't forget to follow us on Facebook for more information.

We'd love for you to sign up for our newsletters, so you don't miss a thing! Stay updated by visiting www.authorkwebster.com, www.authormistywalker.com, or visit Krazy for K Webster's Books and Misty Walker's Thirsty Readers on Facebook. We also have our I Love M/M Romance group where we share recommendations of our favorite gay romances!

Thanks for reading!
K & Misty

ABOUT THE AUTHOR

Misty Walker writes everything from dark and delicious, to sweet and spicy. Most of her books are forbidden in some way and many are age-gap, because that's her jam.

She's lived quite the nomadic life, never staying in the same place for long until she met her husband. They've recently settled in Reno, NV with their two daughters, two dogs, and two hamsters, because everything's better in pairs.

Misty is fueled by coffee and the voices in her head screaming for their stories to be told. Which is why the coffee is necessary, because there's only so many hours in a day and who needs sleep anyway?

If you'd like to keep up to date on all her future releases, please sign up for her newsletter on her website. You can also order a signed paperback of this book, or any of her releases there.

Connect with Misty on social media:
www.authormistywalker.com
authormistywalker@gmail.com
Instagram: www.instagram.com/authormistywalker
Facebook: www.facebook.com/authormistywalker
Twitter: @mistywalkerbook.

ALSO BY
MISTY WALKER

Standalones:
Vindicated
Conversion (also available on audio)
Cop-Out

The Traveler Series:
Bohemian Law
Bohemian Mark
Bohemian Patience

Royal Bastards: Reno, NV
Birdie's Biker

Brigs Ferry Bay
Kian's Focus

ACKNOWLEDGMENTS

Kristi, I love our town and our cute little lobster. It's so fun creating with you.

Ty-bot, thank you for helping to make my dreams come true.

Genevieve, thanks for having my back in all things!!

Sultan, my hype girl! You pump me up and keep me going! Thank you.

Sara, Sarah, Ariadna, & Elizabeth, y'all be the best beta bitches ever.

Amy, you're the best sister I've ever had. And a pretty awesome proofreader. Thank you!

Emily A. Lawrence, thank you for making my words look professional and put together.

Stacey Blake, thank you for making the pages of my books match the words written on them!

Mom, thank you for never making me feel bad when I disappear for weeks on end to get my writing in. I love you!

To my readers & my reader group, Misty Walker's Thirsty Readers, thank you the most! You guys rock my world and motivate me to keep writing. I love nothing more than to get your messages and read your reviews. It's a great big book world, but you choose to read my books and that means everything.

Lorelai and Mabel, without you this book would have been written much faster and with less headache, but I'm so blessed to be your mom and I wouldn't change it for the world.

Printed in Great Britain
by Amazon